ISBN 979-8-9879290-1-8

Written by The LampKeeper

Published by
Debarim Publishing, LLC
807 W Broadway
Spiro, OK 74959
www.debarimpublishing.com

I dedicate this novel to my son, Nathan, my Tod the Fox.

Eighteen years wasn't enough!

Acknowledgments

This novel has been a long time coming. I want to express my gratitude to everyone who helped and encouraged me along the way. Still, before I do, I want to thank my heavenly father for blessing me with the vision of Covenant Cove, the characters that fill my dreams, the talent to write their stories, and the courage to share them with the world.

A huge thank you to Jennifer Hartz for volunteering to be my writing partner and mentor for my first draft. I would've never finished this novel without your advice and encouragement. My sincere appreciation also goes out to my beta readers, Cathy Tuttle and Hailey Bartlett, for always asking for the next chapter. You kept me going when I could've easily given up.

I also want to thank my family. To my husband, Richard, thank you for giving me room to grow and be the woman Yahuah created me to be. To my children, Brittan, Katherine, and Samantha. I know you think your mom is a little weird sometimes, but your loving honor and respect are much appreciated. I love you all.

Lastly, I want to thank my editor and publisher, Sarah Williams of Debarim Publishing, for taking on the work of a novice writer and making it shine!

Eyes of Grace

Dear Reader:

Welcome to the world of Covenant Cove! I'm so happy you stopped by for a visit. Our community comprises people who have come out of mainstream Christianity to follow a simpler way of life. You may see many unfamiliar customs and teachings within the pages of my books. I pray they open your eyes to the truth of our Messiah's sacrifice and the beauty of walking as He walked.

2 Timothy 2:15 "Study to shew thyself approved unto God, a workman that needeth not to be ashamed, rightly dividing the word of truth."

With much Shalom,

The LampKeeper

May YAHUAH bless you

and keep you;

may YAHUAH cause His face to shine upon you

and be gracious to you;

may YAHUAH lift up His countenance toward you

and give you peace.

Numbers 6:24-26

1

Afternoon sunlight streaming through a hole in the blinds bombarded Tamsin's face. The beam drilled through her eyelids, demanding she awaken. Squeezing them tighter against the onslaught caused tiny razor blades to cut into her sleep-deprived eyes. Her hand moved to shield them from the assault. She froze. Better not.

"Tam, get up."

Crud, she woke Viktor. Why was he a light sleeper on top of everything else?

"Mmph. What time is it?"

"It's time to get up. That's what time it is."

Tamsin blinked awake. The numbers on the clock swam before her eyes. The headache started before she rolled onto her back, her muscles protesting every movement. She didn't want to get up because it meant working. Having your husband as your boss isn't a pleasant work environment. More so when the man is Viktor Doroshenko, owner of The Fox Den, Charlotte's biggest gentlemen's club, and you are his fox.

"Tam, I said get up. Now do it." Viktor ordered before entering the bathroom.

She ignored his harsh tone, rolling to her side and closing her eyes again, knowing his methodical grooming lasted for a good hour. He aligned every blonde hair in a side-swept undercut before he ever left the bathroom. She needed a bit more rest.

"Tam!"

Her lids sprang open. She didn't mean to fall back asleep.

"You are so lazy. Quit pretending you're tired. We both slept eight hours."

I am tired.

"Your dancing has been sloppy this past week. I expect to see improvement tonight," Viktor said from inside the closet. Plastic flapped when he ripped it off the clothes he picked up from the dry cleaners yesterday. The hangers thumped against the wall.

Tamsin arched her back, stretching her arms towards the headboard. She could muster the will to rise if she stretched for a minute. Viktor's meaty palm clamped around her wrist.

"I'm up! I'm up!"

She swung her legs over the side of the bed and sat upright in one motion. Her stomach churned. Was she going to be sick? She slapped a hand over her mouth as she ran to the bathroom.

Oh no! Not again! Tears rolled while she emptied her gut.

"I knew you should've got an IUD. You forgot to take your pills again, didn't you?"

"No, I did not. Besides, you said an IUD would make me fat," she said as another wave of nausea hit her.

"You're disgusting."

Tamsin ignored his insult, having become immune to his belittling. She learned long ago that they grew worse if she responded to his degrading comments. She spat out the acidic taste of her vomit and flushed the commode.

"It could be food poisoning... or stomach flu," she said hopefully before turning on the faucet. She bent over, drinking from the tap to rinse her mouth out. "I haven't been feeling well this week."

"That's why I bought this," he said, holding a pregnancy test. He tossed the box on the counter. "Take it." He leaned against the door frame, his unbuttoned shirt revealing his spray-tanned chest.

Tamsin stared at the container. She didn't want to touch it the same way she didn't want to touch the giant boa constrictor brought to her elementary school. Everyone in her class, except herself, lined up to hold part of its long body. The very thought of it disgusted her. She jerked her gaze back up to the mirror before her nausea returned.

"Aren't you going to leave?" she asked Viktor's image, finding his reflection easier to speak to than face-to-face.

He released an audible sigh. "You think I'm unaware you'll run water over it, so it will appear negative?" He moved to stand behind her, pressing in and trapping her hands on the countertop. He glared at her in the mirror. "You're a smart and beautiful girl, Tamsin. A rare combination. They're why I chose you to be my wife over any other girl out there." He lowered his head level with hers to nuzzle her cheek. "But always remember, I'm smarter, and your status in this house is mutable."

Hmm, a compliment and a warning. He must be in a good mood.

Tamsin knew full well what position she played—bait for Viktor's actual money-making business, trafficking. Flesh or drugs, he supplied the vice. Girls or boys. She lured them into Viktor's clutches. He called her smart. She wasn't smart enough to escape the current mess of her life, but at least she could keep herself alive long enough to figure it out. In over her head, her drug addiction kept her compliant, dictating the remnant of her morals. She was painfully aware of what happened to his victims.

Viktor laughed. "Oh, don't look so surprised," he said, misreading her facial expression. "I'll always be one step ahead of you. I even know what you think before you think it." He returned to leaning against the door frame and crossed his arms. "Take the test. I have to leave. I've got an appointment at the club in an hour."

"I need a cup," Tamsin said, squeezing the box in her hand.

He stomped to the counter and unscrewed the lid off the mouthwash. "Use that."

She didn't want to 'use that.' She wanted him to leave so she could think without him standing over her. Viktor pressed the lid into her palm.

"I'm losing my patience."

Another warning. *Shut up, Tamsin, and do what you're told.*

She performed the steps to complete the test. Two blue lines appeared in seconds. She stared dumbfounded at the stick. How could she be pregnant? She was so careful after the last time. Tears streamed.

"I'll take you to the clinic tomorrow." Viktor buttoned his shirt, tucking the tails into his waistband. He admired his image in the mirror, flexing his biceps to pull the sleeve taut before turning around and walking out of the bathroom.

The mundane sounds he made reached her ears. His keys jingled when he picked them up to put in his pocket. His shoelaces zipped through the metal grommets when he pulled them taught. The aglets tapped against the leather as he tied them. Every noise grated on her frazzled nerves.

"I'll pick you up in a couple of hours. Be ready," he said from the bedroom.

The swish of his suit coat fabric reached her ears. The soles of his shoes clicked on the hardwood floor.

"Do you think hiring a driver might help?" he asked, standing in the bathroom doorway with his hands in his pockets.

"Y—yes?" she said, hoping she gave the answer he wanted. *What's he thinking now?*

"Good. You can sleep longer, and my life will be easier if I don't have to chauffeur you around town." He turned and left the room. "I'll start your coffee before leaving." The bedroom door clicked shut.

Tamsin stared after him. He must be bipolar or something. One minute he acted insensitive; the next, he became a flipping barista. She might handle an abortion better if he showed an iota of regret, but his voice lacked emotion. She placed her hand over her abdomen. How did this happen again?

Tamsin moved from the toilet to the inhospitable tile floor, sinking into the despair of her life choices. Leaning on the tub's edge, she held her abdomen while indulging in a good cry. *Why can't I have this baby?*

Viktor stopped her from having the first one because of her age. He said she was too young and irresponsible to be a mother. A year older now, she recognized her husband cared only for the use he could get out of her. This marriage didn't live up to the happy-ever-after hype he proposed. He controlled every moment of her life. Her wardrobe, what she ate, her daily schedule, and even how she applied her makeup fell under his authority.

Tamsin stood up to get ready, wiping away her tears. Though she wanted to wallow in her misery, she couldn't. Viktor became irate when he was kept waiting, and she still wasn't ready.

She checked the clock before turning on the shower. There wasn't enough time to wash and dry her corkscrew curls. Instead, she applied a leave-in curl conditioner and a shower cap before stepping into the glass-enclosed space. The heat from the shower activated the conditioner, making her curls come out silky.

She showered and entered the bedroom to find a tube-style gold lamé dress Viktor laid for her on the bed. Before the club opened, they dined at an elegant restaurant every evening. The stares she received while walking on the arm of her handsome husband catered to her ego until the day he bragged about being able to write off her clothes and their dinners as a business expense. Viktor used her as an advertisement to draw men into the club like the billboards he plastered along the streets and highways leading into the city.

She returned to the bathroom with an old t-shirt over the dress to avoid getting makeup on the shiny fabric. She opened her accordion makeup case and sat on the counter, laying out the brushes and creams she needed for her base layer. Viktor liked her to contour her nose to appear more streamlined. She saw a trivial amount of difference, but he insisted.

Tamsin leaned into the mirror and raised her brush to swipe the side of her nose with a darker shade than her skin tone. Her hand froze. She realized while dressing; she created excuses for getting the abortion. She couldn't raise a baby alone. Now wasn't the right time. And the best one? No baby deserved Viktor for a father. She gasped. Oh, *my gosh!* She dropped the brush she held. She tried to convince herself to have the abortion. She wanted this baby as much as she wanted the last one, but somehow Viktor's wishes became her own. She'd given him complete control of her life until she arrived where she stood today—a seventeen-year-old drug addict forced to dance in her husband's sleazy bar. Viktor kept her broke and supplied her with enough of the drug her body craved to keep her under control, willing to obey his every command and begging for her next fix. Now she let him control her mind, too?

Self-hatred washed over her. She despised the woman she saw. Innocent and honest Tamsin no longer existed. Her grandmother's words returned to her. "If you tell the truth, you don't have to keep track of your lies." Despite the warning, she lied, justified, and compromised, not to others, but to herself. She trapped herself in Viktor's cage, and he blocked her only escape route.

Destructive rage erupted. Viktor brought Tamsin into his world and conditioned her thoughts until she no longer knew herself. *He did this to me!* How dare he use my love against me! She picked up the makeup brush and threw it at the mirror. She threw the other jars and tubes. The plastic containers rebounded onto the floor. The mess didn't satisfy. She picked up the makeup case and threw it. The mirror shattered into a thousand tiny slivers.

She screamed her fury, reveling in the destruction. "I hate you," she shouted to the swirls of glue that once held the mirror to the wall. "I hate you! I hate you! I hate you!"

She panted over the destruction she had created. At whom did she scream? If she were honest, who did she hate? Viktor? Or herself? A wail of anguish spewed forth. This entire time, everything she did, getting married to Viktor, luring other children her age into his grasp, and her child. Everything happened because she allowed Viktor's thoughts and ideas to become hers. She let him in and gave him complete access and absolute control. What on earth possessed her to trust and marry a drug dealer?

She sank to her knees, doubling over and touching her head to the floor. Sobs wracked her body until she choked and coughed on her saliva, ending her crying spell. She rolled onto her back. Reality returned. Miniscule shards of glass covered the counter and spilled onto the floor. *What am I going to do?* She crawled over to the toilet paper dispenser to blow her nose. *When Viktor comes home and finds the mirror broken, he will kill me.*

She flushed the wad of used paper, watching it disappear in the swirl of water. Disappear? Leave? She could solve her problems by packing a bag, walking out the door, and disappearing. The money she stashed without Viktor's knowledge should last a few months. She could find work in another town using the fake ID he made for her.

She straightened her backbone. *Ha! Viktor said he knew everything about me. He'll never expect this. Does he think he has complete control? I'll show him! No one owns me! I won't allow him to take this child from me. I'll run so far, he'll never find me!*

Rushing to the bedroom, she threw her dress on the floor. A giddy laugh escaped her as she stomped on the golden puddle like a child jumping in a mud hole. After donning a pair of yoga pants and a tank top, she shoved a couple of days' worth of clothes in her gym bag before retrieving her money stash from the box springs. The only thing left to get was her ID Viktor kept locked in his office downstairs. She could use the meat hammer on the door handle until it fell apart. She slipped her feet into her tennis shoes, stepping on the heels in her rush to be out the door.

With her bag packed, she scanned the room, ensuring she had packed everything. She tested the drawer where Viktor kept their valuables. *Yes!* The drawer wasn't locked. She raided her jewelry before racing out the bedroom door towards the stairs.

"Where do you think you're going?" Viktor said from behind her.

Tamsin squealed with surprise, stopping at the top of the stairs. *Why is he here?* He shouldn't have returned for another fifteen minutes.

"Where did you come from?" Her voice shook with fright as she turned to face Viktor.

"This is my house. See, I even have the keys," he said with sarcasm, jingling the key fob in front of her for emphasis. "But, to answer your question, I've been waiting for you."

Tamsin's face gave her thoughts away again.

Viktor laughed without emotion. He stroked her cheek with the back of his fingers as he spoke. "My darling. I told you. There's nothing I don't know about you. That's why I waited for you, sweetheart. I realized you might panic. So, I thought I'd stay to help you figure things out. Your future is promising. As your husband, my job is to help you achieve success. So, tell me, where are you going?"

My success? *For your advantage. Not mine!* Try as she might, she saw no way to escape her predicament. The boldness and conviction to leave vanished like smoke with Viktor's confrontation. A reasonable excuse for scurrying out the door without him knowing escaped her. *You have to tell the truth.*

"I'm leaving," she said. There. She delivered the declaration without a quiver though her breath remained suspended in her chest. She couldn't bring herself to meet Viktor's eyes when he was angry.

"Leaving?" Viktor stroked the tops of her arms, his voice calm. "Why do you want to do that? Your life is perfect here—clothes, jewelry, fame. I give you everything you want. You're my wife. I take care of you in every way, and I love you. Why do you want to leave?"

Because you're sick, twisted, and sadistic. She cut her thoughts off before they escaped.

Deception laced his honied words. Tamsin foresaw the outcome of her hasty decision to leave from his tone of voice. His abuse would come, no matter what. She needed to change her strategy to lessen the damage.

"You're right, Viktor. I am confused, and I panicked. Forgive me?"

He gave her arms a slight squeeze. "See, I knew it. That's what I'm here for, babe. To help you see things straight. Logical. We'll get this sorted out. There's no need to run away. Besides, you have nowhere to go, and I'd worry. You mean so much to me."

Wrong! You're worried you'll lose your pawn.

Viktor pulled Tamsin into his arms.

Pay attention. Stay alert

He kissed her on the forehead before looking into her eyes.

Oh, his eyes are so gorgeous. They reminded her of a bright blue sky shining through a sheet of ice. Their unique color camouflaged the vile beast lurking behind their allure.

"You don't understand, but you need to trust me. We shouldn't have children right now. You're still too young. We won't be able to do the fun stuff I promised for your birthday. Remember? We're supposed to go to Australia in a few months and have the big Outback adventure you've been dreaming of." Viktor's gentle voice nearly deceived her into believing he spoke the truth.

"The vacation will end before the baby is born. This is your child, Viktor. Do you really want to kill your child?" she asked, drawing his hand to her abdomen.

He yanked his hand out of her grasp. "Sweetheart, there's also your career to think of. You're on top. I'm getting calls from across the entire country for you to perform. No one wants to see a dancer with stretch marks. Once you turn thirty, then you can have a baby. You said you wanted to be a stay-at-home mom. Once our finances are secure, you won't need to work. It makes more sense to wait."

Everything he said made sense. Except the baby existed now, and she'd never turn thirty if she stayed with Viktor.

"Plus, there's not a baby yet. It's only a bunch of cells—a tiny dot. Ending the pregnancy now is best because it won't feel any pain. You swallow a pill, and boom, no more being pregnant. It's tantamount to being late."

Oh, he made everything sound so simple. Tamsin took the pill he spoke of with her first pregnancy. 'Being late' didn't define the torture she suffered. Once Viktor assured himself she swallowed the pills, he left her alone in the house while the poison designed to eliminate the child from her womb took its course. Pain ripped through her abdomen, making her think she was dying. Waves of cramps worked to expel the fetus from her body. Then there was the blood. So much blood. She didn't know how to dispose of the dead baby. So, she flushed the tiny body down the toilet. "I'll never do that again. Since you don't want a child, I'll raise the baby on my own. Just let me go. I promise I'll never ask you for anything. Don't make me do that again. Viktor, please!" She tried to swallow her tears, but the rest of what she wanted to say burst out in a high-pitched cry. "I can't kill my baby again! Please, Viktor. Please, don't force me to get an abortion." She pulled on his arm, begging him like a petulant child.

Viktor's countenance changed from calm and caring to rage with no warning.

"I promise I'll keep my mouth shut. I promise not to say anything. Please, Viktor. Please! Let me go. Just let me go." Tears streamed over her cheeks; her mind ceased recognizing the danger she faced. The memory of the death of her first child invaded the present. The slimy warmth of blood on her hands, the metallic smell of it, and the gurgling of the toilet when she flushed the body of her child down the drain caused her mouth to spew words unchecked.

"Why do you always make things complicated? I give you an excellent, logical reason, and you defy me." Viktor grabbed her neck, shook her, squeezing her airway, and lifted her off the floor.

She never expected this. Panic gripped her, and she tried to pry his hand away. Her feet strained to find the floor. Heat radiated out from her core and up into her face. Sweat blossomed under her armpits. Awkward choking sounds emitted from her throat when she tried to speak. He was finally going to kill her.

"You know the rules, Tam." He shook her again. "You know the rules! You belong to me! You do what I say when I say it."

He lifted her face to his. Viktor lowered his tone and snarled. "I tried to be nice, and you didn't listen. Now we'll just solve things the hard way. You want me to let you go? So be it." With those words, he flung her backward.

A scream lodged in her throat. She flailed her arms, trying to find something to grab. They only met empty air over the wide staircase. The weight of her bag pulled her backward. Pain exploded in the back of her head and her spine when her body connected with the marble stairs. Her legs flew over her head. The tumble continued, the unforgiving stair edges digging into her pampered skin. A loud snap generated the scream her first shock held back.

She barely clung to consciousness upon reaching the last step. Drawing a breath hurt, and her arm hung at an odd angle. She tasted blood, not feeling the injury from which it flowed. The living room furniture reeled before her eyes. The hard leather soles of Viktor's loafers tapped on each stair as he descended to stand in front of her. He lifted her head by her hair so she could see him.

"Never threaten me again. I own you. The only way you're leaving me is in a body bag."

Tamsin couldn't defend herself when he drew back his fist.

2

Tony clicked on an image of a pontoon boat. He couldn't decide to go with a more practical, less expensive flat-bottomed jon boat or the versatile, pricier pontoon. His wife promised him a boat. Perhaps he could convince her to get both? Tony laughed at his moment of self-delusion. She would never agree to that.

His work phone rang. He swiped the call button without taking his eyes off the computer screen. "Speak."

"Tony? Hey man. You're a hard person to find. Remember me?"

Tingling traveled the length of Tony's spine. The person on the other end of the line was his childhood friend Scott. They both signed up with the armed forces right after high school. He, the Marines. Scott, the army. Despite their different service branches and lighthearted competition, they remained close until Scott married. His wife never adjusted to military life, so Scott left the service ten years ago to save the marriage. Their communication dwindled and then stopped altogether around five years ago. Something momentous must've occurred for Scott to contact him after so many years. But why this number? His personal number didn't change. Who gave him the work number?

"Scott? Wow! Great to hear from you again. How are things going, man?"

"Now that I hear your voice, better."

Tony noted the uncertainty in Scott's voice. The quivers and catches he tried to hide did not match the man of confidence he remembered.

"To be honest, things are not good. Not good at all. Rumor has it you're the man who can help me."

Nothing good ever started with a rumor.

"Really? What's wrong? Your wife ruin another transmission?" Tony's lighthearted joke fell short.

"Naw. Naw, man. That's a simple fix." The voice on the other end trembled. "Tony, they've got my daughter," Scott said, sobbing.

"What do you mean 'they've got my daughter?' Scott, who's got your daughter, and what gave you the idea I can help you recover her? I retired five years ago." Tony feinted at Scott's assumption, not knowing how much he knew or the source of his information.

"Sorry, I'm a mess."

The sound of Scott blowing his nose and clearing his throat echoed over the phone.

"I know I'm putting you on the spot, but I don't have anyone to help me. Traffickers took her. A week has passed, and I've looked everywhere. I can't find her. You're the man who can help me, I'm told. Can you?"

"Traffickers? As in human? Are you serious? Why did you call me instead of the law? Scott, I'm not a police officer. I'm retired from the military. How am I supposed to help? Who told you I could?" Tony tried to sound naïve. Who gave Scott this contact number? He met with the North Carolina State Bureau of Investigation two weeks ago. He signed on as a consultant last week. They asked for help to unravel a case involving Viktor Doroshenko and his web of corruption. Did someone on the state team become compromised? It seemed far-fetched, but every precaution needed to be observed.

"Sorry, I got ahead of myself. I'm going crazy. Gary at the SBI is the one who gave me your number. We used to work together at the Charlotte-Mecklenburg PD. When he suggested I call you, I knew there was hope. Tony, I've got nowhere else to turn."

Could Gary, the team lead, be colluding with Viktor? The timing seemed too coincidental. Tony sighed. This consultation job should've been easy. It took on a life of its own with one phone call. The timing couldn't be worse. In a few months, he planned to separate from mainstream society by moving to a self-sufficient community in the Appalachian Mountains. A town 'where nothing ever happens and everybody likes it that way' offered him the sheriff's position. A quiet life appealed to him. He should've known he wouldn't get out easily.

Tony sighed. "It's alright, Scott. Gary is right; I can help you. I needed to confirm your source before I said anything. Do you know who has her?"

"Yeah. Yeah, it's a local guy named Viktor Doroshenko. Have you heard of him?"

"I've heard of him. Give me every detail you can."

* * * * *

Tony yawned. His wife went to bed hours ago, but he couldn't stop himself once he started. No wonder Scott didn't go to the police. Viktor kept the local long arm of the law fed with incentives and kickbacks. Those he couldn't buy, he controlled with blackmail. The few honest lawmen could not touch him for fear of losing their lives or those of their loved ones.

He pinched the bridge of his nose. The next page held a face of exceptional beauty—a drop-dead gorgeous redhead with the face of an angel. The file labeled her as Viktor's wife, the principal attraction at The Fox Den, Viktor's nightclub. Besides her name, Tamsin Foxx, the woman didn't appear extraordinary. She appeared to be the typical money-hungry trophy wife.

He pulled out another picture of the woman while holding the one of Doroshenko beside her. Though photographed during the same surveillance period, the subjects' attitudes didn't align. Viktor, dressed in slacks and a button-up shirt, seemed ecstatic, displaying a smile so broad his teeth showed. The woman wore a character t-shirt and jeans with holes in the knees. Her surly frown and crossed arms showed extreme unhappiness. He picked up her stage photo again. A seasoned seductress with a come-hither expression stared back at him. Which one portrayed her true persona?

Something in the pictures nibbled at his subconscious, but he couldn't figure it out. He shoved everything back into the package. Tomorrow, he would begin his work in earnest.

He pinched the bridge of his nose again, then leaned back in his chair.

On the one hand, he hated this job. He hated the need for it to exist. At the same time, it called him. Rescuing children fed his soul, but the emotional drain from things he saw could exhaust him beyond his endurance.

Military service introduced him to far-off lands, exotic foods, and ancient customs he thoroughly enjoyed experiencing. His military travels also taught him the fabric of civilization, woven with the threads of laws and statutes, is gossamer thin and often perforated by depraved egos filled with an utter lack of human compassion. The youthful exuberance of heroics he held when first entering the Marines withered with each encounter into the warped realm of the human psyche.

He witnessed sacrifice, slavery, child brides, and bacha bazi, the practice of sexual abuse of adolescent boys by powerful warlords in Afghanistan and Pakistan. Each practice made him realize the depravities of human nature lie behind a veil of self-deception. Featherlight, the veil undulates in the currents of reality. The wearer catches limited glimpses of the horrors on the other side. Most people dismiss the fleeting view, choosing to live in their shrouded worlds where they are carefree and guiltless. You cannot return to innocence from dark to light once you find the courage to face reality. Tony left his veil of self-deception to decompose in the sands of the middle east.

Five years ago, tired of the missing children announcements crossing his news feed daily, Tony assembled a team of ex-military confidants he could trust to combat the rampant contagion corrupting those of low moral standards. They called themselves The White Knights, a throwback to the Medieval era where men of valor rose to protect the weak and guard the innocent. How much did Scott know?

He leaned forward again, resting his elbows on his desk. He stroked the glass shade of the faux Tiffany lamp his wife picked out for his home office and silently prayed to God for placing her in his life. She made his world more beautiful.

He pulled the chain on the lamp, plunging the office into darkness. He said another prayer for the strength to endure and that his memories didn't swallow him alive tonight.

3

Tony steered a rented jon boat into the darkness of the willow trees overhanging the water behind Viktor's house on Three Forks Lake. Despite the shallow depth, the nearly silent trolling motor enabled him to get right next to the bank. He clenched his teeth as branches screeched against the metal hull.

"This clinches it," Tony said, his voice a notch above a whisper. "I'm getting the pontoon boat. I'm not sitting in a bathtub to go fishing."

"How big?" his tech guru asked from underneath the tarp being used to hide the light emitting from his computer screen.

"As big as my wife will let me have."

A loud snort escaped the confines of the cover.

"Shhh!" Regardless of the cacophony of frogs and the lapping water against the floating dock where Viktor kept his boat, he knew the still, night air carried noises far from their source, especially out-of-place noises, such as a voice. The clicking of the laptop keys coming from under the tarp sounded deafening to his ears. "Are you almost done?"

"Yep. A couple more clicks, and now you're invisible."

"You're scary. What can't you do with that thing?" Tony loved technology. With it, he could walk into Viktor's run-down motel and rescue Scott's daughter without being detected. Gadgets made his job easier. Their capabilities frightened him more. A simple Linux program could hack almost any wireless equipment, including a smart car's brake system.

"Want a bigger bank account to go with your boat?"

"Are you offering yours?" Tony asked.

"I thought more like Viktor's assets."

Tony imagined Viktor waking up to an empty bank account. The boat rocked with his silent laughter. "Tempting, but traceable and against the law."

"What we're doing is against the law."

"Yeah, but not for my prosperity." A porch light appeared across the lake, and a dog barked. Time to get moving. "Okay. I'm going in."

The shadows closed around him as he slipped into the gap between the neighbor's manicured bushes and the trees in Viktor's backyard—a privacy fence separating the two yards ended where the foliage began—the moonless night created deep pockets of darkness, making him virtually undetectable in his black attire. He slinked his way to the patio door. Bars over double windows beside a smaller kitchen window caught his attention. He scanned the rest of the house. No other windows had bars for security. Secrets lay behind them.

With a click, Tony slipped the latch on the French doors leading into Viktor's home with his pocketknife. He poked his head through the opening. Light from the coffee maker enabled him to locate places to hide two of four listening devices, one under an end table in the den and the other under a console table against the wall across from the u-shaped kitchen.

The room with the barred windows lay in the dark hall beyond the kitchen. He stepped into the shadows. A regular interior door handle kept the room secure. Familiar tingles radiating from his spine signaled him to be watchful. Given the bars outside, entry into this room seemed too easy.

He used a pen light to peer under the door. He searched for tells and found nothing. Was the door even locked? He reached for the door handle.

* * * * *

Tamsin didn't care who broke into the house. This time Viktor broke not only her body but her spirit as well. He set out to teach her a lesson, and she unequivocally learned it. Do what you are told. There is no escape.

Regardless of her feelings about her husband, she called Viktor to tell him somebody had broken into the house for fear of what he might do to her if he found out she knew and said nothing. He said he was aware and already on his way home. Then the idiot told her to check on what they were doing. She rolled her eyes as she crept down the stairs that almost killed her. Despite Viktor's bravado and flexing, he possessed a coward's heart.

Tamsin raised the baseball bat she retrieved from the closet to her shoulder and tiptoed to the kitchen entrance. Light from a flashlight told her someone stood near the garage door by Viktor's office. She sidestepped into the kitchen, ready to run back upstairs if he pursued her.

"I wouldn't do that if I were you, Mister."

* * * * *

In one seamless motion, Tony turned and pulled his pistol with his right hand, bracing the weapon upon his left wrist while holding his flashlight, using the beam to blind his unexpected guest. He automatically cataloged the details—a baseball bat. Female. Short. Five feet, two or three inches. Red, curly hair. Most likely Viktor's wife. Face too bruised to recognize and broken right arm.

The woman swayed. She used the counter to steady herself. "Are you a cop?"

Her voice reminded him of a small child's. She appeared to be one, with her unicorn pajama bottoms and tank top.

"Are you a cop?" she asked again, pleading for an answer.

Abuse coincided with this line of work. Many victims carried more wounds than this girl. She must've defied Viktor somehow because an accomplice didn't wind up with her injuries. Also, according to surveillance, she wasn't supposed to be here. He had just entered unknown territory and needed to proceed with caution.

"Something like that."

The girl winced as she released her breath. Good grief. Were her ribs broken? Most women stayed in bed to nurse their wounds. She stood defiantly, refusing to yield to her pain. He lowered his flashlight for her to see without squinting.

"Are you a good cop or a bad cop?"

Tony cleared his throat. "I guess that depends on what side you're on."

She laughed but cut the sound off, biting her lip to keep from crying out. A few seconds passed before she responded to his sarcasm.

"You're a good cop."

"How old are you?" Tony asked. The file said twenty-two, but she struck him as much younger.

"Seventeen."

Tony holstered his gun, grabbed her arm, and turned her towards the back door. "I'm taking you out of here."

"You can't. Are you here to catch Viktor?"

"Don't worry yourself over Viktor. I'll take care of him." Tony tried to pull her towards the back door again, but she twisted her hand out of his grasp.

"Did you not see my face?" she asked, pointing towards herself. "I will be worried. You should as well. He knows you're here."

Her statement caught Tony off guard. "What do you…"

"I called him, but he knew you were here."

How can that be? The Wi-Fi signal to the house is jammed.

"Listen to me," she insisted. "I have a doctor's appointment at the Queen City Clinic in two weeks. The doctor takes care of the girls Viktor brings in for treatment. You need to get in touch with the nurse, Ms. Rita. The code word is Fig Newton. We'll have fifteen minutes before the doctor comes in to examine me. I'll give you more information then. You must leave because Viktor will be here in five more minutes."

"How…-"

"Mister, you should trust me. You need to leave before you learn the hard way."

Tony heard the whir of the garage door opening beyond the kitchen entrance.

"Run!"

Tony bolted, not glancing back at the sound of smashing glass. He slid under the trees into the water before rolling into the boat. He slammed the trolling motor into place and flipped the power button to bring the electric motor whirring to life. The boat spun around, creeping along in the opposite direction of Viktor's house. Tony slid onto the floor beside his partner. The larger outboard motor, which operated only in deep water, was a shield.

He saw Viktor run out on the dock and raise his arm, aiming. Tony expected to hear gunshots any second, but Viktor lowered his arm instead, then turned back towards the house.

Tony released the breath he held. That was close. "You can come out now."

His partner threw off the tarp. "What happened? You weren't in there long. What did you find?"

Tony glared back towards the house he narrowly escaped. "An accomplice."

* * * * *

Tamsin leaned against the bathroom counter, picking slivers of glass out of her hand. Maybe smashing the lamp to insinuate she tried to hit the intruder wasn't such a good idea. Viktor shoved her in his pursuit of the man. She lost her balance. Thank goodness only her hands suffered damage and not her face.

"Ow!" She sucked in her breath as she removed another piece of glass.

"You were courageous tonight, my dear." Viktor took the tweezers from her hand and gently removed the glass pieces himself.

"Thank you." Tamsin hated pretending to sound grateful for his compliments, but the platitudes fed his pride. "He still got away."

"The important thing is that you're okay. Tam, you're my wife. I'm supposed to look after you." Viktor dampened a washcloth, wiped the blood off her hands, and wrapped them in gauze bandages. He gave her a gentle hug, but the slight pressure on her ribs caused her to wince and suck in a sharp breath. He released her. "I'm sorry. Your ribs are still healing, and I caused you pain. You should return to bed."

Viktor held the covers aside for her to lie down and tucked them under her arms before sitting on the edge of the bed beside her. His every move put her on alert. His caring actions often concealed cruel intentions. *What is he scheming?* He reached into his jacket pocket and pulled out a syringe. He opened the nightstand drawer and withdrew a piece of rubber tubing.

She hated Viktor for many reasons, but getting her addicted to heroin was the one she hated him for the most. She fought her withdrawal symptoms, hoping each injection was the last. She always caved when her cravings became unbearable. She begged for relief despite knowing deliverance came at a price. No matter what Viktor asked, she complied. The addiction controlled her morals.

"I know you hate this." He wrapped the tubing around her arm, stretching it to cut off her circulation. "So, I have a proposal."

Tamsin, too scared to ask what he had in mind, questioned him in silence. Her eyes widened when Viktor pulled a bottle of pills out of the same jacket pocket he pulled the syringe from, holding both items up in front of her. *What in the world?*

"Tonight, you get to choose whether you live." Viktor shook the bottle of pills. "Or die." The syringe did not create any noise, but its silence was deafening. "

"What are the pills?" Tamsin asked.

"Methadone," Viktor said. "I'm giving you a chance to prove your loyalty. If you do what I say, you'll be drug-free one day."

Die tonight or later? Wow! Tough decision. "What do I need to do?"

"The man who broke in tonight? Tell him exactly what I say when you meet him at the clinic."

"How did you…?"

Viktor held up a small circular device. "Like your friend, I want to know what happens in this house."

Tamsin closed her eyes. So much for escaping, Viktor. She reached up and grabbed the bottle of pills.

"That's my girl."

4

The doctor's office lay on a tree-lined street resembling all the other roads in the medical district. A dentist or eye doctor could occupy the space rather than the women's clinic. The structure blended with the other brick façade buildings built during the same decade. Helping women get rid of their unwanted babies drew enough undesirable attention. They didn't need the advertisement modern architecture offered other medical facilities.

Viktor pulled into a parking space. He handed her a Bluetooth earpiece and a cell phone. "Keep it on. Understood?"

Tamsin slipped the device into her ear, covering it with her hair. "Yes."

"You remember what to tell him?"

"Yes." She bent forward to hide her eye roll.

Viktor grabbed her by the jaw. "Do not cross me this time, Tam. This is your last chance."

"Okay. I understand. I'm supposed to say you're keeping the girls in D building at the old stockyard."

"And?" Viktor prompted, releasing the pressure of his grip.

"You're sending them north this Saturday after the club lets out."

The touch of his hand turned into a caress.

"Tam, I realize you hate me right now. I shouldn't have lost my temper the way I did."

Tamsin squeezed her eyes shut. *Here it comes.*

"Regardless of whether you believe me, I am sorry."

A tear escaped her eye. His words meant naught. He gave the same apology every time, and nothing ever changed. An endless stream of pain and apologies spread before her as long as she stayed with Viktor. How many years before he ended her torment? Could she endure without losing her sanity?

She turned away from him. He wanted to hear words of forgiveness but couldn't bring herself to say them. Instead, she nodded her head, acknowledging his apology.

"I need to be hard to keep us safe. If I get caught, then you get caught."

And whose fault is that? Tamsin stared at the clinic door, remembering how everything began.

* * * * *

The night her mother brought Viktor home, Tamsin immediately knew he was her mother's new dealer. She didn't care. The woman took no interest in her. Why should it bother her if her mother killed herself with the dope she cooked up in a spoon? Her grandmother, who raised her until she passed away a few years ago, was her true mother.

After a few weeks, Viktor asked to play Call of Duty with her after her mother passed out. She shrugged. He interpreted the gesture as permission. Partnering with him against other players became a daily habit. She enjoyed having someone commiserate with her over other online players' stupid moves. It seemed natural when he started showing up at the mall while she hung out with friends at the food court. Young and gullible, she didn't realize he groomed her to accept his will the entire time.

Viktor never acted creepy or set off alarms. He befriended her, caring for her while keeping appropriate social boundaries. He played up to her insecurities, feeding her ego with words. She was prettier than her friends. He called her smile beautiful. Her laugh melodic. Her eyes mesmerizing. He also showered her with extravagant gifts: jewelry, clothes, and games. He paid for her to return to dance class. He bought anything she expressed a desire for. Then one day, he kissed her. Her innocence turned out to be her undoing.

Tamsin thought her marriage life was perfect. He didn't force her to go to school and pampered her with gifts. Viktor requested she address him as her brother to other people because he didn't want anyone asking questions about their age difference. She didn't care

22

what he wanted her to call him if she got what she wanted.

Addicted to gaming, she opened a local online group to make friends. She often invited them over to play on her awesome setup. They crashed in the game room after a marathon night of battles. Yes, she lived the dream life in her self-centered world. She never realized Viktor slipped roofies into their drinks.

While sitting in the clinic, waiting for the nurse to dispense the pills to end her first pregnancy, closed captioning flashing across the bottom of the television screen announced the discovery of the bodies of twin teenage girls in a drainage ditch in South Carolina. They disappeared the night of her last party. Tamsin became suspicious.

She spent six months scouring missing person reports and looking up suspicious deaths. When she confronted Viktor, he hit her. She tried to leave. She woke one week later with him sticking a needle in her arm.

"What are you doing?" she asked, her head spinning.

"Keeping you under control." He explained her job and what he'd do to her if she defied him. She tried to resist, but true to his words, the drug kept her under his control. Over and over, she lured innocent girls and boys into Viktor's house, only for them to disappear.

* * * * *

"I will throw a party for you when you are better."

She shrugged one shoulder.

"Hey, look at me," Viktor said, his voice growing soft. He placed his hand on her shoulder. Tamsin reached for the door handle. Viktor tightened his grip. "If you don't want a party, we'll do something else. You pick."

Tamsin pasted a smile on her face before turning to face him. "You know what I like."

"I'm doing what's best for you." He cupped her neck and pulled him towards him, kissing the top of her head. "You may not see how much I love you right now, but you will someday," he spoke into her hair. "Go. Everything is behind us after this. Okay?"

Before leaving the car, Tamsin nodded her agreement, eager to get this over herself. If praying worked, she'd spend days on her knees to be released from Viktor's control, but the God her grandmother said loved her abandoned her long ago.

She checked in before sitting to watch the muted television in the lifeless waiting room. Instead of scenic pictures, the walls held only informational posters. No live or plastic plants interrupted the monotonous gray color scheme—no magazines to peruse.

"Tamsin," Nurse Rita called from the doorway leading to the exam rooms.

The kind, elderly woman offered to help her leave Viktor after her 'tragic fall' down the stairs. She declined, not wanting to put the woman at risk.

Tamsin rose from her chair. *Here we go.*

She stopped the nurse before she opened the door. She raised her finger to her lips and then pointed towards the room, questioning silently if anyone was waiting for her.

Rita shook her head, then turned the handle.

Relief flooded her. She needn't ruin another life.

"How are you feeling today, Tamsin?" Nurse Rita laid a paper gown, a cell phone, and a folded scrap of paper on the countertop.

"A lot better than last week."

"Good. The bruising will disappear. Your foundation is fantastic, by the way. I wouldn't suspect a thing if I didn't already know."

"Thank you. Viktor hired a makeup artist to teach me. If you're interested, I can show you how to make yourself appear ten years younger."

"Thanks, but I'm proud of my wrinkles. I've earned every one of them. Hop up on the table."

Tamsin read the note while Rita placed a blood pressure cuff on her arm. The mystery intruder kept the message simple. *If you want me to trust you, you must prove yourself. I know Viktor is there. Phone active. Say what you need to say. Get rid of the phone.*

Tamsin scribbled in the air, showing she needed to write something. Nurse Rita handed her a pen. 'Can't talk. Where can I hide this?' she wrote on the note. Nurse Rita placed the black phone in the shadows under the seat of the exam table.

"Okay, you're alive and well. You know the routine. The doctor will be here soon," Rita said, acting normal.

Tamsin grinned. Nurse Rita made everything sound like a typical doctor's visit, but she winked in parting before closing the door. The woman reveled in the subterfuge.

She hurriedly hopped off the bed to change into the paper gown. At her last appointment, her slow movements enabled the doctor to catch her in her underwear. Being caught in the middle of changing creeped her out.

She sat in silence for a few minutes before Viktor spoke.

"Why aren't you talking?"

"There's no one to talk to," she said.

"Where is he?"

She could tell by the tone of his voice the news irritated him. "How am I supposed to know?" she answered with sarcasm.

"I swear, Tamsin, if you're lying to me."

"I promise, Viktor. No one is here. Come see for yourself if you don't believe me."

"Good afternoon, Tamsin," the elderly doctor said, shuffling into the room. "Nurse Rita was right. You are looking much better."

"Thanks, Doc."

"How're the ribs? Any tenderness?"

"Only when I bend wrong."

He slipped his hand inside the gown, applying pressure on her ribcage. "How about now?"

"A little, but not that bad."

The doctor scribbled on the clipboard he held. "It'll probably be tender for a while. And your arm? Any pain there?"

"No, but it's itchy, and I can't use my game controller properly. I keep dying."

"We'll remove the cast in a couple of more weeks." He continued to scribble on the board. "You play video games?"

"Oh yeah. My favorite game is The Legend of Zelda, but Viktor prefers war games like Halo. There's a huge online community, so I'm never short of gaming partners."

"That's nice," the doctor said, making small talk. "Lay back on the table so I can check your abdomen."

Tamsin stared at the ceiling while he pressed random places on her stomach, asking if she felt any pain. When the pressing turned to caress, she lifted her head to stare at him. The perv had his eyes closed.

"Hey, Doc?"

"Hmm?" he hummed, continuing his ministrations.

"Viktor pays you a lot to treat the girls at the hotel, but does he pay you to fondle his wife?" The click of Viktor hanging up the phone sounded in her earpiece.

"Oh, everybody has a price. How much did you cost, Viktor?" He couldn't hide the maleficence undertone in his voice. Tamsin shivered with aversion. Incredulously, this man scared her more than her husband.

The sound of breaking glass, followed by a startled scream, came from beyond the closed door. The doctor stared wide-eyed as he jumped away.

"A pittance. Viktor seduced my mother into signing the marriage license with the promise of a lifetime supply of drugs. She died a week later from an overdose."

Viktor burst into the room. The doctor backed against the wall at the sight of Viktor's fury. "I told you, Doc! Not her!"

The doctor turned turtle, ducking his head onto his shoulders. "Viktor, I… I… I swear. I only touched her abdomen and ribs."

Viktor glanced at Tamsin for affirmation.

"It's not where but how he touched me that matters."

Viktor turned back to the doctor. "I clean up your messes at the hotel, Doc. If you overstep again, they will find the next one with your DNA all over it. Do I make myself clear?"

The doctor nodded. "I apologize, Viktor. I don't know what possessed me."

Viktor rolled his shoulders and twisted his neck. "When can she return to dancing?" he asked in a much calmer tone.

"In a couple of months. She needs to build her strength. If she pushes too hard, she could have a setback."

Viktor clenched his fist. "Fine. Tam, get dressed. The doctor and I will finish this talk in his office."

Tamsin waited for the sound of another door closing before she retrieved the phone from the exam table. "Did you hear everything?"

"Every word. You did well. Now get rid of the phone before Viktor returns and catches you." The click of the call ending echoed in her heart. He hung up. She wanted to commiserate, celebrate their victory, and make more plans. She one-upped Viktor, and the mystery man left her hanging. Men!

Tamsin tore off her gown and dressed. By the time she finished, her disappointment had faded. If the man helped her get free of Viktor, it didn't matter how he acted. She deposited the phone into the biohazard box with a giggle. Nobody would look for a phone there. She walked out the door with renewed hope and an extra bounce in her step.

5

The Fox Den passed through a dozen owners before falling into the hands of Viktor Doroshenko. Originally designed to be a steakhouse, the building maintained the aura of a lodge-style restaurant, though ceasing to function as such several years before Viktor procured ownership. The exterior corresponded well with its name despite the uninviting fresh coat of Pepto Bismol pink exterior paint, mirrored windows, and a fuchsia neon fox with a flashing tail out front. Inside, rope lights lined the ceiling's perimeter, highlighting the vulgar purple walls of the vestibule where Tony stood waiting in line to pay the entrance fee. He glanced towards the floor, where the age of the structure became glaringly evident. No buffing and shining could hide the worn black and white checkerboard tiles.

The blood in his veins throbbed to the beat of the music permeating the thick wooden doors separating him from the entertainment going on behind them. He moved forward after paying. The throbbing increased when he placed his hand on the door, causing reverberations up his arm and into his chest, repeating the tempo of his pounding heart. He loved being face-to-face with his prey. He believed firmly in the adage, keep your friends close and your enemies closer. The threshold in front of him separated him from Viktor's inner circle. A familiar shiver ran across his spine, but excitement instead of apprehension caused the feeling this time.

For this operation, he chose the role of a middle-aged Little Italy transplant. His hooked nose and Brooklyn accent, gained by binge-watching The Godfather, added authenticity. To complete the transformation, he bleached the tips of his chestnut hair and shaved off his graying beard. Brown contacts hid his blue eyes. The memory of his wife's scream when he sprang the disguise on her brought a crooked, wolfish grin of a man on the prowl to his lips. He even found a dirt cheap, eighties model Camaro. The car possessed a showroom gleam thanks to a body wrap, but the engine sucked oil like a fish gasping for water on dry land. His smile broadened. The middle-aged man in him didn't care.

Tony pushed open the door, stepping into a den of decadence where passions overruled common sense, and a pocket full of money made you king for the night. He gave Viktor credit for the interior workings. The man possessed excellent business acumen. A prominent center stage with a dancer's pole drew the customer's attention upon entrance. Two side stages, also with poles, ran the length of the back wall. Bars serviced each end of the building. The setup heightened the entertainment factor for club patrons. The diversions being offered didn't include his purpose for being here. He prayed for covenant eyes. To see what he needed and nothing more.

Scanning the tables, he spotted an empty one near a group of college students. One wore a cone party hat with the words "Birthday Boy" printed in gold lettering. Exactly who he wanted to see.

Earlier in the day, he passed a boxing club. On a whim, he stopped in to watch the action. Before leaving, he overheard a group of young men discussing their plans for the night. When they mentioned The Fox Den, an idea formed; he and his team devised a plan that, if executed correctly, should land him a security job working for Viktor by the end of the night.

Tony sat behind them. A topless waitress sashayed over to get his order. He laid three one-hundred-dollar bills on the table, ordered a whiskey straight for himself, and a round of drinks for the birthday boy's party.

When the drinks arrived, he raised his glass in a salute with the young men and watched them down their shots without taking a sip of his own. He bought them another round. After the sixth round, their celebratory cheer escalated to the level of boisterous.

The music ceased. Tony caught movement from a darkened corner. Viktor emerged, pulling his wife behind him while walking toward the stage. He carried a wireless mic—time *to light the fire.*

"Oh, wow, they're getting ready for an auction," he said, his voice just loud enough for the party in front of him to hear.

"Sweet! Wish I had money." The birthday boy slurred his words. He turned to face Tony. "I'd bid on her in a heartbeat. She's slammin'."

"Hey! It's your birthday, right?" Tony opened his wallet and handed one thousand dollars to the young man. The money assuaged his guilty conscious for using the group. "Hope you have your best birthday ever." Tony clapped him on the shoulder.

"Sweet! For real? Thanks!" he said, fanning the money to count the bills.

Viktor, now on stage, raised the microphone to his mouth.

"Five hundred dollars!" the birthday boy shouted, leaving the room silent.

Here we go. Tony sat back in his chair, waiting for the show to unfold.

"Six hundred!" a person on the other side of the stage hollered.

The birthday boy's eyes grew wide. "Seven hundred!"

"Eight hundred," a third voice of competition burst from behind Tony.

"Nine hundred!" the birthday boy screamed, desperate to win.

"Nine-fifty!"

"One thousand! One thousand!" The birthday boy waved the money in the air, waiting for other bidders to provide a counteroffer. He jumped after a brief silence. "I won! I won!" Cheers, clapping, and catcalls erupted across the building, congratulating him.

Tony snuck a peek at the stage occupants. Viktor seemed amused. His wife's mouth hung open. The inebriated birthday boy staggered up to the stage, holding the fanned-out cash up high while his buddies cheered him on with whoops and hollers.

"Can you believe this guy?" Viktor spoke into the mic before he grabbed the money. He then used his foot to shove the birthday boy away from the stage, causing the drunken man to lose his balance and fall on the small pedestal table where his friends sat. The table tipped over, and the birthday boy landed at Tony's feet.

His plan unfolded better than he thought. He assumed Viktor would throw the man out, at which point his team planned to step in and escalate the scene into a fight. He never expected Viktor to snatch the money right out of the guy's hand. "Are you going to let him treat your boy that way?" Tony asked them while the other party members helped their friend to his feet. "If it were me, I'd get his money back."

Tony glanced up at the stage where Viktor waved the fan of money. Tamsin, with bright red cheeks and crossed arms, appeared embarrassed.

"Candy from a baby," Viktor bragged into the mic.

After a round of questioning gazes, the group rushed the platform with roars of outrage. Thunking sounds emitted from the speakers when Viktor tried to hold back his attackers by using the mic for a weapon. Bouncers converged to help their boss. The melee of males shifted over the center peninsula, grappling for control and throwing punches.

The birthday boy and his friends clearly knew how to fight. Tony enjoyed the show until Tamsin nearly fell off the stage while backing away from the fray. He caught her, spinning her out of the way before two bouncers careened off the stage behind her.

"Time to take out the trash. Are you in?" he asked, winking at Tamsin. Tony chuckled at her shocked expression when she recognized his voice. He waited for her nod of commitment before confronting the brawlers.

One by one, he removed each member of the birthday party by tapping them on the shoulder. Once becoming aware of his size, they dropped their fists. He escorted them to the exit, opening the door until only Viktor and the birthday boy remained. The bouncers were either unconscious or nursing bloody noses.

The birthday boy and Viktor slowly circled with fists raised, sizing each other up. Viktor threw the first punch. The birthday boy easily dodged the clumsy strike and returned two rapid-fire punches squarely to Viktor's nose. Blood poured out of Viktor's nostrils, staining his shirt. The man's pugilist abilities were impressive. The birthday boy pried his money out of Viktor's clenched fist before turning towards Tony with a wide grin. He then hopped off the stage and exited the building.

Tony's attention returned to Viktor. A bloodied bar towel now covered his face, and he continually hollered for Tamsin to assist him, even though she held the towel and guided him towards a door at the far end of the stage. His bouncers dutifully followed. *What a wimp.*

Tony returned to his seat. Pleased with how the evening events unfolded, he downed his drink and waited. Viktor should ask to speak with him soon.

His thoughts turned to Tamsin. In the eyes of the law, snatching her away constituted kidnapping. He debated committing the crime anyway, but he needed her to remain close to her husband for the time being. Using her weighed on his conscience, but she knew Viktor's secrets. She could expose the things he kept hidden from the rest of the world.

He checked into her background and found the typical child-of-a-drug-addict history. Her grandmother raised her until the age of twelve. Tamsin inherited the house when she died, but her mother moved back in, causing her stable and healthy environment to fall apart.

According to the neighbors, one man after another passed through the home. Tamsin exchanged her childhood friends for less influential companions. Throughout her elementary years, she kept straight A's. By the time she reached the age of fifteen, she had developed a penchant for skipping school. Her grades reflected the downfall of her home life. A more positive role model may have helped her overcome her mother's negative influences. Instead, Viktor showed up and exacerbated her downward spiral into seedier behavior.

Over the past couple of months of research and surveillance, Tony learned much about her. He probably knew her better than she knew herself. She had a favorite meal at every restaurant. He discovered what stores she shopped in and her favorite colors. He kept her company while she watched sunsets on the dock and replenished the candy she kept hidden in the bushes by the guest house. She never cried when Viktor scolded her publicly, but tears poured when no one watched. Her everyday actions led him to believe the real Tamsin to be the young girl raised by her grandmother, not the seductress Viktor paraded around town. Tony wanted to set the real Tamsin free, but her freedom had to wait for now. The knowledge she possessed mattered more.

The waitress returned, bringing Tony out of his reverie. She served him another drink and an invitation to meet the boss. He brought his glass with him. She led him through a black curtain separating the front of the house from the dressing rooms and Viktor's office.

The size of the room surprised him. He expected something more elaborate. No bigger than a walk-in closet, the aura of a restaurant office remained, even down to the terracotta-colored tiles. A filing cabinet, a desk, and a few chairs barely fit inside the small room. Viktor sat behind the desk. Tamsin stood by, holding a clean bar towel. Her expression gave Tony no clues about Viktor's mood. His eyes caught movement on the oversized television screen displaying images from each security camera.

"Ah, here he is." Viktor rose, holding out his hand.

"Viktor Doroshenko. This is my wife, Tam."

Tony nodded towards Tamsin before returning Viktor's offered shake. "Tony Pelletti."

"Mr. Pelletti. Tony, please have a seat. You're probably wondering why I've asked you back here."

Tony pulled the chair closest to him at an angle where he could escape or block the door if needed. He propped one foot on the opposite knee, then slowly leaned back before answering. "I assume this concerns what went on tonight," he said, using his New York accent.

"It does." A large image of himself appeared on the television screen. Viktor spun his chair to face the image. Tamsin backed against the wall to keep from being hit. "I reviewed the footage. Your ability to diffuse the situation with no violence impressed me. Have you worked in security before?"

Viktor brought up the subject Tony wanted. Working in the club should afford him access to Tamsin and the other employees without suspicion. Co-workers shared secrets. He planned to uncover them, and what they didn't know, Tamsin surely did.

"A time or two."

Movement outside the office caught Tony's attention. Tony turned towards the sound only when Viktor showed interest in their visitor. A bouncer shook his head. Tony returned to leaning back in his chair. The silent communication didn't concern him, but Tamsin shrinking further into the corner alerted him that something more lay beneath Viktor's niceties.

Another man joining the first added to Tony's unease. With a few more clicks, the image changed to one of himself handing money to the birthday boy. "Does your experience also include instigating others to create the very scene you so magnanimously diffused?"

The image surprised Tony. Surveillance informed him of the front-of-the-house camera locations. Per the information relayed to him, the angle needed to capture the footage now on the screen shouldn't exist. The faulty intelligence confirmed Tony's suspicion.

Someone on the state's side appeared to be compromised. Thankfully, he developed a cover story.

"You think by giving my nephew money for strippers on his twenty-first birthday; I somehow instigated what happened tonight?" Tony wanted to laugh when Viktor's jaw dropped. His attention turned to Tamsin when she coughed. She refused to meet his eyes, but her compressed lips and raised eyebrows told him she held back laughter. "I didn't realize he'd use it to bid on your wife?"

"Your nephew?"

"Yep, my sister's son. Don't tell her what I did. She'd skin me alive." Tony shifted position before continuing. "I came for the kid's birthday, but I've decided to stay awhile. I'm living with her until I find a job, and you know how family can be. I'll never hear the end of her griping if she finds out. If she tells my mother too...." Tony shook his head, then pulled his wallet out of his back pocket, flipping it open to display his New York driver's license. "Look, I'll pay for any damages." Tony snapped his fingers. "Or I could work it off if you're hiring."

"Tony. There's no need for compensation. I apologize for accusing you." Viktor clicked away the image on the television screen. "Honestly, I thought you might be one of the people snooping around, trying to cause me trouble. A couple of months ago, someone even broke into my house."

"You don't say. I'm a lot of things, but I'm no thief. Plus, I've only been here for three weeks." The tingle reappeared. Does Viktor suspect him? "Any idea of who they could be?"

"I wish I did. Then maybe I could stop them. My wife was home alone. Nearly scared her to death."

Tony didn't remember her acting frightened. In fact, in his opinion, she acted pretty boldly during her confrontation with an unknown burglar. "I can imagine." Tony rose to leave, thinking the night's work to be a bust. "Well, I hope -."

"I'm not hiring for the club, but I have the perfect job for you."

"You do?" Tony returned to the chair. What position did Viktor think a man of his stature could fill other than security?

"Yes, I do. I need someone to take care of my wife."

Tamsin, silent until now, gasped and started coughing. "Viktor! We don't even know him," she said between coughs.

"Nonsense. He's perfect for the job."

"Excuse me? What do you mean by 'take care of my wife?'"

"Allow me to explain. After falling down the stairs, Tam has been convalescing for the past few months. The doctor says she's healed enough to return to the gym to rebuild her strength. I can see from your physique you're experienced in physical fitness. You could be her trainer. Get her back into shape. She also needs someone to drive her around and stay with her while I'm away from home."

"So, you want me to babysit your wife?"

Tony glanced at Tamsin. She glared back, making her thoughts obvious. She didn't want him to be involved in her daily life. Why?

"Viktor, I don't need a babysitter."

"Of course not, my love. You need a trainer, though, and I promised you a driver so you could sleep later. Remember? He can take you shopping as well. Somebody staying with you until I get home is for my peace of mind. Tony here can fill every one of those positions. The pay will be worth all his time away from his family."

Tony caught the undertone of mockery in Viktor's voice.

"But-."

"That's enough, Tam."

Tony watched the color drain out of Tamsin's face before breaking eye contact with him. He didn't think it was possible, but she retreated further, seeming to fold into herself to escape the anger in Viktor's voice. Her reaction ignited his protective instinct. "How about this?" he said. "I'll try the job. We'll give it a few weeks. If it doesn't work out, no hard feelings."

"Agreed. You can start tonight." Viktor dug a set of keys out of his pocket and laid them on the desk. "Take my wife home. She's not feeling well. I won't return until early morning. There's a guest house by the dock. Sleep there."

"You're the boss." Tony snatched the keys off the desk and turned towards the doorway. The two bouncers blocked his exit using their collective size for intimidation. Tony smirked. "Hey, Boss. You want to call your goons off, or is this a test?"

Viktor waved them away.

"Tony, you forgot your drink."

He didn't forget his drink. He didn't trust its purity. "One's my limit."

"A man with principles. I like that. People are weak when presented with temptation." Viktor picked up the drink and downed the brown liquid in one gulp. "Of course, temptation is a lucrative business."

Tony's skin crawled. His instincts told him the business Viktor spoke of didn't refer to the club. The man even exonerated himself by blaming others' inability to control themselves. He wanted to punch the smirk Viktor displayed off his face. He quieted his temper, reminding himself of the impending collapse of Viktor's empire.

"Tam, you can leave. I have work to do," Viktor said, dismissing them.

Tony stepped aside, permitting Tamsin to lead the way.

* * * * *

Outside, Tamsin followed the mysterious intruder named Tony to his car. Up close, wearing regular clothes, he didn't intimidate her as much as he did when he broke in. His larger-than-life build seemed approachable. The absence of his beard exposed loose skin around his jawline. His dark brows enhanced his eyes. She saw the wisdom gained when you've seen too much in them. The same expression stared back at her whenever she looked in the mirror. She recognized him as a kindred spirit instead of an imaginary hero outside her reality.

She must keep Viktor from discovering his identity. She tried her best to deter him from taking the job. Why did he ignore her protests? He said to trust him, but could she? The man couldn't take a hint. He didn't know Viktor the way she did, either. *This will be a nightmare.*

"The car's over there," she said, pointing. Her frustration over this recent development enhanced her southern accent.

"Hang on. I need to get my bags."

Ugh! She stomped her foot on the pavement. He sounded so nonchalant. How could he be so aloof? "Look, Mister."

"Tony."

"Look, Tony. You do not know what you're getting into."

"Oh?" He slung a large duffle over his shoulder. "Why don't you enlighten me," he said before shutting his trunk and walking away.

Tamsin stepped quickly to catch up to him, practically running to keep up with his long strides.

"I don't want-"

"What you want doesn't matter. Your husband wants you chauffeured around town. I needed a job to get close to him. Now I get to play nursemaid to his barely legal, spoiled rotten arm candy. Lucky me."

Barely legal? How did he know it's my birthday? "Wait a minute. What do you mean, spoiled rotten?"

"Mrs. D, Tam, or whatever I should call you, I've been up almost twenty-four hours, and I am tired. I don't feel like hashing this out tonight. Can we talk after I get some sleep?"

The exhaustion in his voice made her feel guilty. She didn't want to argue, but he needed to leave. "I didn't realize-"

"There's a lot you don't realize, but we can discuss everything later. No more arguments. I'm taking you home."

He begged for understanding with his eyes. She wondered what he spent his day doing for him to be this tired. What kind of stress must he be under to develop such deep eye bags? She gave in to his request with a nod, knowing nothing but disaster would follow.

6

Tamsin jolted awake. Uneasiness toyed with her memory, prohibiting further rest. The clock on the nightstand told her she slept an hour later than usual. She rolled onto her back. The covers lay smooth on Viktor's side of the bed. His not returning home last night didn't bother her. He often stayed at the hotel after her fall.

Fall? The man threw her down the stairs. She needed to quit adopting Viktor's thinking and words. Though now aware of the habit, breaking the cycle proved difficult. She tried to erect boundaries between her thinking and Viktor's mind control, but the lines kept blurring. Did she know her true self anymore? If she ever escaped Viktor, she... then she remembered who brought her home from the club. Despite her protests, the mysterious man agreed to work for Viktor. She pressed two fingers against the space between her eyebrows. Great. Another day starting with a headache.

"Not feeling well, my dear?" Viktor asked as he entered the bedroom.

Tamsin jumped. "Viktor, you startled me. And no, my head hurts."

"That's what happens when you sleep too long." He sat beside her, taking out her pills from his coat pocket. "These will help, but before I give you one, I'm asking again, are you sure you don't recognize him?"

Tamsin hated her body's reaction. The bottle and its contents distracted her. The clicking sound of the little white tablets when Viktor moved his hand triggered a cerebral addiction response. She missed the euphoric feeling the heroin supplied. The methadone eased her suffering. As long as Viktor dispensed the medication on schedule, she could be drug-free soon.

Getting clean came with a price beyond measure. If she betrayed Tony, she lost the one chance she had left to escape, but if she crossed Viktor, she would lose her own life. Either way, she ended up losing. "I told you last night. Whoever broke in had a beard."

Viktor pinched her chin and turned her face towards him. "And since you've spent time with him?"

Focusing on Viktor's question required the whole of her willpower. Like the heroin, he used the pills to control her, withholding them until he got the desired results. She couldn't afford mistakes. Tony's life depended on her keeping his identity a secret. "He doesn't sound the same either. Tony's voice is deeper, and he speaks with a New York accent. The guy who broke in spoke with a southern drawl."

Viktor searched her eyes. She dared not move. Any hesitancy, and he would know she didn't tell him the complete truth. "You heard his voice on the recordings from that night, didn't you? They're not the same guy."

"Alright." He opened the bottle and doled out her pill. "Keep me informed if he does anything odd."

Tamsin nodded before popping the tablet in her mouth and running to the bathroom to wash it down. Did Viktor catch her evasion? She knew Tony disguised his voice while sitting in the office last night. How long before she slipped up and exposed his identity? Too bad Tony didn't possess enough sense to stay far away. She hoped she could convince him to leave soon. Until then, he needed what little protection she could provide.

Viktor followed her into the bathroom. "I'm meeting with my broker in a couple of hours."

Tamsin inhaled the stream of water coming from the tap and began choking. By 'broker,' he meant partner, which told her he was planning something. Likely, something to do with Tony. Was Viktor setting Tony up? She turned off the faucet before meeting his challenging expression in the mirror. He knew bringing up his partner always triggered her anger. He wanted a fight. She added a dollop of toothpaste to her toothbrush. "Okay," she said before sticking the brush in her mouth. *I'm not giving you what you want.*

"I'll start your coffee."

"Mmm hmmm." She forced herself to continue brushing her teeth once he left. She needed to calm her nerves and control herself. Tony couldn't afford for her to panic and do something stupid. While dressing, she contrived a plan to oust him from her life before whatever Viktor was scheming unfolded. She'd try to convince him to quit one more time, and if she failed, she'd tell Viktor that Tony had made a pass at her. Viktor's possessive nature might cause the man a beating, but bruises had to be better than dying if Viktor discovered his true identity.

Resolute, she hurried towards the smell of freshly brewed coffee. Her giant mug waited on the counter to be filled with decadent Irish Cream creamer and the black liquid that warmed her soul. This ritual became one of her few enjoyments after marrying Viktor, and she rarely deviated from the routine. She stuck her nose to the carafe and inhaled. Movement across the yard caught her attention. What on earth?

She returned the coffeepot to the burner before pouring her coffee, moving closer to the kitchen window, astonished by what she saw. Tony danced around the backyard, swatting an unseen enemy.

"What's he doing?" Viktor asked from behind her.

"Something odd," she replied before she could stop herself.

"Oh, haha. One of those days, huh?" he said, referring to her uncontrolled sarcasm.

"Apparently so."

"Well, it's a good thing I'm leaving. Otherwise, you'd be in for a rough day."

Tamsin grimaced a reply. She knew better than to goad him. While getting ready, she roleplayed arguing with Tony in her mind, and the mood never left her. "Sorry. I guess my head still hurts a bit."

Outside, Tony defeated his unseen attacker and turned towards the French doors.

"Drink your coffee. You're happier when you're full of caffeine and sugar. I'm gone. Remember to keep your phone with you if you go somewhere."

Before she could form a reply, Tony knocked on the back door. Viktor headed in the opposite direction. Maybe she imagined the urgency of his exit, but he appeared to be avoiding his new employee. Before opening the back door, she shrugged off Viktor's odd behavior.

"Oh, good. You're up," Tony said, pushing his way inside.

"Yes, I'm awake." She followed Tony into the foyer.

"He upstairs?"

"You just missed Viktor." She turned towards the kitchen and her yet-to-be-poured coffee.

"Your husband's a coward. I think he was aware of the wasp nest over the door."

"So that's what you were doing. We thought you were practicing a weird mating ritual." The words sprang out before she could stop them. What made her say such rude things? She didn't know this man and, despite not wanting him here, knew he worked to expose Viktor's crimes. He deserved respect for his effort, if nothing else. She turned to apologize but became distracted by the large welt on his arm. "You got stung. I have something for the pain." She grabbed his wrist to pull him along. He remained in place.

"It's only a bee sting. I'll live."

"There's no sense suffering. I know stings hurt." She tugged on his arm, to no avail. "Come on." She pulled again.

"I don't need to be doctored for a wasp sting." He jerked out of her grasp.

Tamsin retreated at his tone of voice. Viktor spoke with the same level of irritation when he tired of her nagging him. "I… I'm sorry. I only wanted to help." She turned and walked to the kitchen.

Tony sighed in exasperation. "What are you going to do?" Tony asked.

"Nothing weird. My grandmother taught me a simple home treatment."

"What? Tobacco? I've tried that one before, and like most folk remedies, it didn't work."

"I know. That's why this is my remedy." She pulled an onion from the cupboard, holding it up for him to inspect. "When spring arrives, I always buy onions for bee stings, just in case." She placed a cutting board on the counter. "My grandmother used to tape slices to the bottom of my feet when I was little. I got stung a lot because I never wore my shoes. One time, a hornet got me on the rear end. I was sitting there, drinking Kool-Aid, minding my business, and bam! Right on my left cheek. I screamed bloody murder. When my grandmother applied the onion, I went from a screaming banshee to 'ahhh' because it works quickly." She cut a slice, bringing out the juices with the knife's edge. "Here, try it. The onion cools while easing the pain."

Tony extended his arm for her to lay the slice on the welt. "Wow. Amazing. The pain just disappears."

"I know, right? I'll get you a bandage. The longer you keep it on, the better."

"There's no time. We need to go."

"Go? I haven't even sipped my first cup of coffee."

"We'll stop on the way."

"Well, I should get my purse."

"You won't need it," he said, grabbing her arm and pulling her out the door.

* * * * *

"Are you taking me to Carowinds?" Tamsin's jaw dropped. She sat straighter in her seat when they joined the line of cars entering the amusement park. Every summer, she begged to go when she saw the commercials on TV. Her grandmother could never afford it, her mother didn't care about anything she wanted, and Viktor always said he was too busy. She barely contained her excitement.

"Yeah. I planned to go before I got hired to be your babysitter."

Tamsin stuck her tongue out at Tony.

He laughed.

The queue moved quickly, and Tony parked the car. Tamsin opened the door before Tony cut the ignition.

"You're not excited, are you?" he asked.

"A little. I've never been before." She smiled and left the car. Tony met her at the bumper.

"To be honest. I'm pumped too. I haven't been here since I was a teenager. Let's get our tickets."

Tamsin walked a few steps before stopping. "You dropped your accent," she blurted out.

"I don't need to keep up the pretense when I know Viktor isn't listening."

His statement caught her off guard. Did he know about the listening devices? "Wow, you're not as dumb as I thought." The words flew past her lips before thinking. Ingrained to respond to Viktor's

42

chastisements with regret whenever she made careless statements, she backed away from Tony before giving him a chance to react. "I'm sorry. I shouldn't have said that. Viktor hates when I don't think before speaking."

Tony stopped her retreat by laying a hand on her shoulder. "For starters. I'm not Viktor. Your teenage sass doesn't faze me. I will never hurt you. Ever. Don't be afraid of me. Understood?"

Tamsin nodded. "I am sorry, though."

"Apology accepted. Also, you are correct. I am not dumb, but I have unanswered questions about how Viktor's operation works. I brought you along in the hopes you can fill in the blanks. The quicker you're out of danger, the better. Today, we'll talk business where no one can overhear us. Every other day, I'm only your trainer and chauffeur. Okay?"

She nodded. "You should know something about me before we talk."

With a smile on his face, Tony started walking again, his long strides eating up the pavement in front of him. "Oh yeah? What do I need to know?"

Tamsin skipped to keep up with him. "I'm not a good liar. Viktor still suspects you're the man who broke into our house. I told him you didn't look or sound the same. I think he believed me, but I'm not sure. Also, he told me to inform him if you exhibit any odd behavior."

"Noted. I have a trick you can use to make Viktor think you're lying when, in reality, you're telling the truth. I'm aware I'll be under intense scrutiny. He may suspect me, but he will never be one hundred percent sure," he said with a shrug.

"But you don't understand. If he finds out who you are, he'll kill you."

Tony halted. "Look. What do you want me to call you? Tam? Mrs. D?"

"Tamsin. I've never liked Tam, and Mrs. D sounds old."

"Tamsin, this is not my first rodeo. I understand the dangers involved. I can handle whatever Viktor throws at me. Okay?"

She crossed her arms and cocked her head to the side. He thought he knew Viktor better than she? Ha! He didn't have a clue. "Oh? You're aware? You can handle Viktor? If I didn't stop you from going into his office, you'd be dead now."

"Oh? How so?"

"After I tried to run away, he rigged the office door to electrocute anyone who touches the doorknob."

"You tried to run away? Is that the reason Viktor beat you up?"

Tamsin nodded in silence. She should've realized Tony would have questions about that night. She wasn't ready to revisit the memory of her injuries, nor did she want to tell Tony or anyone else that, after Viktor threw her down the stairs, he punched her in the abdomen until she miscarried. He told her that he'd ensure she could never have a child if she defied him again. Tamsin retreated from Tony, crossing her arms and looking away.

"How does he get in?"

"Remote control."

"See. That is the type of information I need to know."

Tony sounded upbeat, but she still reeled from her re-surging memories. She kept her head bowed to hide the tears in her eyes.

Tony leaned down, peering into her face. "You ready to go inside, or do you need a minute?" he asked teasingly, trying to coax a grin from her.

Tamsin tried to resist.

"Come on. Today is the last day to ride Thunder Road."

"What's Thunder Road?"

"The first roller coaster I ever rode. It will be the last too."

"The last one? Why?"

"The reason is personal. I might tell you one day. Let's enjoy ourselves and forget everything else for a while. Okay?"

Maintaining his wide grin, Tony crooked his arm out to escort her. She hesitated. Forget everything else? The possibility enticed her. Tony wiggled his brows. Could she forget her worries? He believed you could. She hesitated a moment before unfolding her arms to take his elbow. "For a while," she said, faking her confidence.

7

The impulsive decision to include Tamsin on his Carowinds trip was one of Tony's better ideas. Initially, he wanted only to get her to a location where they could discuss Viktor's activities uninhibited by listening devices, such as the ones he found in the guest house.

Spending time in an amusement park with a sassy teenager did not appear on his bucket list. His wife and he, unable to have biological children, chose not to adopt because of his life in the military. After just a few hours with Tamsin, he realized how much they had missed. Her childlike enthusiasm over the attractions renewed his timeworn soul.

His ruse to get her alone became a day of firsts for her: her first roller coaster ride, funnel cake, and carnival games. Seeing and experiencing the rides and entertainment through her unrestrained energy brought Tony a joy he never knew he lacked. He didn't have a name for the feeling until one carny needled him to win a prize for his daughter. Then he understood the sentiment to be what a parent feels for their child. It also explained the ridiculous amount of cash he spent shooting targets only to wind up with the tiny, pink stuffed dog she now cradled in her arms.

He contemplated this foreign emotion while they went to the cabana he rented, where they could eat lunch and talk in privacy. He picked an open-faced tent between the wave pool and the roller coaster. Tony figured the constant drone of the waves and the excited chatter of children playing should keep their conversation from being overheard.

"Is that the roller coaster you were talking about?" Tamsin asked.

"It is. I have fond memories of riding it." He chuckled. "I got my first kiss on that thing." He stared at the ride, lost in the memory of the first time he kissed his wife.

"Did you love her?"

"Still do," he said without thinking. "What I mean is-." He sighed in frustration, putting his hands on his hips, so much for keeping his private life private. Her lighthearted manner transgressed his defenses. He couldn't afford slips of the tongue. He wanted to trust her, but, considering Tamsin's admission that Viktor could detect her lies, he thought it best not to divulge details of his real life.

"You still love the first girl you ever kissed? That is so romantic."

The wistfulness of her voice eased Tony's apprehension. She's lovelorn. He couldn't blame her for latching onto the sentimentality of his memory. Given the cold-hearted man she married, she must crave loving affection. From his observation, the only time Viktor paid attention to his young wife was when he benefited from her work.

An idea formed in his head that went against every boundary he set to keep from becoming invested in his job. He knew better than to become attached to any of the girls he rescued. It always led to heartache. Acting upon his current thoughts would extend the investigation. Despite all the internal arguments he raised, he spoke the words to start his course of action. "Tamsin? Have you ever been to the zoo?"

"No."

"Biltmore House?"

Again, she answered no.

"Grandfather Mountain? Hanging Rock? Anywhere in the mountains? The beach?"

With each question, she shook her head.

"My grandmother wasn't well, and we never had enough money for extras. I didn't realize it, but she used almost her entire savings for my dance lessons, my one indulgence. When she passed away, there was barely any left to pay for her cremation. My mother didn't even buy her an urn. She just stayed in a cardboard box on the shelf. I don't know what happened to her after Viktor sold the house." Tears formed, spilling across her cheeks. She erased their tracks with the palms of her hands. "I miss her."

Tony didn't mean to stir her memories. With an awkward hand, he patted her shoulder until she composed herself. His practical nature leaned towards problem-solving. He couldn't fix grief and never felt comfortable when it arrived. "It wasn't my intention to make you sad. Since we have to spend time together, I thought I could take you to places you have never been."

She sniffed and wiped the remaining moisture from her eyes. "You'd do that?"

"Well. Sure. We can do training outside of a gym. We should be able to pull off a few day trips without raising suspicion."

Fresh tears formed, and she threw her arms around his waist. Tony stiffened. His hands hovered above her shoulders, not sure what he should do. He didn't expect her to have such a physical outpouring of emotion.

"Thank you for caring about me." She raised her head to look at him.

Her tear-filled eyes broke Tony's heart. How long has it been since she felt love without an agenda? After her grandmother's death, he guessed never. Tony grimaced at her upturned face, her eyelashes laden with moisture—poor girl. Without thinking, he wiped her tears. "This will not be fun and games. Viktor hired me as your trainer, so you will have to train. It's going to be work." He grasped her shoulders, pushing her away. "Speaking of which," he said, turning her around and pointing her in the direction he wanted her to go. "It's time for our talk. Meet me in the last cabana. I'll be back with lunch soon."

"Tony?"

"Yeah?"

"You.... I...." She sighed. "Nevermind."

"Don't worry, Tamsin. Everything will be okay. Wait for me in the cabana. I ordered a pizza for our meal."

When she entered the little blue and white striped tent, Tony left to find his contact. He figured she doubted his plan to chaperone her around the state. Determination quickened his steps. He would not let her back out. She needed more enjoyment in her life, and he planned to give it to her. He already had some destinations in mind.

Tamsin paced the open end of the tent. She tried relaxing on one of the chaise loungers, but her thoughts and nerves kept her active. Tony's offer to take her sightseeing made her forget any danger he might face if he remained working for Viktor. She swayed between keeping her mouth shut because she really, really wanted to go to the places he mentioned and to do the right thing by convincing him to quit. She wanted both. Maybe she could visit a few destinations before mentioning him quitting again?

She spotted him approaching from several cabanas away, holding a large pizza box up in the air. Children darted between the other tents and the wave pool. He smiled at their antics. He appeared to be an ordinary man enjoying a day of fun. Then she thought of Viktor, and her decision became clear.

"It's a minefield around here with all the kids running everywhere," he said, laughing as he reached her. "Hope you're hungry. I ordered a large." He sat on one of the lounge chairs, placed the box on the side table between them, flipped the lid open, and rubbed his hands together. "Mmmm. Philly cheesesteak with the works. Dig in while it's hot."

Tamsin teetered on the edge of the chair across from him. "Tony-."

"Eat," he said around the food in his mouth. "Have some water."

She waited until he dug a bottle out of the bag he brought back and handed it to her before she started again. "Tony, I-"

"Can this wait until after we eat?"

"This is important, and I need to say it before I change my mind."

Tony sighed, removed an electronic device from the bag, and laid it in the space left vacant from his eaten slice of pizza.

"What's that?"

"Recorder." He lifted another slice of pizza out of the box. "So I don't forget anything," he said, explaining the need for the equipment.

"Tony, I appreciate your offer to take me places I've never been, but you must quit. It's--"

"I'm not quitting," he said around a mouthful of food.

"But you have to quit. You don't understand."

Tony gulped his water, making the plastic crack as he inhaled the contents. "I'm not quitting," he said before starting a third slice. "You said that Viktor believes I'm the man that broke into his house. That means that he suspects you're lying to him. It will make him suspicious if I quit right away. In his mind, it'll be confirmation you lied about my identity. What do you think he'll do to you?" He finished the slice he held. "No. The best course of action is to continue this charade. It'll confuse him when nothing happens. If he does discover you lied, I can be there to protect you."

His logic frustrated her. She wanted him to be wrong. He wasn't, and it angered her. She shot to her feet. "If you don't quit, I'll make you get fired."

Tony burped. "Sorry. That came out of nowhere." Through eating, he leaned back in the lounge chair, resting his head on his forearm. "What are you going to do? Say I came on to you?"

Tamsin's mouth dropped open. How did he know?

"Stop trying to get rid of me. You're safer with me around."

"You don't understand," she pleaded.

Tony shot up from his resting position to tower over her. The move spawned her flight response, and she jerked backward, tripping over the edge of the lounge chair. Tony's arm shot out, catching her before she fell.

"Then make me understand, Tamsin. You're the one that asked me to trust you. Your offer to help is why I'm here, but now, all you're doing is trying to get rid of me. What are you not telling me? Why are you keeping his secrets? Help me to help you escape. Give me something to put him behind bars where he belongs."

Fresh tears welled in her eyes. His plea cracked her shell of self-preservation, but Viktor's threats kept her lips sealed. She wouldn't live long if Viktor found out she had revealed the mechanics of his enterprise. Did it matter when she died, though? Eventually, he would sell or kill her once her usefulness ended.

"We've been digging for months. We know he's trafficking, but we can't produce any physical evidence. He appears to be a normal, everyday businessman. We even planted listening devices most everywhere he goes, and we've got nothing." Tony sat back, rubbing his spikey, short hair. "There must be something we're missing. At this rate, we'll never be able to stop him."

Tony's frustration seeped into her. She understood how he felt. In the past, she felt discouraged over her inability to escape. She was powerless. Today might be her only opportunity to end Viktor's reign of terror over her. He wasn't here to intimidate or stop her from telling Tony what she knew, and Tony couldn't stop Viktor without her revealing all of Viktor's secrets. If she kept silent, she became a willing accomplice. Her gut recoiled in horror at the thought. She'd never be able to live with herself if she didn't reveal the details of Viktor's operation. A surge of bravery coursed through her.

"That's because he speaks in code."

"In code? How? Give me an example."

Tamsin sat on the lounger and picked up a slice of pizza. The aroma awakened her hunger. "Take today, for instance. He went to see his broker."

"We've listened to their conversations. They center on investing. Stocks and bonds and such."

"They might use investment terms, but the stocks and bonds they're discussing are people. Dividends are his profits. Penny stocks are the strung-out women turning tricks at the motel. Viktor is their supplier. He gives them as many drugs as they want and a place to live while taking all their earnings. If they become disobedient, he cuts them off until they come running back, willing to do anything he says for a freebie fix. Next is common stocks. The kids labeled as runaways. Nobody tries to find them because they have a history of trouble at home or are in the foster care system. There are brothels full of those kind of kids in the city. The big money makers are preferred stocks—Mommy and Daddy's precious babies that make the news. Disease free and easily intimidated into submission because they've had everything handed to them on a silver platter. They're chosen because they fit a specific criterion. They are auctioned, and Viktor rakes in the dough."

She took another bite of the pizza, chewing it ferociously, watching him, waiting for all the details to click into place. It didn't take him long. His face turned red with anger.

"And bonds," he growled.

"Those are clients. There are different levels of those too. Corporate bonds are average businessmen. Municipal bonds are people like mayors and judges." She licked the little salty crumbs off her fingers before picking up another slice. She didn't realize how hungry she was.

"Are there higher levels?"

"Mmm hmm. Treasury bonds are senators, presidents, princes, and sheiks." She tore off a massive chunk of the slice with her teeth, devouring it. "This is good pizza. I've never had pizza with white sauce before."

"You've got sauce on your chin." Tony handed her a napkin. "So, what are you?"

"What do you mean?" she asked, wiping her face.

"Does he have a name for you in this code language?"

The food in her mouth turned to sawdust. She swallowed before laying the rest of the slice back in the box. "I'm equity."

"Meaning?"

"It means I'm worth more to him than the money he invested."

"I'm not following. Besides dancing at the club, how do you make him money?"

"You know how Viktor said you could take me shopping last night?" She waited for his confirmation. "Well, shopping also has another meaning, and that's why you must quit. He's setting you up."

Tony nodded his head, digesting what she had told him. "Humph. He can try. Tell me what shopping is and how it factors into his scheme."

Tamsin launched into the story of how Viktor encouraged her to start a local online gaming group for teens. Once a month, they held meet and greets at the mall in Concord. The club grew fast. One time, they had over fifty members attend.

She enjoyed the camaraderie of the gaming community. There was always someone to keep her company when Viktor left her alone for extended periods. Before long, he suggested she invite her friends over for gaming parties. The parties turned into sleepovers because her big brother let them have alcohol. When she woke up the next day, someone was inevitably missing.

"Viktor said, 'oh, they went home.' I became suspicious when they discovered the bodies of the twins."

"So, Viktor is using your social media account to target his victims? And every one of his targets was in your house?"

"Yep. Didn't you catch my hint? I mentioned gaming on the phone call at the doctor's office."

Tony shook his head. "I wish I had. I paid more attention to what Viktor said about the doctor."

"Well, Viktor hasn't been active since you arrived on the scene, but you watch; in a month or two, he'll suggest a party. You'll take me to the mall for a meet and greet. I announce I'm having a gaming party. After everyone is out of it, he'll do a live video stream, and his client picks out which one they want. He calls it shopping."

"And with me staying in the guest house, it'll be easy to make me the fall guy if anything happens. Knowing Viktor, I'm sure he plans for something to go wrong. There are only a few organizations that operate undercover to fight human trafficking. With mine out of the way...." He quickly locked the bag in the lock box the park provided. "Well, that is not going to happen." He rubbed his hands together, then stretched his shoulders. "All right, the discussion is over. Let's go ride a roller coaster."

Tamsin couldn't believe it. She just informed him that his life was going to be ruined if he kept working for Viktor, and he acted like it was a game. "Are you insane?" She believed it might be a distinct possibility. "I told you how much danger you're in, and you're like, 'let's go ride a roller coaster,'" she said, mocking him. "For real?"

Tony returned to sit in front of her. He picked up both of her hands, covering them with his own. "Tamsin, I know you don't understand, and I know you don't know me, but if we're going to come out of this alive, I need you to trust me. If we're going to stop Viktor, you must let me do my job."

Tears welled in her eyes again. She held one piece of information that Viktor didn't know she knew. With the variety of drugs the doctor prescribed her after Viktor threw her down the stairs, she should've been asleep, but the medication had the opposite effect. So, she lay wide awake when the sound of arguing reached her ears. The porch light on the guest house illuminated Viktor and another man she'd never seen before. The argument turned into a scuffle. Viktor pulled out a knife and sliced the other man's throat. Blood splattered across the side of the guest house. Tamsin covered her mouth to keep her scream from escaping before running to the bathroom to vomit.

"Tony. He will kill you. I... I've seen him do it. Please, quit before it's too late." Her voice, tainted with fear, came out in a tearful quiver.

Tony's calmness evaporated. His gentle clasp turned into a tight grip. "You watched him kill someone? Are you sure?"

"I know what I saw," she said. "He took the body off in his boat. The next day when I woke up, he was painting the guest house."

"Would you recognize who he killed if I show you a picture?"

"I think so," she nodded.

Tony retrieved the bag and pulled out a black-ringed notebook. He flipped the pages to the one he wanted. "Is this him?"

"Yeah, that's him. And that's Scott. He was a regular at the club. He was always so nice. I wonder why he stopped coming."

"You know him?"

"Yeah. Well. As much as possible. He didn't come in often until the night he got drunk. Viktor was going to throw him out. He started yelling. 'I know who you are. I know what you do. Do you think you can throw me out? I know somebody that can shut this club down, shut you down, and shut down this whole town.'" Tamsin mimicked the gestures made by the drunken Scott. "Then he goes, 'All I've got to do is make a phone call.'" She splayed her thumb and pinky and held it up to her ear.

"Next thing you know, Viktor and he are best buddies. I spent many nights falling asleep in a booth after closing while they drank until dawn."

Tony cleared his throat before speaking. "Did you overhear any of their conversations?"

"No. Although, one night, their laughter woke me. They were talking about knights in shining armor or something to that effect. I rolled over in my booth and went back to sleep."

"Could it have been White Knights you heard?"

"Maybe. I didn't pay that much attention," she said, shrugging one shoulder. "I'll never see one of those." When Tony appeared, she hoped he might be the person to get her out, but he was determined to remain in Viktor's clutches. It was only a matter of time before Viktor figured out his identity. If Tony didn't end up in jail because of Viktor's machinations, he'd die and be hauled off in Viktor's boat like the other guy. Such a waste. She sighed and flipped the page in the notebook.

"Don't!" Tony said too late.

"Oh. It's them." The pages before her held the pictures of dozens of missing children. The faces she knew jumped out at her. "This one," she said, pointing to the image of a chubby teenage boy with curly, dirty blonde hair and freckles.

"Tamsin, you don't have to do this today. It can wait."

"Don't you need to know?"

"Yes, but it can wait," he said, reaching to take the notebook.

"No," she said, snatching it out of his grasp. "It needs to be done now." Nobody would know which children were missing if she died because of Viktor. She jabbed her finger at a girl with brown hair and braces. "This one too."

Tony started placing stickers next to each picture she pointed to. It didn't take her long to identify almost twenty children. She slammed the cover shut and shoved the book at Tony.

He took her hands in his again. "Tamsin, thank you. You've been very brave today."

She wiped tears from her eyes and sniffed. She didn't feel brave. Identifying those kids exhausted her emotionally. She remembered their laughter and the things they said. Now they were gone. Most likely, all of them were dead. "Tony, I think I need to ride your roller coaster now."

8

"Ugh, I am exhausted," Tamsin laughed as she entered the house through the garage door entrance. "I wasn't aware having fun could take so much out of you." She kicked her shoes off by the console table before laying her stuffed dog on the peninsula and turned to open the fridge, sticking her head inside. "You want something to drink?" she asked.

"Yeah, water."

She handed him a bottle without looking. For herself, she took out a Starbucks Frappuccino. Before she removed the lid, Tony grabbed it, put it back in the fridge, and replaced it with water. "Hey! I wanted that."

"Drink this instead. We will begin your training tomorrow. You need to get hydrated." He brought his own bottle to his lips. His eyes drilled into hers.

His stare reminded her of their conversation before leaving the park. To mislead Viktor, they needed to continue playing their roles. He, the bully trainer. She is the spoiled rotten trophy wife.

"Fine." She tried twisting off the lid. When it didn't budge, she slammed the bottle on the counter. She'd never admit to needing a trainer, but her broken arm's disuse caused more strength loss than she thought. She braced herself against the counter. "You were a lot more fun at the park, despite putting me on a roller coaster I nearly flew out of." She picked up the knife lying on the cutting board, intending to clean up the mess left when Tony rushed her out the door.

"You weren't in danger of flying away." He twisted the lid off for

55

her and made a scoffing sound. "It's not like you're an angel or something."

Using the knife as an extension of her finger, she pointed it at him. "Well, at least I don't have horns like you."

"Touché." Tony pointed at the onion. "I am impressed by your southern doctoring skills, though. I thought everyone down here slapped tobacco on whatever ails you. Perhaps you're an angel of mercy. Cut another slice of that onion. I'll tape it on this time, as you suggested earlier."

"I don't think it will work as well."

"It doesn't hurt to try."

She braced the knife against the onion before applying pressure to cut into it.

"Well, it's nice to see you returned my wife in one piece," Viktor said out of the darkness of the hallway.

Tamsin's hand holding the knife jumped, slicing the blade into her finger. She sucked in her breath, grabbing her wounded appendage. Tears welled in her eyes. Her bottom lip quivered. She didn't know if she had nicked herself or almost sliced off her finger. All she could do was stand there holding it while her heart pounded.

Tony yanked off several paper towels from the nearby roll.

"Tamsin, you are such a klutz," Viktor scolded as he hurried over to them. "How bad did you cut it?" He grabbed the wad of towels from Tony. "Here, let me see."

Viktor led her to the sink, turning on the overhead light to inspect the wound. He clucked over her worse than a mother hen. Like the night he broke in, his solicitous conduct toward her injury warned her he held a hidden agenda. *What was his game?*

"Well, it's deep, but I don't think you need stitches." He wrapped the towels around the wound and applied pressure. "Tony, will you fetch the first aid kit from under the hall bathroom sink?"

With Tony's back turned the pleasant expression on Viktor's face disappeared. He squeezed her finger harder. "When I get you alone...," he whispered in her ear.

She knew an ulterior motive lay behind his solicitous behavior. Something had angered him. Did it have to do with the broker? Or worse? Did someone follow them today? Did Viktor know what she told Tony? No. No, that couldn't be it. There's no way he could know. Something else triggered his anger.

"Here you go, boss," Tony said, re-entering the kitchen area. "And this cell phone was lying on the vanity."

"Thanks, Tony. Just lay them here," pointing to the countertop."

"Alright, boss. If you need nothing further, I'm calling it a night."

"I think I can handle this. Thank you for keeping my wife entertained today."

"No problem. See you in the morning, Mrs. D."

"See you in the morning." Her voice was quiet. Now she knew Viktor's anger stemmed from not knowing what she had said to Tony. He set her phone up to listen to her conversations when he wasn't with her, and she left it at home after he reminded her to take it with her.

"I'm sorry. I won't forget it again," she said as soon as Tony closed the back door. Her eyes pleaded with Viktor for forgiveness.

"My dear Tam. I'm not mad because of the phone." He ran his fingers deep into the thickness of her hair. "Tony left a message at the club that he took you to Carowinds."

"Then why are you mad?"

He twisted her hair in his clenched fist, causing her to wince. "Because you seem to have forgotten to whom you belong. When I give you an order, you are to obey me. Not that overgrown ape with more muscles than brains."

"Are you jealous?" She gasped. Her mouth! Saying things before her brain processed it. She held her breath, waiting to see how Viktor reacted. She expected him to explode any second. Instead, after a few moments of intense staring, he kissed her. She touched her fingers to her lips when he pulled away. Except for a few quick pecks, he showed no physical affection towards her since throwing her down the stairs. Could it be that he left her alone because he felt guilty? She questioned him with her eyes.

"There is no reason for jealousy if my wife remembers who she belongs to."

She shook her head. "No, there's not." He kissed her again, then pulled her into his arms. *What is up with him?*

"Want to hear a story I've never told you?"

She nodded. Viktor did nothing without it benefiting him. She just needed to bide her time to figure out his game. Maybe his story held clues.

"Remember when I started hanging around your mother?"

"Yeah. I always wondered what you saw in her."

He leaned back against the opposite counter, pulling her with him. "I wasn't there for her. I was there for you."

"What do you mean?" she asked.

"My orders were to obtain you for a client. I used your mother as a ruse to get near you. Once I spent time with you, I wanted you for myself." He cupped her face in his hands. "So, I kept you. I defied my orders, and I've paid dearly for it. I risked everything and married you to keep you safe. You're that special to me." He pulled her against his chest. "I love you, Tam. Everything I do is for our future."

Alarm bells went off in her head. He never professed to love her without motive. Oh, he was definitely up to something, but what?

Only one way to find out. "Really?" She squeezed him tight when he nodded. "Oh, Viktor. Knowing you married me to protect me makes me love you even more."

He pushed her shoulders back so he could look at her. She pasted a smile on her face. He studied her, seeming to search for something. He returned her smile. She didn't know whether he had found what he was looking for, but he kissed her again. She wasn't in imminent danger.

"I'm glad to have my old Tam back. You looked at me differently after... Well. Let me finish cleaning your wound. We can put the nastiness behind us. Okay?"

"Okay." She placed her hand in his open one so he could clean and bandage her finger.

"So, what did you and Mr. Overgrown Ape talk about today?"

There it was. He buttered her up with words he thought she wanted to hear so she would lower her guard. Thankfully, Tony coached her on what to say in case Viktor questioned her.

"Well, we talked only a little. We spent most of the day waiting in line. Oh, he said you owe him one hundred fifty dollars for my part of the costs for today."

He tore off a strip of tape to wrap around the gauze he placed over the cut. "Huh! I don't owe him a dime. I didn't ask him to take you to Carowinds. He could've left you at home and gone by himself." With the bandaging complete, he started cleaning up the mess. "What else did he say?"

"He wants to visit the zoo and the beach. Can I go with him? Please?"

"No. Look at the trouble today caused."

"Please," she coaxed. "You're always working, and I don't want to sit home alone. I promise to always keep my phone with me. Please." She poked her bottom lip out. "Please," she said again, twisting back and forth while holding his hand, playing coy.

He rolled his eyes at her antics. "Fine, but the first time I call you, and you don't answer —"

"I'll be in big trouble." She hugged him. "Thank you, Viktor. You're the best husband ever." *The best at being the worst.*

He returned her hug, keeping her locked in his embrace. "Tam, you're not keeping anything from me, are you?"

She drew back. "Keeping something from you? What on earth could I not be telling you?"

"What did you say to him, Tam?"

The teasing tone from earlier was absent from his voice. Tony said to use sarcasm to make Viktor believe she lied. She needed to walk a fine line to pull off the deception.

"You mean, did I reveal any of your secrets?" She drew away from him. The incredulous look on his face fueled her sarcasm. "Oh, yeah. Spilled everything to a complete stranger. The words went 'whoosh,' right out of my mouth." She held up a bare wrist as if checking the time. "Oh, wow. It's getting late. We should try to sleep before the cops show up to arrest us."

She turned towards the front hall, then looked back over her shoulder to gauge his reaction. Livid described him to perfection. Returning, she wrapped her arms around his waist. "Please don't be mad. I'm teasing. I have no desire to go to jail any more than you do." His expression didn't change. "Fine. Do you want to know what I said? I told him how much I missed my grandmother. I argued with him, trying to make him quit because I don't want a trainer. As I said, we spent most of our time waiting in lines. He acted a fool on the merry-go-round doing stupid riding stunts, and I almost levitated out of a roller coaster car. I screamed bloody murder while he laughed at my fright. I'm glad they're tearing down the wooden monstrosity. It's dangerous." Still, his expression didn't change. It worried her. "Viktor, please don't be mad," she begged, tears of fear forming.

"That's everything?" he asked.

"Yes. I've told you every subject I discussed with Tony today."

"How did you get this stuffed animal?" Viktor asked, nodding towards the counter.

Tamsin glanced at the toy in disbelief. "You are jealous! Viktor! He's old enough to be my father."

"You forget what business I'm in. Age has nothing to do with lust." He wrapped his arms around her. "You're my most prized possession. Of course, I'm jealous of the time he spent with you today." Viktor claimed her lips in a possessive kiss. "But I can see how doing something frivolous has brought my wife back to me. I'm willing to compromise if it mends the rift between us."

"You're too good to me, Viktor," Tamsin said, laying her head on his chest. She yawned, the exercise she received today catching up with her. "Oh, wow. I'm more tired than I thought."

"Go on to bed. I need to make a call first."

Tamsin left the room, stopping midway on the stairs to overhear Viktor's conversation. She peaked over the railing. Viktor stared out the kitchen window towards the guest house.

"He's tucked in for the night." Pause. "I've set the spyware up on Tam's phone. Anything they say will automatically record in the database. If he is the guy, he'll question her the first chance he gets, and then we'll have him." Pause. "No. Tamsin knows to keep her mouth shut." Pause. "Right, I'll see you then. We'll discuss the details where she can't overhear."

Tamsin hurried up the steps before Viktor caught her lurking. Giggling, she closed the bedroom door. She didn't think using duplicity in telling the truth to cover a lie would work. Viktor always detected her deceptions. But Tony said to trust him, so she did. He turned out to be correct. Viktor believed her every word. "I'll never doubt you again, Tony."

"I told you to trust me," Tony said, his voice coming through on the earpiece her hair hid.

9

Tony mused over the barrenness of the vacant club while flipping chairs onto the bistro tables. Under normal occupancy, the room pulsed with electrifying music and held a dark ambiance that spawned seductive energy. Beneath bright fluorescent lights, void of its jubilant spectators, the atmosphere turned depressing and repugnant. The secrecy of shadows obscured the multitude of sins, the sharp lighting unmasked. With the flip of a switch, alluring furnishings transformed into grotesque monuments stained with the taboos of fleshly desire and drunken debauchery.

He didn't know why he bothered with cleaning tonight. In less than twenty-four hours, The Fox Den would forever close. What did it matter if he vacuumed the carpet or mopped the stage? Tomorrow, after months of evidence gathering, once Tamsin and he left her house, the coordinated arrests of Viktor and his cohorts, along with multiple prominent figures in the city, would begin. Weeks ago, he secured a safe house, so they could watch the saga unfold on television until the trial. He stocked it with plenty of popcorn.

He stomped towards the utility room in the back of the building. He knew his problem. Nerves. They planned everything down to the tiniest detail. Copies of the digital evidence and Tamsin's deposition existed in multiple secure locations. They overlooked nothing, but he could not shake the sense of foreboding, causing the tingling of suspicion in his spine.

He rolled his shoulders to release the tension. This same feeling of doom came over him on his first reconnaissance mission. Everything played out as planned during that assignment. This one should be the same.

He stopped outside the dressing room door that held the young woman he'd come to love as a daughter. He hesitated to knock. What was she doing? She usually didn't take this long. Once she removed her stage makeup and changed into street clothes, she was ready to leave. Unbidden, a myriad of possibilities flew through his mind. Did she get choked? Or fall? Did Viktor return without him knowing? Tamsin, the star witness in the case, would be Viktor's primary target if he discovered her participation. He rushed into the room.

She sat with her bare feet braced against the counter in front of her, rocking gently back and forth on the hind legs of her chair. Her file picture, which once evoked anger and loathing, didn't do her justice. A row of uncovered bulbs on each side of the mirror she faced highlighted her long, red, corkscrew-curly hair. Not the orange-red either. Her auburn curls matched the splash of freckles across her nose and cheeks in otherwise unblemished skin. Her eyes, framed by dark lashes, flashed a mesmerizing bright green before transitioning to a yellowish hazel towards the center. Her nose flared slightly when taken by surprise. The unconscious trait alerted him to Viktor's deception on multiple occasions.

She stared off into space, unaware of his presence. He wondered where her thoughts took her. These past few months, he tried to give her happy memories. Did she remember the things they did together?

He took her everywhere within driving distance. At the Biltmore House, he watched her eyes glisten in wonderment over the luxurious estate's fine furnishings, beautiful architecture, and vibrant gardens. There, he discovered her passion for everything botanical.

Then came Grandfather Mountain. He showed her the rock silhouette for which the mountain received its name. He coaxed her onto the mile-high suspension bridge, showing her the majesty of God's creation below them. She told him of her dream to travel the world.

Their next adventure landed them in Kitty Hawk for a walk on the beach to collect shells after a storm. He witnessed her discovery of making damp sand bark when you scuff your bare feet across the surface just the right way. She played in the surf, and he helped her build a sandcastle. They both forgot the sunscreen.

Every week, he planned fresh adventures, both big and small.

Sometimes they simply walked in a garden, enjoying the serenity of their surroundings. On other days, they slid over slippery rocks or raced through the trees on a zipline. They lost themselves in corn mazes and picked out pumpkins at the farmer's market. He gave her the childhood she missed out on.

He tracked the whereabouts of her grandmother's ashes. The family who bought the house surrendered them to a funeral home, which buried them in a field set aside for unclaimed remains. She complained over the barrenness of the open land. She demanded he buy a bag of wildflower seeds so she could scatter them. He didn't have the heart to tell her they would be mowed down before blooming.

Her world escaped Viktor's regulated confines to a vast wonderland full of discovery. Oh, how he was going to miss her once this assignment ended. But she vowed to cut every tie with her past. "People, places, everything. I want everything gone so I can forget," she said. He didn't keep track of the other girls his team rescued from human trafficking, leaving the healing process to others, but the thought of Tamsin moving on with her life without him witnessing what she made of it bothered him.

Tony cleared his throat to get her attention, and she jumped, pushing herself backward. He rushed to catch her before she toppled over. "Whoa. Careful."

"Tony! Why do you keep doing that to everybody? It's nerve-wracking."

"I honestly wasn't even trying this time. You were off in another world. Why are you so deep in thought?" He rested his arms on the backrest of the chair he straddled.

"Just thinking. Daydreaming."

"About what?"

"What to do with my life? How do I decide? What if I choose wrong?"

The dilemma worried Tony as well. He'd seen women fall back into the familiar habits or lifestyles from which they fought to break free of. It happened too many times to dismiss the possibility. Tamsin falling into the trap of familiarity terrified him. He resolved to be a positive influence in her life until the moment she pushed him away. "Do you have any ideas?"

"I thought maybe I could be a nurse. Rita seems to enjoy her job.

What do you think?"

"Helping people is rewarding, but I believe you should do whatever makes you happy."

"And if I don't know, what makes me happy?"

"Take the time to learn. With the prosecutor willing to return the money from the sale of your grandmother's house, you'll have the means to do so." He pointed towards her reflection. "I don't think you'll find the answer staring at a mirror, though."

Tamsin gave a short bark of laughter. "You're right. They lie."

"Maybe you're looking in the wrong mirror."

"The wrong mirror? Don't all mirrors work the same?" She scrunched up her nose in confusion.

"Every mirror shows your reflection, but only God's mirror will show you the truth," Tony said, his voice taking on a solemn tone.

Tamsin sat up straight, turning to face him. "God's mirror?" she asked, her curiosity piqued. "What is that? A crystal ball or something that can tell me my future?"

Tony erupted with laughter over the accuracy of her description. "In a way, it is a sort of crystal ball. Around two-thousand Bible prophecies have been fulfilled."

"Wait. You're talking about the Bible? The Bible is God's mirror?" Tamsin said, shaking her head. "You're a Bible Thumper? I didn't realize you believed in God."

The offensive title of "Bible Thumper" irked him. "I'm a believer in the good news of the Gospel. I don't pound on doors to share what I know." He raised his finger and shook it at her. "And there's a lot about my life I haven't shared with you."

"Like what?" She turned sideways in her chair, resting her chin on her folded arms across the back. "And don't tell me something generic. Tell me an obscure memory or secret."

"Hmm," he said, pretending to think, waiting until her foot began tapping in irritation. "When I was a young boy, my best friend and I loved re-enacting the western heroes we watched on television. I even had a stick pony named Silver my mother kept corralled in the umbrella stand by the front door. Our favorite show was The Lone Ranger. I always played the role of The Lone Ranger, and my friend played his sidekick Tonto. Tonto called The Lone Ranger, Kemosabe.

Every other word out of my friend's mouth was Kemosabe. The nickname stuck and turned into my callsign."

Sharing the memory of Scott and himself carried his thoughts to another problem. After rescuing Scott's daughter, Tony lost track of him. Despite all his connections, he still couldn't find any trace of him. After Tamsin implicated Viktor in the murder of a state field agent, Tony feared his friend may have met the same fate.

He pushed that thought aside. He could think of hundreds of other worries for the next twenty-four hours. Keeping the woman in front of him safe was the most pressing. He noticed her staring at him in the mirror.

Tamsin's eyes held an odd gleam. She rested her head on her fist, a secretive smile pasted on her face. "What?" he asked.

"I'm trying to picture you as a child. I bet you had chubby cheeks and blonde hair." She sighed again and giggled under her breath. "I can imagine you galloping around. I wonder if—." Tears welled up in her eyes. "Never mind. I don't want to discuss things that aren't part of my future."

"Alright then." He never asked her the details of her painful memories when they surfaced. If she wanted to talk, he'd be here to listen. "Your turn. Tell me something no one else knows. Then we must leave. We have a long day ahead of us tomorrow."

"I do have the perfect story for you. Do you want to know why I chose fig newton for my password?"

"I wondered about your safe word. Nobody could ever guess a brand of cookie."

"Not unless they knew the story, and even Viktor doesn't know this one." She fiddled with the elastic of the fox face mask she wore while on stage. "Growing up, my grandmother made it a tradition to dress up every Sunday for afternoon tea. We even donned hats and lace gloves. She'd set out her blue and white Bombay tea set on the front porch. The pot was shaped like an apple. The lid had a stem with an attached leaf. All the cup handles had butterflies. Sometimes she'd invite people over, but most of the time, it was just us."

Tony enjoyed watching Tamsin tell stories. He didn't know if she realized it, but she became animated, using hand gestures and even changing her voice to tell them. She painted a picture of a young girl wearing a yellow dress, and when she twirled in circles, the dress fanned out around her. On her feet, she wore ruffled socks with black patent leather shoes. A woven straw hat, trimmed with a lace ribbon and daisies, sat atop her curls. He added two missing front teeth and a skinned knee to complete his mental image.

Tony jumped when Tamsin's hand waved in front of his face. "I bet you were an impish child," he said.

"Of course." She returned to rocking on the hind legs of her chair. "But back to the story. My grandmother's favorite cookies were Fig Newtons; she served them at every tea. As a selfish, small child, I preferred chocolate chip and always begged my grandmother to serve them instead." Tamsin dropped the chair to the floor with a thud. "Well, one day, she caved to my begging. She said, 'Alright, Little Miss Gotta Have Everything My Way, but I'm warning you, whatever happens, you must face the consequences of your choice.'"

Tony gave a bark of laughter. "Your grandmother sounds wise."

"She was, but I didn't appreciate what she tried to teach me until after I married Viktor, and then it was too late." She frowned. "Anyway, the next Sunday afternoon was so hot. You could see the heat waves rising off the pavement, and the cicadas' songs drowned out other noises. We dressed in our finest clothes, including fancy lace gloves. My grandmother placed the tray holding the tea set and the plate of cookies on the table, but this time, instead of Fig Newtons, my requested chocolate chip cookies lay on the plate. I was so excited. I finally got my way. I dug into the cookies and gobbled every single one up myself." Tamsin sat straighter up in her chair. "Now, picture this. Nice fancy dresses. Hats. Lace gloves." She motioned towards each part of the attire. "Almost one hundred degrees outside, and here I am, eight years old, eating chocolate chip cookies."

"Oh no. Chocolate everywhere," Tony said.

"Everywhere. There were spots on my dress. Smeared on my face and gloves. I somehow got chocolate on my hat and socks as well."

"What did your grandmother do?"

"Well, once I realized I ruined my clothes and the entire afternoon because my grandmother was right, chocolate chip cookies do not go well with tea, I did what I'm best at. I cried. My grandmother got a wet washcloth to wipe away the chocolate and my tears. 'Tamsin,' she said. 'You're just like your mother, won't believe dog mess stinks until you stick your nose in it.'"

Tony gave a hoot of laughter. "I agree with your grandmother. You're definitely hardheaded."

Tamsin stuck her tongue out at him before shooting to her feet. "Time to go. The sooner I sleep, the quicker this will end. Who'd he leave with?"

"Don't worry," Tony said, waving his arms and snapping his fingers. "He's with the amazing Ginger Snap!" He directed his men to keep an extra close eye on Viktor tonight. If he did one thing out of the ordinary, they'd notify him immediately, and the entire operation would be called off. "He drove her to her house, and there's been no reported change."

Tamsin gave a bark of laughter. "You know, I don't blame him. She has a much better personality than Copper Candy and Cinnamon Twist. At least her hair color is natural."

"Hey, you forgot the Asian girl he brought in, forced her to dye her hair bright red, and gave her the name Mulan Rouge. I liked her."

"Oh, yeah? I forgot about her. The way she throat punched that frisky customer was surreal." Tamsin imitated the action.

Tony's eyebrow rose. "I've been wondering. How did you get away with using your real name when every other girl who works in this joint uses a synonym for the color red as their stage persona?"

"My last name is Foxx. He said we were 'destined' to be together." She made a sound of disgust. "What a load of bull."

"And your first name? Tamsin? I've never heard it before." Tony held her jacket for her to slip into.

"Oh, that. My mother read a smutty romance novel, and the heroine's name was Tamsin. She liked it, so here I am." She shrugged into the coat. "Supposedly, it's Scottish or Gaelic or something to that effect."

"You poor kid. School must've been pretty rough."

"You have no idea." Tamsin started playing with the curls in her hair. "I dropped out of school after the teasing became unbearable. Then Viktor happened, and everything went from bad to worse."

"We should get going."

Tamsin's hand hovered above the fox mask before snatching it up. She gave the room one last inspection.

Tony followed wherever her eyes landed. Stained flooring.

Graffitied walls. "Are you certain you can let go of this? I mean the glamor, the lights. You won't find a posher gig anywhere else. You'll be holed up for months when you go into witness protection." Tony followed her out the door.

She wrinkled her nose in distaste. "There won't be a Fox Den after your boys finish with Viktor." She spun on her heels. "And there never was any glamor. Viktor lied, and dumb me believed him."

They exited the building, and Tony locked the rear door for the last time. His watch said three-forty-five in the morning—only twelve more hours in the danger zone. Once Viktor was behind bars and Tamsin tucked away in a safe house, he could relax his vigilant guard.

He looked forward to his life returning to normal. The job of sheriff in a sleepy little community still waited for him. Tamsin could move forward with her life after the trial without fear. Her annulment came through a couple of days ago, and the DA chose not to pursue charges against her, considering Viktor forced her to take part in the abductions while she was still underage. A lump formed in his chest. He'd thought of everything except how to say goodbye.

"Tamsin?"

"Yeah, Tony?" she replied over the car's roof, a smile lighting up her face.

Tony tucked the vision away. *I'm going to miss you. I'll never forget you.* He couldn't bring himself to say the words he wanted. "After tomorrow...," he said with a gulp. *If there is a tomorrow.* "In case I neglect to say it, thank you. We couldn't have solved this case without your help."

"Tony, believe me, it's been a pleasure," she said before sliding into the passenger seat.

10

Tamsin opened the passenger door and slid onto the buttery soft, tan leather seat of the Mercedes Viktor purchased for Christmas, their first year together. She skimmed her hand over the suppleness; she remembered being marched outside, Viktor's palms covering her eyes. His eagerness to surprise her fed her excitement. She squealed with delight when he removed his hands to reveal the silver sedan with a giant red bow atop the roof. He bought her a car!

She imagined people staring, envious of her, sitting in the passenger seat beside her handsome and rich husband. No more was she the poor kid with a weird name and a drug-addicted mother. She now wore boutique fashion instead of hand-me-downs collected by the church to give to the less fortunate. No more being beneath everybody else.

Envy is a powerful influence. It clouded her judgment. How Viktor made money to buy the car didn't enter her mind. She craved everything ever denied to her. She wanted everything he gave her and more.

Tamsin jerked her hand off the seat as if it burned her. She vowed to herself never to fall into the trappings of materialism again. Her youthful dream of being rich and famous fled after being thrown down the stairs. What good did a closet full of clothes, an expensive ride, and a nicely padded bank account matter if you lived a miserable existence? Now, she wanted nothing more than a quiet life, making memories to dwell upon in her old age.

Tony started the car. "You don't look happy. What are you thinking?" he asked.

"Wondering what kind of car I'll own in the future. I doubt it will be as pleasant as this one."

"Cars are for getting you to your destination. Although I admit, the running air conditioner has been nice."

Tamsin laughed with cynicism. "Yeah, but the price those kids paid for this car. I can't forget. How do I live the rest of my life knowing?"

"Everyone has done things they wish they hadn't. Even me," Tony said, putting the car in reverse and backing out of the parking space. "You need to forgive yourself. If you keep beating yourself up over the past, you'll never move forward."

"That's easy for you to say. You've never actively lured anyone into the clutches of a human trafficker."

"You didn't have a choice. Viktor had cops on his payroll. He would've killed you if you said something to the wrong person."

Tamsin turned, staring at her reflection in the mirror without really seeing herself. She knew he spoke the truth. It didn't stop her from feeling like a coward. How many people could she have saved if she'd spoken up? How many lives did she destroy? Parents, brothers, and sisters, never to see their loved ones again because she preserved her own life.

Tony put the car back in park. "Your circumstances are not who you are."

"Then who am I?" she asked, her voice raised. "All I see is someone too focused on her own pleasures. I asked for this car. I desired all the clothes and jewelry. It was never enough. I kept shopping despite knowing where the money came from to pay for everything." She threw her head back against the headrest. "If only I had done something."

Tony laid a hand on her shoulder. "You did the best you could in impossible circumstances. You have your entire life to become the person you want to be," he said, returning his hands to the steering wheel.

Tamsin noticed his nervousness. He ground the pad of his palm over the leather.

"I'm partial to the Tamsin I know. She's witty, has a good sense of humor, is resilient, and has a kind soul. If I had a daughter, I'd want her to be like you."

Tony's admission brought bitter longing. A mentor like Tony could have changed the course of her life. At least he came into her world. She might've already died without his instruction and guidance. "If I were your daughter, Viktor would be dead."

"This is true."

"I wish you could've been my father. I wouldn't be in this mess."

"Ha! I wouldn't have let you out of my sight."

A moment of silence hung in the air before she spoke again. "Before you return to your life, can you help me with something?"

"Tamsin, you've never asked me for anything. If it's within my power, yes. What will you have me do?" Tony glanced towards her; merriment curled the corners of his mouth. "It's nothing illegal, is it?"

"Would you still do it?"

"Probably."

"Well, it's a good thing it's not. In fact, fathers do this for their daughters."

Tony turned his torso towards her, leaning back against the car door. "Now I'm more suspicious. What do you want?"

"Teach me how to drive," Tamsin wheedled, placing her hand together in prayer.

He choked on the breath he inhaled. "I rescind what I said. Anything but that. You'll give me a heart attack."

"Too late. You already agreed."

Tony let the automobile roll through the parking lot. He stopped before pulling onto the street. He turned to Tamsin with a gleam in his eye.

"Are you sure you want me to teach you how to drive?"

"Well, yeah. Who else is there?"

A cagey sneer spread across his face.

Seeing it, Tamsin developed second thoughts about her decision to ask him. Tony's fondness for startling people could be nerve-wracking. He planned on getting a rise out of her. How?

"Okay, you asked for it." He stomped on the gas, squealing tires swinging out of the parking lot.

* * * * *

Ten minutes later, Tony slowed the car before turning into the gated community where Viktor's house was located. The normal time lasted

71

at least fifteen minutes.

Tamsin congratulated herself on robbing him of hearing her cry out in fear. She didn't make a sound the entire trip — though she screamed 'we're going to die' in her mind whenever he drifted around a curve.

"Still want me to teach you?"

She unlocked her knees, where her feet were jammed into the floorboard, and released the death grip on her seatbelt. "You enjoyed that entirely too much," she said, huffing her irritation.

A wide grin spread across Tony's face. "You're right. I did." He turned into the driveway. "You should be proud. You handled it far better than my wife when I pulled it on her."

"And you're still married?" Tamsin asked in disbelief. Tony never disclosed the details of his private life before now.

"I guess I have too many other endearing qualities."

The sound of skepticism escaped her. "Name one."

Tony's expression turned smug. "I rescue little girls from big, bad wolves."

Tamsin pursed her smiling lips and rolled her eyes. "Touché."

The car fell silent. She stared at the mini-McMansion she had called home for the past two years. Most houses in the neighborhood were similar in size and architecture. She wondered if any of the neighbors suspected what had happened inside this one. Tomorrow, a swarm of reporters would crawl over the manicured lawns. They would wonder how they never saw what was happening in front of them.

"You're procrastinating," Tony said, bringing her out of her contemplation.

Tamsin drew a deep, cleansing breath. She didn't want to give away that her stomach was in knots. Tomorrow, her life would forever change. If Tony or she made one misstep, they could lose their lives.

"Yep." She removed her seatbelt. "Tony?"

"Yeah?"

"After tomorrow, in case I forget to say it," she said, repeating Tony's words back to him. Though he didn't speak the words, she knew he meant 'if I'm not here after tomorrow.' "Thank you for being my white knight."

"Aww, you make me blush," Tony said with humor, trying to ease her somber mood.

She heaved a sigh. "You're right. I am procrastinating." She opened the door to look for her barrel-style clutch purse, finding it under her seat. She stepped out of the car. "Good night, Sir Lancelot!" she said. Standing in the light of the open door, she brandished her handbag like a sword. "We have dragons to slay on the morrow."

"Good night, Maid Marion."

11

Tamsin stood in the kitchen. As was her habit, she laid her purse and phone on the counter before kicking off her shoes. Tony said to keep her routine. When Viktor came home, he wanted nothing to be different. 'Keep everything the same. The slightest deviation could alert him,' he warned her.

A few minutes won't hurt. She needed to say goodbye to the house. Some memories made here were good. There was laughter and love before Viktor destroyed her innocence and trust.

She ran her hand across the smooth glass-top surface of the stove. She seldom cooked anything. Her grandmother taught her to make basic foods such as scrambled eggs and an easy chicken casserole, but more complex meals were beyond her experience. At the start of her marriage, she tried to impress her husband with simple meals she learned to cook by watching videos. He insisted on eating out before going to the club, leaving the food she made untouched. After work, they ate at a twenty-four-hour diner, so she gave up trying to learn.

She came to the sink. Every day she stood here drinking her coffee while she stared out the window, lost in daydreams. During the summer, she'd see people on the lake water skiing or fishing and wondered how they lived. They appeared to be carefree, but did they have secrets too?

Viktor took her out in his boat once. When he learned she couldn't swim, he threw her in, telling her to sink or swim. She almost drowned and refused to step foot in the boat again.

She turned away from the window, moving out of the u-shaped kitchen, past the breakfast table to stand in front of the French doors that opened onto the patio where she planted her grandmother's peonies. It was the one thing she insisted on bringing with her when she moved in with Viktor. She didn't know her mother had died until after he sold the house with its contents. She cried because her grandmother's ashes were gone. His effusive apologies comforted her, fooling her into believing in the sincerity of his love. Later, she could dig up the bulbs.

She reversed her steps, bypassing the table to enter the game room. Viktor brought in an interior designer to help with the layout. Bookshelves flanked a gargantuan television hung above an elongated lava rock gas fireplace. A special mantel with a flip-down face hid several consoles and extra charging stations for wireless controllers. Viktor overruled Tamsin's choice of gaming sofa and chairs for seating and insisted on an oversized sectional sofa. She understood his reason once she discovered his underhanded use of her addiction.

She moved from the game room into the unused living and dining rooms. Although they held comfy furniture and high-end whatnots, they lacked personal touches, creating an antiseptic atmosphere.

The curved marble stairs Viktor threw her down separated the space. The fear she felt falling through the open air still haunted her sleep. Many nights, she awoke with a scream. Cold sweat gathered on her forehead and trickled down her back. Viktor pulled her into his arms to comfort her and whispered, "It's over," until she relaxed and fell asleep again.

The action, so inconsistent with his disagreeable nature, baffled her. During the day, he ordered her around like a soldier. Yet, when she lay at her most vulnerable, weeping and afraid, the man that hurt her most tried his best to comfort her. What purpose did his pretense of loving her serve at that moment? He wanted nothing from her. Why?

She shook the question away. She didn't need to be concerned about Viktor's hidden motives any longer. Why stress herself with unanswered questions now that she was close to gaining her freedom? Tomorrow, Viktor and everything associated with him would become her history. The thought brought a surge of adrenaline. *I will be free!*

She ran up the stairs. A few months ago, she caught another dancer folding a few bills into a secret pocket on her G-string. When Tamsin asked why, the girl said it was to hide from her boyfriend. She learned how to sew and did the same thing to her stage costumes. She held back at least twenty dollars of her tips from Viktor each night she worked. The money was in her grandmother's Bible she kept in the guest suite. The last time she counted, she had one thousand bucks.

Of course, that was before the lovely Miss Ginger Snap began working at the club. She had long legs, an hourglass figure, and hair falling past her buttocks. Once she hit the stage, Viktor's scrutiny over how much money patrons tipped her became lax.

The night she met Ginger, Tamsin knew why Viktor hired her and was relieved. It meant sleeping alone for a while. She didn't have to pretend to love him when he wasn't there.

It didn't take long for Viktor to work his wiles. He started stepping out with the woman within a week of her being hired. It wasn't his first affair. He didn't hide his habit of sleeping with other women. He expected Tamsin to accept his ways. The first time she caught him, she exploded. He brushed off her anger, explaining it did not differ from grocery shopping. If one store didn't have everything you needed, you went to another. At sixteen, she didn't possess the ability to combat his logic. After two years of marriage, she realized he had manipulated her.

A month ago, she didn't care about their relationship until she walked into the dressing room and caught them together. Viktor had his head buried in the woman's neck and didn't see her, but Ginger met Tamsin's reflection in the mirror. The woman's smile did not meet her eyes. She pointed her finger toward Tamsin and pretended to be shooting a gun. Tamsin shivered and shut the door on them. The woman was pure evil.

At the top of the stairs, she glanced at the entrance to the master bedroom and stopped. Viktor insisted on closing the interior doors whenever they left the house. Tony's warning sounded in her head throughout the day. *Do not deviate from your routine.* She knew she had closed that door.

It stood wide open.

Tamsin figured she had five seconds to choose between running or facing what was coming.

Viktor's voice came from beyond the doorway. "About time you got home."

Scratch that. She had no choice. Crippling fear seized her. *I'm not getting out of this.* Viktor disliked being kept waiting. The club closed at two o'clock. It must be around four now. He'd been waiting a long time. *What is he doing here?*

"I thought you were out with Ginger," Tamsin said, her voice wavering with fright. The courage she possessed walking into the house, knowing it would be her last night here, evaporated.

"Is that an explanation or an excuse?"

Viktor sounded calm. Sometimes she couldn't tell if he was happy, angry, or indifferent. His ability to mask his emotions was one reason for his success. He led people into a false sense of security and then pounced. It hurt to breathe.

"Well, what are you waiting for? An invitation?"

She wanted to say divine intervention but, from experience, kept her mouth shut. Smart-aleck remarks made everything worse. Besides, she knew she'd receive no help from that department. With trepidation, she entered the bedroom and shut the door.

12

Tony slipped the latch on the French doors. He thought Tamsin should've unlocked them before his arrival. Her purse and shoes were missing from the counter. Who moved them?

"Hey! It's awfully quiet for a party," he said with a raised voice. No one answered. *Where is everybody?*

He didn't feel the need to panic yet. Everyone tiptoed around Viktor's volatile temper, so the silence wasn't unusual. He expected the house to be livelier because of the large gaming party planned for the evening. The lack of epic instrumental music emanating from the Bose surround sound speakers worried him. Making no noise, he stepped into the game room. He found Ginger lounging on the sectional, dividing her attention between the TV and text messages on her phone. A headset covered her ears. *Prime target.*

With the quietness downstairs, Tony partook in one of his favorite forms of entertainment. Startlement. He could never resist the chance to scare someone. He crouched low so his reflection didn't appear on the TV screen, then duck-walked towards the couch. *This is going to be glorious!*

"Whatcha watching?" Tony's voice roared as he jumped over the couch.

Ginger screamed, throwing her phone up in the air.

He caught it before it crashed onto the hardwood floor.

"Tony! Why do you keep doing that?" she asked in exasperated indignation. She tore the headphones off and paused the video on the television.

"Wow. That was awesome. I finally got you to scream. Good thing I have quick reflexes, or you wouldn't have a phone," he said, handing it back to her. The frozen image on the TV distracted him. "Hey! Isn't that 'There Goes, Ian?' I love this guy. Everywhere he goes, something weird happens. It's hilarious."

"Yep, He's one of my favorite channels to watch. Did you see his last video?"

"Where he stayed at the crazy cat lady's Airbnb?"

"That's the one. I laughed the entire time. The situations he gets himself into are just too funny. The best part was at the end. He said..."

"'Well, that was a cat-tastrophe!'" they said in unison.

Ginger pressed play on the remote to resume the show. The sound came through the headset loud enough for them to hear. Tony sat beside her, engrossed in the images flashing across the screen.

"I'm sure that most of his stuff is staged, but this one appears real," he said, fear coloring his voice.

They watched in fascinated horror as the star's treehouse adventure turned into a saga of tornado survival. Windows exploded as flying shrapnel punctured the structure's three-hundred-sixty-degree views. The tree swayed, tossing poor Ian to and fro as if he were aboard a ship at sea. He ran around, searching for a safe harbor, only to find more danger. Desperate, he hugged a large branch, bemoaning his imminent death.

"They're all real, Tony," Ginger responded in quiet disbelief as she watched the screen with bated breath.

"They can't be. The man would be dead by now."

"Well, aren't you two getting cozy?"

Ginger and Tony both jumped at Viktor's voice behind them. Tony ignored the implied meaning of the comment. Viktor leaned against the hallway entrance. He held a glass in one hand and a vodka bottle in the other. Liquor always made tongues loose.

"I'm surprised, Tony. I took you to be the loyal type."

"Hey, boss. Getting the party started a bit early, huh? Where's everybody else?"

"Oh, my gosh! Viktor! Baby, is that blood on your hands? Are you hurt?" Ginger leaped to Viktor's side, fawning over him.

Viktor twisted his wrists to look at his hands, spilling the contents of the glass on the floor. "It appears so." He sighed audibly before weaving over to the counter, where he set the empty glass and bottle. He braced his elbows against the sink edge for support while he washed the blood away.

The man is drunk! Tony spied the blood before Ginger. He could tell it didn't come from any injury Viktor had sustained. The smeared stain covered the entire back of his hand, showing the man tried to wipe it away. Did he do something to Tamsin? Was she hurt? How soon could he get to her? *Please, God, let her be alive.*

Ginger ripped off a wad of paper towels to dry Viktor's hands while she searched for his injury. "Did Tamsin do this to you? I swear if I see that—"

"Speaking of your wife. Is she almost ready, Boss? We should leave to pick up the decorations and deli trays soon."

Tony stared Viktor dead in the eye, praying the man provided an answer to verify Tamsin's safety. Viktor returned his gaze in silence, confirming Tony's fear. The plan had gone awry and now spiraled towards a terrible end.

"You like her, don't you?"

You have to be kidding. He's jealous? What brought this on? "Mrs. D? Yeah, she's nice. What's not to like?"

Viktor sighed again. "You're evading the question. I'm going to ask you one more time." He stared Tony down, his eyes flashing with rage.

"You like her. Don't you?" Viktor's anger punctuated every word.

"Whoa. Boss. Why are you mad? I said, 'Yeah,' but you've jumped to the wrong conclusion. Your wife and I are friends and nothing more."

"Really? Friends, you say?" Viktor poured himself another glass of vodka. "Funny. She's under the impression your relationship is more... intimate. She even admitted as much to me after you brought her home late this morning. Tell me, Tony, what were you and my wife doing in the club for over an hour after it closed?"

Oh, no! He was here? How did he slip past the guard? And she what? Why did she say such a thing? At least Viktor said, 'thinks' instead of 'thought.' His use of the present tense meant even though he may have hurt Tamsin, she still lived.

"Wait. She told you she and I?" Tony asked, not admitting to anything.

"Yeah. Can you believe it? You know what's sad?"

Tony watched Viktor, trying to read the man's mind. The only problem is Viktor lacked morals, making him unreadable and thus unpredictable. Tony was flying blind.

"I assume you'll tell me, and I won't like what you say?" He maintained his composure, sitting on a barstool to appear relaxed. He didn't want to give away any information without knowing what had happened. "Let's get this over with."

Viktor walked to the console table next to the dining room entrance. He removed one of the many guns he kept hidden around the house from the top drawer.

"What's sad about this situation is that I know who you are."

"Oh? And who am I?"

"Mr. White Knight. Rescuer of damsels in distress? Sound familiar?" Viktor pointed the gun at Tony's head, sighing. "I hoped my Tam would see the errors of her ways before this masquerade came to the finale, but she protected you instead. She believed she could save you by directing my anger towards her. She knows I don't share my women. Not their bodies or their loyalty, so I did away with her. I will do away with you, too, in a few moments."

Tony's attention stayed fixed on Viktor and his gun as he stood up and backed away. He raised his hands, showing he had nothing to hide.

"How'd you find out?"

"It's amazing what information comes to you when you have the right leverage?" Viktor said, grinning. "And since you'll be dead pretty soon, I guess letting you in on all my secrets won't hurt." Viktor feigned laughter. "You heard from your ol' buddy, ol' pal, Scott, after rescuing his daughter? Unlike you, one drink wasn't his limit. He told me everything. I even know the name of your pet toy horse. Hi. Ho. Silver." He giggled his amusement.

Tony lowered his hands to his side. Thank goodness he sent his wife away before going undercover. "You let this play out for months? Why? So, you could have this moment?"

Viktor laughed more. "Yep. You know?" He gulped the contents of the glass. "The more I think about it, the funnier it becomes. The hours of planning Tam and you did? All the evidence gathering. It's useless without you two as witnesses." His laughter turned to snickers. "And the best part is that you've exposed every single one of my next targets. Thanks to you, I'm going to own the entire state."

Tony sighed. Time to end the show. "Viktor Doroshenko. You're under arrest for human and drug trafficking. You have the right...."

Viktor's roar of laughter cut off Tony's recitation. Tony laughed with him. He had an ace up his sleeve.

"... to remain silent," Ginger said, finishing the first sentence of the Miranda Rights while she pressed her service pistol into Viktor's neck.

Viktor didn't do his homework when he chose his victims. It didn't take Tony long to find a relative in law enforcement. With much persuasion on Tony's part, Ginger agreed to go undercover as an exotic dancer. He told no one, not even his own team, who she was.

Tony walked over and snatched the gun out of Viktor's hand. "You know what I think is funny? You assumed I was stupid. As if I'd take the chance of you getting your hands on a loaded weapon? I replaced the bullets with blanks." He made a sound of disgust. "Viktor, my backup plans have backup plans. Now, turn around so I can cuff you."

Viktor complied. Rage exploding the veins in his temple and neck.

Ginger, now pointing her gun at Viktor's face, snickered herself and resumed citing Miranda Rights.

Viktor remained motionless while Tony placed handcuffs on his wrists.

"Do you understand the rights I have just read to you?" Ginger asked with a mocking smile.

Viktor kept silent.

"You might as well answer her. A simple yes or no will suffice."

"Yes," Viktor replied through clenched teeth.

"Where's Tamsin?"

"I'm not telling you a thing."

Tony grabbed Ginger's gun, pressing it to Viktor's head. "I can guarantee you that this gun has bullets in it, and I'm sure Miss Ginger here will be more than happy to watch the man who killed her baby sisters die. Where is she?" Tony said, baring his teeth in a sneer.

"Trunk of my car."

"She alive?"

"You forget. 'I have the right to remain silent,'" Viktor said, mocking Tony's concern.

Tony punched Viktor's gut, causing him to fall to his knees. He grabbed Viktor's hair, wrenching back his head. "You better pray she's alive. If she dies, you'll never get your day in court." He handed the gun back to Ginger.

Tony rushed towards the garage, praying the turmoil in his gut was wrong about what he'd find.

13

Curled into a ball, the hospital bed swallowed Tamsin's diminutive frame. Even in sleep, she protected herself. Tony wondered how she survived the brutal beating Viktor unleashed with his baseball bat. Black, blue, and purple bruising edged with the mustard yellow of healing, garish colors against the backdrop of white sheets, covered every inch of her exposed skin and bore witness to the number of blows she received. Her rhythmic breathing eased the tension dogging him over the past couple of weeks.

Her injuries entailed a collapsed lung and several broken bones, including her jaw, arms, and several ribs. They compared little to the brain swelling caused by a cracked skull. One week in an induced coma and surgery to mend her jaw healed her body, but the long-term effects of the brain injury remained unknown.

Tony inhaled, calming his temper. The doctor credited her powerful spirit with keeping her alive. He disagreed. Dozens of trafficked girls experienced the same beatings and didn't live. Yes, Tamsin possessed a will to survive; but he knew a higher power intervened. She wasn't breathing when he found her stuffed in a suitcase in the trunk of Viktor's car.

He rose to stare out the window, shaking off the memory. The doctor cleared her from round-the-clock monitoring yesterday and moved her out of the ICU. With Tamsin out of danger, the focus now turned to her recovery. Would there be brain damage? What would he do if she came out of it and Tamsin wasn't herself anymore? The potential outcomes plagued him.

The rustle of sheets drew his attention. Tamsin mumbled something but returned to the steady breathing of sleep. He choked back tears, imagining what she went through. Her choice of death rather than exposing his true identity humbled him. She didn't know Viktor already knew and was merely testing her loyalty. She failed the test to keep his identity secret. The decision almost ended her life. The Bible verse, John 15:13, came to his mind. "Greater love has no one than this than to lay down one's life for his friends."

Tony returned to the bedside chair. Hanging his head, he pressed his knotted hands against his forehead. He should've told her Viktor might know more than it appeared. Instead, he kept her in the dark, fearing she might become too scared to help him. He should've told her to protect herself, even if it meant exposing himself. The blame for her injuries lay upon him. He didn't deserve her loyalty. He prayed for the chance to repay her sacrifice.

* * * * *

Tamsin watched the man who saved her life through the crack of her eyelids. Even though she had no recollection of what transpired between realizing Viktor was home and waking up in the hospital, she perceived she survived because of him. While working together, they formed a bond that transcended the boundaries of mere friendship. His presence calmed her.

Watching him, she realized she knew less than a handful of details about his personal life. He revealed he was married, but did he have children? Wait, he didn't have a daughter, but did he have a son? What did he enjoy doing? Did he prefer dogs or cats? What kinds of food did he like? She bet he could rattle off her likes and dislikes, but she knew next to nothing about him. She never thought to ask. Now he sat by her bed, catering to her yet again, probably losing sleep worrying over her. Was Tony his real name? She took him for granted, assuming nothing and no one existed for him outside of her and her problems. How selfish could she be?

Tears formed. A sob escaped her.

"Hey. Hey. Hey. It's okay. I'm here." Tony patted her arm. "Why are you crying? Are you in pain?" Tony asked in a soft yet gravelly, sleep-deprived voice.

"Noooo!" Tamsin wailed, sobbing harder. *Why does he have to be so nice?* She wouldn't feel so guilty if he treated her the same as everyone else in her life. Deep, gulping sobs wracked her body. She wrapped her arms around her rib cage, trying to ease the pain the deep breaths caused.

"Tamsin, calm down. Tell me what you need, and I'll get it for you. Please, stop crying. You're hurting yourself."

She hid her face. She couldn't stop. The concern in Tony's voice compounded her guilt, and she felt sorry for herself, too. She didn't know what had happened. Was Viktor in jail, or was he coming to kill her in her sleep? Relief at seeing Tony. Anger over what Viktor did to her. Dozens of emotions flooded her at once. She released them with her tears.

"It's okay, Tamsin. It doesn't matter. If you need to cry, cry," Tony said in a soothing voice. He squeezed her hand in reassurance. "We'll still be here when you get done."

Tamsin let her tears flow a few moments longer before she couldn't stand the sound and shut down the tear factory, her breath coming in, halting gasps until her breathing regulated. "Ow."

Tony sprang from the chair to help her.

"No, you need to go home and be with your wife," she stated without emotion once she gained control of herself. She used her feet to push herself up higher on the bed. "You need to stop worrying about me and—." The words he spoke finally registered. "Wait. You said, 'We'll.' Who's 'we'll'?"

"My wife and I," Tony answered with a grin crinkling his eyes.

Tamsin's eyes bulged in disbelief. *His wife is here?* Why on earth did he bring her to the hospital? He must be joking. "Are you serious?"

Tony pointed to the opposite side of the bed for his answer.

Apprehension seized her. What plausible excuse could she give the woman for monopolizing her husband's time for months on end? A simple 'I'm sorry' seemed inadequate. 'Thanks for lending me your husband. You can have him back now.'? No. Too flippant. She needed to face her, regardless. The woman deserved an apology, and a thank you. She hesitated to roll over, not knowing what to expect.

"Hello dear. I'm happy to meet you finally. Tony's told me a great deal about you."

"You're a hippy!" Tamsin slapped her hand over her lips. *Ow!* She forgot about the hardened fiberglass covering of her cast until she bumped it against her jaw. *It serves me right for saying that.* She thought she had mastered her runaway mouth during the past few months. Thinking before saying helped keep her out of Viktor's line of fire. She attributed her lapse to shock.

A head taller than herself, the woman standing before her radiated 'good vibes.' A wide band of colorful fabric covered her salt and pepper, wavey hair, except for two thin braids at each temple and the big poof of a ponytail. Chandelier earrings with multi-colored stones dangled from her ears, and several long, beaded chains hung around her neck. Her clothing was a tie-dyed t-shirt and a blue jean skirt. Multiple leather bracelets and a pair of round, mirrored sunglasses hanging from the neckline of her shirt completed the impression.

Tamsin removed her hand from her mouth. "I'm sorry," she whispered. She rolled over to apologize to Tony as well. "Your beard is back," she said instead. "How long have I been out?"

Tony and his wife laughed. Tamsin bristled but kept her emotions hidden. Not knowing what happened worried her, and they laughed at her.

"Tony, you're right. Her spirit is delightful and charming. I think I'll enjoy having her for a daughter."

Wait. What? She narrowed her eyes toward Tony.

"Dear. We should ask her first. Remember? I said it's up to her. She is an adult and can make her own choices."

Tony's wife sat on the edge of her bed with her hip, placing Tamsin's hand in hers. Tamsin turned her head towards her, but the woman's eyes remained focused on Tony.

"Of course, we'll ask first, but I'm sure she will say yes. I know the lifestyle may not be what she's used to. Once she's there for a while, I know she'll love it." She turned her focus to Tamsin. "Isn't that so?" she asked, her expression expecting an answer.

"I." Tamsin's stare of bewilderment passed between Tony and his wife. *What are they getting me into?* "Guess."

"See, Dear," the woman said, turning back towards Tony. "Everything will be fine."

The smugness of her voice proclaimed her confidence. She reminded Tamsin of her grandmother when she wanted to get her way.

"You'll stay with us on our ranch in the mountains. We'll move there once you're out of the hospital. When the trial ends, you can decide whether to stay or go, but I hope you stay."

"But—"

"Oh, please say yes. I promise we'll have loads of fun. There are horses, cows, and chickens. There's a stream running through the property and a separate cottage where you can live. Doesn't that sound nice? Hmm?" she asked, patting Tamsin's hand. "And the best part is, if you stay with us, we get to change our names. I've always wanted to change my name. Oh, please say yes."

The woman's face held a hopeful expression. Tamsin didn't want to disappoint her, but she wasn't sure she should live with Tony and his wife, even temporarily. What if Viktor found her? She could never put them in danger. She needed to know what transpired while she was out of it before she decided.

"Tony, what happened? The last thing I remember before the nurses drew blood this morning was you taking me home. Where's Viktor?"

"He's in jail without bond. You're safe, Tamsin. You'll never see him again."

"What if he looks for me when he gets out? If I'm staying with y'all—" Tony's words relieved her immediate apprehension, but what of the future?

"He'll never find you. Technically, you died. Your death certificate shows you passed away from severe blunt-force trauma a week ago. The nurses and your doctor think you're a Jane Doe, and we're the concerned couple who found you."

"I'm dead!" The coil squeezing her heart unfurled. The weight of fear lifted away. She gasped at the unexpected feeling of lightness. Tony's words sang through her mind. *I'm dead! I'm dead!* "I'm free?" she asked in disbelief.

"Yes, you're free of Viktor. You don't need to appear in court. You can erase him from your life."

Tears formed, but she wiped them away before they escaped. She should celebrate instead of cry. She never believed she could be one-hundred percent free of him. The knowledge she didn't need to spend the rest of her existence on this earth expecting him to pounce at any moment released tension keeping her in bondage. Her death changed everything.

"He'll never get out? Are you sure? You're positive?" Her eyes begged Tony for more affirmation.

"Viktor has enough charges to keep him locked up for three lifetimes," he said.

Tony's assurance broke the dam. She turned to Tony's wife, seeking a woman's comfort even though they had just met. "I'm free," Tamsin said, tears forming again.

Tony's wife drew her into her arms, patting her on the back. "Yes, you are, and you'll stay with us while you get better. I'll take good care of you. You'll get the rest you need, and when you're ready, you can start your new life."

Tamsin brought herself under control. Her earlier crying caused her chest to ache. She was getting tired too. She pulled away and wiped the wetness off her cheeks. "Thank you for opening your home to me. I was afraid of being alone, but I didn't want to tell Tony. I didn't want to burden him when he'd already done so much for me."

The woman waved Tamsin's gratitude away. "Having you come live with us pleases me. I get to play mother hen, and I can change my name. It's a win-win."

"What is your name now?"

The woman made a face of disgust and rolled her eyes. "Tonie. Well, Antoinette. I've always wanted something mystical. Maybe Juniper or Rayne?" She sat up straighter. "Oh, those sound nice together. What do you think, Dear?" she asked, turning to Tony. "Doesn't Juniper Rayne sound like a good name for me?"

"Wait." Tamsin pointed her finger at the woman. "Your name is Tonie?"

Tamsin waited for her confirmation before turning her pointed finger toward Tony. "And your real name is Tony?"

He nodded.

"It's why we call each other dear most of the time. Using our names to address each other feels weird, so we stick to terms of endearment."

"I can imagine," Tamsin said, incredulous that two people with the same name married each other. She didn't blame Tony's wife for wanting a different name.

She kind of fancied the idea of renaming herself now that she thought about it more. She could be an amnesiac. No past. She could make herself over. Get rid of her bad habits. She liked the idea of changing her personality. "What about you, Tony? What will your new name be?"

"Well, I'm more of a traditionalist. I lean towards Biblical names. Maybe something Western?" He snapped his fingers after a few moments. "Jeremiah Johnson? Jeremiah and Juniper Johnson. I'm satisfied with the sound of them together," he said. "But, so you know, I'm calling you Momma Jun," he added.

Tonie gasped. "Jeremiah! You may not call me that! No sir! This is not a reality TV show, and Tamsin bears no resemblance to Honey Booboo. I can't believe...."

Tony escalated her irritation, needling her with nonsensical counterarguments.

Tamsin listened to them teasing each other without focusing on their words. She could tell they loved each other by their tones. Neither of them raised their voice in anger. The few married couples she knew yelled and screamed at each other whenever one of them got mad.

She always wanted a father and mother like the ones in the reruns her grandmother watched on TV. Tony's wife said she could live as their daughter. But for how long? Did she really want to cut ties with Tony as she had planned?

"Mother. Father. You shouldn't argue in front of your child."

"... and you're a John Wayne wannabe...." Tonie's voice trailed off.

They stared at Tamsin.

"Tamsin, did you say what I think you said?" Tony asked.

"Yes, Ton... uhh, Father," Tamsin said, grinning in amusement at their shocked expressions. "I'll be your daughter, at least until I get better. Afterward, we'll reassess. Agree?"

"Well, hot dog then! One more question needs to be answered before we can discuss concrete matters."

Tamsin gave him a puzzled look.

"What will your new name be... daughter?"

Her face fell in bewilderment. She never considered a new name when she daydreamed of her future life. She always pictured it as adjectives. Calm. Peaceful. Fulfilling. Successful. The perfect name popped into her head.

"Grace?"She glanced at Tony for confirmation she had chosen an acceptable name.

"It's your decision."

Tamsin thought for a few more seconds. "Yes. Grace. It was my grandmother's name."

"Ohhh. Grace Saffron Johnson. They flow, don't you think?"

Tamsin didn't care for the name Saffron. Wasn't it a spice or something? Should she agree to the name since her new mother picked it out? She opened her home to her, after all. A knock on the door interrupted her thoughts before she could decide.

In unison, they turned towards the entrance with either anticipation, suspicion, or fear. A middle-aged woman poked her head inside before pushing the door wide open. She wore a white doctor's coat.

"Good afternoon. My name is Dr. Kirkton. I've joined your medical team. I'm glad to see you're fully awake."

"Thank you." Tamsin didn't elaborate further, not knowing how much the woman knew.

Before continuing, the doctor scrutinized each of Tamsin's visitors. Her new parents didn't budge. Tony crossed his arms, defying the doctor's unspoken request for them to leave the room.

"Is it alright to discuss your medical information with your visitors present?"

"Oh. Uh. Um. Yes. They've offered me a place to stay until I can get back on my feet. This is Jeremiah and Juniper Johnson. They should know the extent of my condition, don't you think?"

The doctor nodded her head in greeting before continuing in a concerned voice. "As one of your doctors, I think it's my duty to ask if you know and trust these people. If not…"

Tony interrupted. "Doctor, I'll be happy to provide my credentials and personal references to assure you of the safety of your patient once released to our care. You can also contact Director Gary Thomas with the State Bureau of Investigations if you need further information."

The name drop appeased the doctor. "Thank you. I'll be waiting for that information." She started flipping through her clipboard.

"It seems they admitted you as a Jane Doe. What is your real name?"

"It's Grace." The name came easily. "Grace… Saffron… Johnson," she said, halting over the additional names. They felt fake. She wondered if the doctor believed her.

"Okay. I'll make a note so we can get your records updated. I like your middle name."

The doctor's compliment eased Tamsin's misgivings about accepting it.

"Are you married?"

Tamsin shook her head. Her apprehension rose. Did the woman know she lied? What if Viktor found out she still lived? Did he send her?

The doctor made some notes before continuing. "Okay. Miss Johnson, they added me to your medical team because your lab work showed some unusual results this morning."

The doctor's statement sucked the earlier merriment out of the room. Her new mother and father grabbed each of her hands. Their show of unity and love brought tears to her eyes. *This is how it feels to have loving parents.*

Is it going to last? How long do I have?

"I'm not sure you'll care for what I have to say."

Tony squeezed her hand harder, reassuring her of his support.

"It's alright, Doctor. I'm ready." *She's going to tell me I'm dying.*

"You're pregnant."

Tony flopped into his chair.

Tonie started doing a little happy dance, hopping from one foot to the other. "A grandchild. A grandchild."

"Grace? Are you okay?" the doctor asked with concern in her voice.

Tamsin's eyes rolled up into her head. Convulsions threw her back onto the bed.

14

Five years later…

Ian MacGregor lowered his car window, leaned over, and screamed. "Why am I here? I despise it here!"

His experiences in North Carolina fostered a love/hate relationship inside him. Unpleasant childhood memories still loomed in the recesses of his memory despite his efforts to suppress them. During his last visit, he nearly died. While filming an episode of his tree house adventure series, a small tornado formed during a summer storm, almost directly hitting the treehouse where he stayed. He vowed never to return. His agent, Abigail, had a different idea. With themes for his traveling adventures running short, she latched onto what she termed the 'Barbecue Hop.' It involved eating a lot of meat in all the lower forty-eight states, but instead of flying, he was driving. Alone. He agreed out of his passion for driving the car he inherited from his grandfather, a convertible, nineteen-fifty-four, lemon yellow Buick Skylark.

Ian turned off the car's antique radio to call Abigail so he could complain for the third time. What he wouldn't give for the automobile to have Bluetooth capabilities. The frequent commercials were wearing on his nerves.

"Tell me why I'm doing this again."

"Because Ian, your stats dropped significantly. Something needed to be done, and you didn't offer better ideas. I don't know about you, but I enjoy getting paid, and your sponsors are paying well for this trip," the agent's disembodied voice quipped.

"But, why barbecue? Barbecue is where travel shows go to die."

"Because barbecue pays the bills. We need this series to keep us paid for the next six months. This is a goodwill tour. The shutdown is hurting small restaurants. You're doing them a favor. Remember to wear your mask." She spoke in a singsong voice.

"But I'm in North Carolina. The last time I returned to this state, it almost killed me. I told you not to send me back."

"You know what? I don't like big, whiney social media stars. You are three-quarters through. What do you think can happen before you reach the border?" Abigail asked.

"Did you forget who you are talking to?" He didn't keep the sarcastic tone out of his voice.

"You'll be fine. In the fall, during the Lexington Barbecue Festival, is when you have to stay overnight."

"Abigail! That's hurricane season!"

"Quit being a big baby. Lexington isn't anywhere near the coast. I'm working on a skiing series for the winter. We should consider different mountain ranges in each hemisphere to keep the show running for a year. I'm in negotiations with a major network. If they pick the show up, it will financially set both of us."

"Are you trying to kill me?" Ian asked, incredulous she even suggested he ski. Given his penchant for getting into absurdly ridiculous accidents, putting his feet on two sticks and sliding across the snow while descending a mountain was not a sound idea. Although his accident proneness made him famous, he didn't have a death wish.

"I'll never tell," she bantered back.

"Oh, ha-ha."

"On short notice, I came up with barbecue. It's only a few months to keep the money supply rolling. I've blown through my trust fund and have bills to pay."

Ian gave a bark of laughter. Though they both attended the same private high school, it was through a scholarship program. Right before graduation, Abigail conceived the travel show "There Goes Ian." She said he only needed to act the part, and she'd handle everything else. With no better prospects than fast-food joints, the local mill, or the military, the same as his grandfather, he went along with her idea.

Abigail turned out to be a social media guru. The channel became an overnight success. After only a few episodes, sponsors started contacting her. Admittedly, they staged a few of his 'accidents.' He couldn't be a complete buffoon twenty-four-seven. Unfortunately, the unstaged mishaps sometimes ended in pain, as did the last episode of his wild west series. Driving cattle, something he had always dreamed of trying, landed him in the emergency room, getting stitches in his thigh. He requested a simple assignment this time. He never considered he'd wind up back in North Carolina during tornado season for a second time.

"Alright. Fine, I'll do the series, but those better be extremely nice ski resorts," Ian conceded, despite his feeling of apprehension.

"I promise they will be. Don't forget to upload footage regularly and send context. I'll pull your photos from the Cloud."

"Yeah, yeah. I know what to do." Ian said, grumbling his response, no longer in the mood for talking. He wanted out of the state. Foreboding dark clouds built across the sky. Being the middle of April, peak tornado season, the sight of them set off his anxiety. Chattanooga, his destination, loomed two hours away. He mashed the gas pedal a little harder.

"Have fun. Talk to—."

Ian checked the bars on his cell. No signal. Figures.

He tossed the phone onto the passenger seat and turned the radio back on, resolved to ignore his fatalism psychosis and enjoy the early spring scenery along the highway. The song on the radio, one of his favorites, lifted his spirits enough for him to tap the beat on the steering wheel. His bright mood faded fast. The radio's volume dwindled before stopping altogether. The car engine fluctuated between racing and nearly stalling despite him pressing the gas pedal to the floor. Ian pulled into the breakdown lane, inching at a snail's pace, determined to make it to the exit ramp a few more feet ahead.

He turned right onto a two-lane road, hoping to roll downhill to a gas station where he could call for help. The car stalled a few yards out of sight of the highway. He coasted to the roadside. Great! Just great. Ian checked his phone. Still no signal. Abigail jinxed him.

He couldn't sit here. He tried getting the car started by turning the ignition off and on. A truck blasted past him, blowing a train horn. Ian jumped at the alarming noise and dropped his phone. He opened the door to maneuver beneath the oversized steering wheel to reach the phone, which landed underneath the gas pedal. The sound of a motor whirring to life gave Ian hope he could get the car started until he saw the soft-top roof lift away from the windshield and fold itself behind the back seat. He left the ignition switch in the on position, then hit the roof switch while retrieving his phone.

No! No! No! This can't be happening. Ian flipped the switch to make the roof return to the closed position, to no avail. He tried starting the car again. Nothing. What else can go wrong? He crossed his arms over the steering wheel, resting his head on his forearms.

A few rain drops fell before turning into a drizzle. Maybe it won't be much rain. The bottom fell out, drenching him in seconds. I should've known better than to ask what could go wrong. Abigail is going to love this. His fiascos were Abigail's favorite stories to post and received the most views. Might as well do some work. He dug out his waterproof GoPro from the trunk and shot A and B-roll footage of himself sitting in the car, water rivulets pouring over his face. He set up the camera and tripod for footage of him pacing, trying to find a cell phone signal while shivering from the chilling rain. With nothing left to do, he sat in the driver's seat, cold, wet, and miserable. Help should arrive eventually.

The spring downpour lasted less than half an hour. Ian's drenched clothes clung to his body. He grabbed a set of dry ones from his bag in the trunk before digging around in his grandfather's emergency kit to see what it provided. He rolled his eyes when he pulled out a blue tarp. I wish I'd known that was here before it rained. He ducked into the roadside brambles to change, popped the hood to signal his distress, then spread the tarp over the front seat. He'd start walking if no one came to help in the next hour.

The double toot of a horn startled Ian awake. He sat up, disoriented. The plastic underneath him crinkled. His head throbbed. His neck ached. He blinked against the sun's glare. *How long did I sleep?*

"Need help?"

Ian turned his head towards the voice. A black form outlined by the westerly sun stood by the driver's side front wheel. Ian stared gape-mouthed at the featureless figure, waiting for his brain to function.

"Dude. You alright?"

"Yeah," Ian said, his voice croaking. He ratcheted his fingers against his eyes, rubbing the sleep from them. His cheeks tingled when he brushed them. *Great! Now I'm sunburnt too.* "What time is it?" he asked, yawning.

The man moved out of the sun's glare, enabling Ian to see his features. Attired in a typical dark blue mechanic's uniform and ball cap with Casey's Garage embroidered across the front, Ian figured him to be somewhere between fifty and sixty years old. His friendly face wore a concerned expression.

"Four o'clock, nearly quitting time," Casey said. "Have you been out here awhile? Your face is red."

"Ever since it rained," Ian responded, his voice still hoarse. "Do you have any water?"

"Sure thing. Wait right here."

Ian watched the man walk back to his truck. He seemed to be a nice guy. The gap between his two front teeth and his stocky bulldog build gave the man a friendly appearance. He checked the call log on his phone. Four hours? No wonder he didn't feel well. Thank goodness somebody showed up. If Ian had walked now, all the shops would be closed when he reached them.

"Here you go, man," Casey said, handing Ian two cold water bottles.

Ian chugged the first one. The second he rubbed against his face, the droplets on the outside soothed his heated skin. "Ahhh. Thanks, man. I can't believe nobody stopped to help me before now."

"It's a good thing I came along then. What's wrong with your car? She's a beaut, by the way. You don't see them like this anymore." Casey traced the rounded curve of the fender as he walked toward the front of the car.

Ian knew precisely how he felt. Nothing beat the design lines of classic cars. He spent many hours polishing the finish before a show. His grandfather entertained him with stories from the war in Vietnam while they rubbed and buffed every inch until the paint gleamed. The man tried to get him interested in mechanics, but Ian preferred disc drives and game rooms over screwdrivers and wrenches. Now he wished he'd taken at least a rudimentary interest in repairing the car.

"Thanks, my grandfather left it to me after he passed a few years ago," Ian said, following Casey to the front.

"Your grandfather had good taste. This engine is clean too. What happened?" Casey asked, bracing his hands against the open hood of the car.

"Well, everything died. First, the radio quit, then the engine began acting weird. The power steering stopped working, and then everything died altogether. The last thing working was the blasted roof switch."

"Hmm. Sounds like the alternator. I'll check it out, but if I have to order the part, it will take a few days before it arrives."

"Dude, as long as you can fix it in time for me to be in Chattanooga by next Saturday, the delay won't bother me. I can stay in a motel—no big deal. I need an actual vacation," Ian said with a shrug. Used to dealing with setbacks, he learned waiting usually turned out to be worth the wait. Many of his best and most memorable adventures happened while waiting.

Casey removed his cap, rubbed his shaved head, then replaced the hat. "See, here's the thing. We don't have a motel," he admitted with a sheepish expression.

"Okay. What accommodations are there?"

"People stay in the sheriff's cabin occasionally. I'll call him once we get back to the shop," Casey offered before returning to his tow truck.

Ian waited for Casey to get the car secured onto the rollback before speaking again. "Umm, what if the sheriff says 'no'?"

"In that case, you can stay in the shed behind the shop."

"No problem. As long as there's wi-fi."

"That might be a problem."

Ian climbed up into the passenger seat. "There's no wi-fi?" he asked, with raised eyebrows.

"Well, there's the internet, but it's mostly connected directly to computers. People in town try to use as little technology as possible. We're considering adding municipal wi-fi when we finish the library."

What sort of town doesn't have at least one motel? And no Wi-Fi? "Where are you taking me?" Ian asked after Casey started the truck.

"Covenant Cove. Where nothing ever happens, and everybody likes it that way."

15

Abundant spring vegetation separated the hodgepodge of houses and driveways as they traveled toward town. Large tree limbs loaded with bright green foliage provided shade from the setting sun. Ian spotted purple and white flowers bursting forth from the carpet of dead leaves in the woods, but their rate of travel prevented identification. The colors brightened his mood. Casey kept up the conversation by asking a plethora of mundane questions.

The mechanic admitted to watching none of his channel's videos but promised to check it out when he found the time. He volunteered his ten-year-old son to lend Ian a hand during his stay because 'he seems to be into that sort of thing.' All talk ceased as they topped a hill, and Ian received an elevated view of the town.

"Is that where we're going?" Ian marveled.

"Yep."

Picturesque seemed an inadequate word to describe the village community below him. Nestled on a rolling basin and surrounded by a natural horseshoe of high hills, the micro town delighted Ian with its provincial charm. Small buildings led into a few taller ones that designated a downtown area. Or was it just a neighborhood? Tiny bungalow-style houses sitting on spacious lots with plenty of flowering trees completed the scenery. Beyond the rows of buildings lay a park with a large pond, playground, and community building with an attached picnic shelter. He never encountered a town he felt an immediate connection to in all his travels.

An overabundance of solar panels detracted from the town's postcard perfection. They dotted the landscape like swollen ticks on a dog. Roofs. Yards. Poles. A large cluster beyond the pond marred the park scene. Why did they need so many? "What's with the solar panels?" Ian asked.

"Most of the town uses them for electricity." Casey's tone implied that Ian should know the purpose of solar panels. "There are a few exceptions. The mail center, the doctor's office, and my shop are all grid-tied. The original houses on the outskirts also have electricity. When the sheriff arrives, he will go over how everything operates."

By this time, they pulled into Casey's garage, a simple cinder block building with two bays and a waiting area. The gambrel roof and red paint imitated a barn. A beat-up, green Ford pickup truck occupied one open bay. He expected Casey's shop to be a gas station, but it lacked pumps. *Where do people get their gas?* Cracks in the concrete sprouted weeds, but the building appeared cared for. Sleeping in the shed might be okay.

"Nice setup you have here."

"Thanks. When I arrived, it was a dump. Paint peeling. Roof caving in. But my wife urged me to have more faith; it looks great now. Have a seat inside while I unload your car."

Ian ventured into a glass-fronted waiting area. Signs for mountain bike and kayak rentals hung on the back wall. Casey was quite the industrious fellow. He was a mechanic and kept a couple of side hustles. Abigail would love the footage of him kayaking rapids.

Thinking of her, he checked his phone to see if the signal had returned. He had full service. Ian opened his texting app to inform Abigail of his current circumstances.

Movement outside the window caught his eye before he could finish typing his message. A young woman rode an adult tricycle toward the front of the shop. Thanks to Casey's cleaning habits, the clear window gave him an unadulterated view of her smiling face.

Ian's jaw dropped. He journeyed worldwide, meeting exotic women and even dating several as a wow factor for the show. He knew the women used him as a stepping stone on their climb to fame. After a few hours of them fawning over his notoriety, he became fatigued with their artificial interest. He'd rather sit alone in his hotel room than have his emotions exploited by a sycophant. He left them with feigning heartbroken when he boarded a plane for a new destination. Their pouty faces didn't fool him into thinking they had lasting affection for him. He made sure to let them know he wasn't interested in a long-term commitment, but their efforts to lure him into one never ceased to amaze him.

Still, their painted lips, long nails, and high heels drew him like a magnet. He enjoyed the envious looks men gave him with a beautiful woman hanging on his arm, and their company alleviated his boredom. He preferred women who took care of themselves over the freckle-faced girl next door type standing outside. Nevertheless, the purity of her smile captivated him. She looked untainted, her expression almost childlike. He saw no guile lurking in her eyes.

With smooth, lithe movements, she dismounted the bike. Precise and controlled, efficient in execution despite the long boho style overdress and ruffled underskirt she wore. A colorful scarf covered her head except for a cascade of red curls billowing out the back. The word enchanting entered his mind.

Instead of texting Abigail, he took a picture of the girl while she stood talking to Casey. He snapped his jaw together when he realized his mouth still hung open. He remembered the time he went para-gliding. When he first jumped off the cliff, his heart did a flip. It did the same now.

Casey's bulky form doubled hers. The two chatted momentarily before Casey pointed towards the building, showing they were discussing him. Ian spun on his heel before she caught him gawking. He counted to thirty before turning back around. The woman was gone.

"The sheriff will be here soon. I just got done with his oil change. I sure hope he lets you stay in the cabin. If we have to clean out the shed, it'll take over an hour, and I'm already hungry."

Ian's stomach emitted an embarrassing growl at the mention of food. "I know what you mean," he said, rubbing his belly while staring down the street. This town's structure baffled him. When Casey spoke about the sheriff, Ian didn't miss the timbre of respect in his voice. He wondered if keeping the peace was all the position entailed. Could he have stumbled upon a cult similar to Jonestown, and the sheriff be their cult leader? There weren't many people or cars. This thought brought another question to mind.

"Casey, I've been wondering something. We've been here at least fifteen minutes. We were near the highway for at least half an hour. I had been waiting for someone to stop since before lunch. The only vehicles I've seen this entire time are a truck blowing a train horn, your rig, and a woman riding a bike. How did you know I was there?"

"Train horn? Coming or going?" Casey asked with concern, seeming to be disturbed by the information.

"Yeah, train horn. I think it came this way. Why?"

"I need to tell the sheriff." Casey pulled out a flip phone before returning to the bays.

Ian wondered about the age of the old-fashioned device. It appeared no one here wanted to take part in the twenty-first century. No wi-fi? Why did a truck with a train horn cause such an alarm? How did everyone cook without electricity? Where are the people? These thoughts brought him back to the sheriff with the godlike status. Should he lodge in the cabin? Was it safe? Do any guests get to leave? What if this was some kind of bizarre Stephen King town and...? Ian shook the thought away. Casey didn't strike him as having a 'Children of the Corn' persona, but his anxiety remained. Abigail is going to enjoy this adventure.

He called her.

16

Ian smashed his thumb against the hang-up button. Abigail laughed at him. He might laugh, too, if he weren't the one in the middle of this downward-spiraling escapade. Her laughter scraped at his inflamed nerves. Good thing he liked her. She did a fantastic job managing his life, but sometimes she could be insensitive.

They formed their friendship when they both started Elon Christian Academy, a private school between Greensboro and Burlington. Newcomers, both quirky in appearance, found it difficult to inject themselves into the long-established cliques their classmates forged in elementary school. Abigail's sturdy build towered over most of the ninth-grade boys, and he wore braces to correct a pronounced overbite. He also suffered from facial eczema. A few classmates teased them about their appearances, but not nearly as many in the public school he attended. Still, the unwelcome atmosphere whenever he or Abigail tried to take part in group activities, deterred them from trying to nurture other friendships.

In eleventh grade, the orthodontist finally removed his braces, and they discovered his dairy allergy. His eczema cleared. Girls started noticing him. He became popular, but Abigail grew to six feet in height, standing eye-to-eye with him and most other boys in the school. Her weight remained above average no matter how many diets she tried. He stayed friends with her, preferring to hang out with someone more genuine than the fickle classmates who first shunned him for his appearance.

The night they graduated, instead of attending one of the after-parties, he sneaked his grandfather's whiskey out of the house, and they went camping. It didn't take them long to get thoroughly wasted. The conversation turned toward their tragic histories and the unlikelihood of finding somebody worth marrying. Then Abigail suggested they agree to marry each other if neither found anyone to love by the age of thirty. He agreed.

Over the past couple of years, the looming cutoff age seemed to come quicker. Two years remained. Should he marry a woman who controlled every aspect of his life? The redhead popped into his mind. He wanted to know her better. He wondered if she was spoken for. *Oh, I hope not.*

For the first time since starting his social media channel, he regretted how much he traveled. He never stayed anywhere long enough to form more than momentary friendships. Though he dated, nothing lasted longer than a few nights out to dinner. He was due in Chattanooga by the end of next week. Can a relationship develop in a handful of days? Certainly not something lasting. She likely has a husband or, at least, is seeing someone. So why bother?

Ian switched his focus toward the room's contents: three chairs, a table, and a Bible. The table held a display of Covenant Cove Honey. No television blared annoying ads as most service stations did while you waited for your oil to be changed.

The variety of colored jars drew his attention. Most were the standard orange-yellow signature color of honey. Others were a deep red. With the light shining through them, they reminded him of the redheaded woman when the late afternoon highlighted her hair. He sighed his frustration. *Why can't I stop thinking about her?*

The darker jars' labels read Chipotle Infused Clover Honey. *How do you make hot honey?* Movement on the other side of the parking lot caught his attention. The redheaded woman reappeared. His heart raced into double time before plummeting when a man appeared behind her. *Please, don't let that be her husband.*

The man towered over her slight frame. Ian estimated him to be at least five inches taller than himself. A khaki button-up shirt conformed to his bulging arms and chest. Blue jeans, boots, a ball cap, and a walk like he owned the ground beneath him identified him as the formidable sheriff. *Please, please, please don't let that be her husband.*

The sound of Casey cranking the truck reached Ian's ears. He flopped into the nearest chair, pretending to be engrossed in his phone. He didn't want to be caught gawking.

Thankfully, his sunburn hid the heated blush caused by his racing heart. The thought of meeting this mammoth sheriff and not staring at the pixie-like woman standing next to him produced perspiration despite the cool evening air of spring. *Let me pull this off.* He inhaled. *I can pull this off.*

The door opened with a swish. Ian stared at his phone harder, determined not to lift his head. A delicate, spicey scent reached him. *It's her!* Ian tensed when the heavy clump, clump of boots followed. The scent wafted stronger towards Ian with the breeze from the closing door. *I'm doomed!*

"Ian MacGregor." The man's voice demanded his attention.

Ian casually raised his head to make direct eye contact with the man. *That's it. Don't let him know you're nervous.*

"At your service," Ian said, standing and holding out his hand to be shaken.

The man clutched it, giving a single, rigid shake. Not enough to hurt, but Ian understood the unspoken message: 'Don't mess with me.'

"You've met Casey. This is my daughter Grace. And my name is Jeremiah Johnson, the town's sheriff. Welcome to Covenant Cove."

Ian glanced at Casey and then Grace as he introduced them. When his eyes rested on her, he couldn't pull his gaze away. Up close, her delicate features entranced him. He found her lack of makeup leant an aura of honesty, which relieved him in a way he couldn't explain. He smiled, and her face flushed. *Her name is Grace, and she's not his wife!*

"Ian?" Jeremiah coaxed, clearing his throat for emphasis.

Casey's nudge on Ian's arm broke his trance. "Fitting," he blurted, returning his attention to the sheriff. Ian tensed, feeling the wetness spread in his pits. *Oh, good grief. I just stared at his daughter right in front of him.*

"What's fitting?" Jeremiah asked.

"The name G… uh… I… uhhh… Jeremiah Johnson," Ian stammered. "Excellent western. I watched the movie with my dad a long time ago. It fits you."

"Yeah? I said the same thing to my wife," Jeremiah preened.

Grace stifled a snort, drawing Ian's attention. The edges of his mouth turned up. She caught his gaze, blushed, and turned her focus to the floor. *Did she feel an attraction too?*

"Grace." Jeremiah drew out her name in warning.

"Yes, Father?"

"You stay here with Brother Casey while I take Mr. MacGregor for a quick ride. I'm sure Sister Rebecca will be along shortly with the baby." Jeremiah's voice, while not raised, held authority.

Oh, great. I'm in for it now. Guess I'll be sleeping in the shed tonight.

* * * * *

"Ian, I'm not going to beat around the bush," Jeremiah said, putting the truck in gear and heading away from town. "I know who you are and enjoy your channel in my spare time. I figure you will want to film while you're in town. There are rules you need to follow while you're here. Not everyone in our community will want to be in your videos."

Whew! No sleeping in a shed. "I understand," Ian acknowledged. Footage often needed to be edited to omit individuals who objected to being on camera.

"Rule number one: never put my family on any social media. In fact, don't take any pictures or videos of us," the sheriff warned. "Rule number two: get permission from everyone else."

Ian casually turned towards the window before Jeremiah caught his deer-in-the-headlights look. He felt a pang of remorse over the picture he'd snapped of Grace without her knowing. It was right to erase the image before Abigail posted them, but he wanted to keep them. He checked his watch. After five o'clock. Abigail wouldn't check his cloud account until Monday. He decided he'd wait and erase the picture later tonight once he analyzed his emotions further.

"Understood. I have release forms for anyone agreeing to be on camera." Ian said, talking to his reflection more than the man beside him.

"Great. I knew you'd be easy to get along with," Jeremiah proclaimed, clapping Ian on the shoulder. "Now that's out of the way. We need to address the horn issue. The name of the boy who owns the truck is Dean. He gave Grace problems last year, and I banned him from entering the town. We'll review the rest of the rules once I finish with him."

He finished speaking as he pulled into a driveway of a double-wide

106

trailer with small garden sculptures, birdbaths, and a myriad of flowering plants cluttering the yard. It looked like a bomb exploded in a bougie garden center. Where every chipped statue landed is where it remained, with no order to be seen. They reminded him of his grandparents' backyard. Other memories surfaced. He pushed them away.

Jeremiah ascended the steps with bold authority to knock on the wooden screen door. Ian opened his window a crack and heard the high-pitched barking of several miniature dogs inside the house. A lanky man stepped out onto the porch. His relaxed stance contradicted Jeremiah's, who braced his fisted hands on his hips. Ian couldn't hear what they said, but when Jeremiah jabbed his finger toward the man's face before leaving, he knew it wasn't a casual conversation.

"Okay, that's taken care of," Jeremiah said, returning to the driver's seat.

"You don't like him?" Ian asked with a hint of sarcasm. What might happen if he got on Jeremiah's wrong side?

"I don't care for how he treated my daughter. Whether I like or dislike him has nothing to do with how I treat him," Jeremiah grimaced, backing out of the drive.

Ian waited for him to continue with more of an explanation. He wondered what the nature of the crime committed was to deserve banishment.

"Now, back to town," he said, backing out of the drive. "There are more rules you need to know about."

"I'm all ears," Ian said, trying to keep his frustration out of his voice. Too many unanswered questions swirled in his head. Vague answers were given to the questions he asked. He didn't want to be pushy. Being without a means of escape limited the amount of assertiveness he could exercise.

"The idea of Covenant Cove began after the housing crash of 2008. It's not an official town; it's a perpetual trust set up by the founder, who passed away almost five years ago. The mailing center is only address for the entire community."

"Wait," Ian said, his curiosity piqued. "Are you saying nobody here owns their property?"

"Not in the town proper, no. There are some community members whose land adjoins the property," Jeremiah said. "But you're getting ahead of me. You need to understand the purpose of the town before understanding how things operate."

"Okay, what's the purpose?" Ian asked with just a hint of his mounting frustration.

"Let me ask you this first. What do you know about the Bible?"

Ian suppressed a groan. *Oh, good grief.* A religious community. He didn't look forward to being pestered to accept Jesus into his heart. *Just what I didn't need.*

"Sheriff, I'm not trying to be rude. Really, I'm not, but I'm kind of on edge here. My car broke down in the middle of nowhere. Casey appeared out of nowhere to pick me up from nowhere when I didn't even call him because nowhere doesn't have cell service. How did he know I was there? A guy driving a truck with a train horn is cause for alarm, and you will ban me for giving your daughter problems. Does that include staring at her? Because if it does, I'm up a creek without a paddle. And to top off an already horrible day, I probably just made you angry. I'm going to be stuck in a shed without a toilet or running water for the next few days because there's no hotel in this town that's not a town." Ian's voice rose with each word he spoke.

Ian propped his elbow up against the window, placing his head in the palm of his hand. *Well, I just did it. I'm sleeping in a shed or getting kicked out.*

Jeremiah released a long whistle. "Son! You have had a rough day. Bet you're hungry too."

"Starving," Ian confessed, ashamed of his outburst. "Sorry to go off on you."

"Don't worry. I get angry for no reason when I'm hungry, too," Jeremiah admitted. "We'll get you fixed up when we get to the house, but I need to explain the town laws first. Everyone must follow them while staying here."

"Can you give me the shortened version? I haven't eaten since seven this morning," Ian confessed.

"Sure. This is a Torah-keeping community. The basic rules are to observe The Ten Commandments, including the seventh day Sabbath, which starts at sunset. That means you can't do any filming or picture-taking tomorrow if you'll use them for money-making purposes. Also, mind your manners and keep your hands to yourself. I saw how you stared at Grace."

"Understood. Wait. Did you say Torah? Like in the Old Testament Torah? You're Jewish?" Ian asked in astonishment.

"Nope. We're Natsarim or what the Bible calls Watchmen," Jeremiah said. "We believe in Jesus and following the commandments of the Old Testament to the best of our ability, but let's hold off on the rest of your questions until after supper because, honestly, I'm getting hangry too."

Although questions raced through Ian's brain, he agreed to postpone asking them. He had never heard of Christians keeping Torah. The Christian academy taught that the Old Testament Laws were for the Jews only. He found the foreign concept intriguing.

"Hope you like Chipotle Honey BBQ chicken because that's what we're having," Jeremiah said, interrupting Ian's thoughts. "Let's pick up Grace and your gear."

So that's what it's for. "I haven't tried the flavor before, but it sounds delicious." *Ha. Barbecue. Figures.* Well, at least Abigail can't say I'm slacking.

17

The braying of several hound dogs greeted the truck when Jeremiah pulled onto his property, located a mile past the pond and park. Both men refrained from speaking during the ride, each suffering the pangs of empty stomachs. Grace did not volunteer to fill the silence.

"Grace, see how long before supper's ready," Jeremiah said, turning the truck off. "I'll show Mr. MacGregor around a bit."

"Yes, Father," she replied before exiting the truck to navigate the onslaught of animals vying for her attention.

Ian stared in wonder after her. He couldn't help himself. On the ride here, even though she sat behind him, thoughts of her kept him occupied. Her unique scent kept him aware of her presence.

"She's beguiling, isn't she?" Jeremiah asked.

"Yeah," Ian sighed before realizing who had asked the question. He coughed. "Well, what I mean is…"

"Don't worry. So long as you remember, she's not on the menu." His gruff voice conveyed a deeper warning.

"Sheriff, I'm not like that," Ian said, protesting Jeremiah's assumption.

"Oh? You're a man, aren't you?" Jeremiah challenged. "Even I can see her allure. She has a rare and enchanting spirit, but she's suffered more than you can imagine. She's distrusting of men. Getting to know Grace better will depend upon the type of man you are. Are you a lion or a swan?"

"Excuse me?"

"There are two types of men: lions and swans. A lion needs a harem to survive. He surrounds himself with side chicks to support his ego. Swans have one mate for their entire life. The male's sole purpose is to take care of his mate. You'll have to prove yourself to Grace if you want to stand a chance with her?"

"Papa!"

Ian's jaw dropped. A rambunctious little boy with wavy red hair, the same shade as Grace's, leaped off the porch and crawled through the open window into Jeremiah's lap.

"Momma said to tell you supper's ready. Who are you?"

Shocked, Ian didn't answer. *He's the mirror image of her.*

"My name's Joshua. I'm going to be four years old in September." He held up two chubby fingers on each hand.

Ian gained control of his surprise. "Nice to meet you, Joshua. My name is Ian, and I'll be twenty-eight next month."

"And that's Mr. MacGregor for you, little man," Jeremiah admonished. "Tell the women we'll be there in a couple more minutes. Off with you."

"All right, Papa." Joshua exited the truck through the window and ran up the steps.

"She's not so interesting now, is she?"

The goading in Jeremiah's voice irritated Ian. Grace, having a child, didn't bother him. The assumption that it would affect his view of her annoyed him. People watching his videos thought they knew him. Even Abigail didn't know his private thoughts anymore. Should he try to convince Jeremiah he wasn't a fickle person?

"Where's his father?"

"He's not in the picture."

"Will he ever return?"

"My most fervent prayer is she'll be completely free of him one day," Jeremiah said. He bumped his fist against the steering wheel. "Time to eat. I'm starving." He launched himself out of the truck.

* * * * *

The meal included the spicey honey barbecue chicken, along with homemade potato salad, green beans, crusty sourdough rolls, and limited conversation. Exhausted from the day's activities, Ian didn't mind the silence. He wondered when Jeremiah would take him to the cabin. He just wanted to sleep. Then Grace set a plated apple pie slice in front of him and asked if he wanted coffee to go with dessert.

"Yes, please." He needed the caffeine.

"Mama, can Mr. MacGregor help me put a puzzle together?" Joshua asked.

"Well, I don't know, Joshua. I've never seen him put one together before," Grace replied, a teasing smile lighting up her face. "Shall we ask him?" Grace turned towards Ian. "Mr. MacGregor, are you capable of helping Joshua assemble a puzzle?" she asked in a haughty tone.

"Well, I don't know," Ian said. "I am getting senile in my old age, but if you get the puzzle, Joshua, maybe we can figure it out together."

Joshua giggled and ran to retrieve the puzzle from the cabinet underneath the window in the dining room.

"Does he run everywhere?" Ian asked Grace.

"Pretty much," she replied. "The only time he is completely still is when he's asleep."

Grace left the room. Joshua scrambled back into his chair. Ian's hand shot out to steady the booster seat when it shifted. Joshua opened the wooden box and dumped the contents onto the table. Pieces slid everywhere. Ian caught a piece before it fell on the floor.

"Is this wood?" he asked, fingering the thick puzzle piece.

"Yeah! This is my favorite puzzle. It's got all kinds of cool pieces," he said, digging through the pile. "See!" He held up a flower.

"Oh, wow. Cool. My turn," Ian said with excitement, digging into the pile himself. He discarded a few pieces before holding up his find. "A chicken!" he exclaimed. "Or is it a rooster?"

"Look, Mr. MacGregor! A lion. Rawr," Joshua giggled, making claws with his fingers.

Juniper caught Ian's eye when she placed a coffee cup before him.

"You know, we've never put this puzzle together," she said, combing through the pieces herself. "Look, Joshua, I found the hummingbird again."

The scene before him prickled his memory. He forgot how it felt to be surrounded by family. Many Sundays, his parents and he ate lunch at his paternal grandparent's house after church. Each person present could be a member of his own family. He became Joshua. Jeremiah and Juniper stood in place of his grandparents. Grace, doing the dishes, became his mother, and he replaced himself with his father.

The make-believe memory evoked a longing that pulled him deeper into an artificial reality. Smells and sounds associated with his childhood visited his senses. He closed his eyes, inhaling the burning smell of his grandfather's pipe. His mother sang with the radio in the kitchen, and he could hear the faint clicking of his grandmother's knitting needles.

"Dad, Dad!" He shook his father's arm, trying to get his attention.

"Mr. MacGregor! Mr. MacGregooorrr!" Joshua exclaimed, waving his hand in front of Ian's face.

Ian jumped in his seat. The abrupt return to reality left him bewildered for a moment.

Everyone at the table stared at him. Heat crawled up his neck. "Sorry, Joshua, you caught me in a daydream." To cover his embarrassment, he raised his mug, only to realize he had drunk his coffee while he was zoned out.

"That's okay, but it's not daytime anymore. See, it's tomorrow," Joshua said, pointing towards the window.

Ian turned to see darkness overtaking the remnants of the reddish-orange hue of the setting sun. An unexpected joy filled him. He couldn't remember the last time he felt the comfortable peace surrounding him now. "So, it has Joshua. So, it has." Grace's peppery scent pulled his attention away from the window.

"That's right. It's tomorrow," she said, setting a glass with an unnamed but delicious-smelling concoction and a small, lidded jar in front of him. "Which means it's time for little men to get ready for bed."

"But, Momma, we haven't found your favorite puzzle piece yet," Joshua protested.

"Mr. MacGregor is holding it in his hand."

Ian raised his hand to see the shape of a fox between his thumb and forefinger. "I'm a hound dog. Arooroorooo!" he said, bouncing the wooden figure through the air to tickle Joshua with it.

Straight away, Joshua started mimicking him. His chubby cheeks puckered up, imitating the same noise, bringing Ian to laughter. He turned to the other adults to share his enjoyment. Grace and Juniper looked amused. Jeremiah wore a deep frown of anger.

"Not in this house, you're not," Jeremiah warned.

Jeremiah's understanding of Ian's words caused him the most embarrassment yet. He knew his videos didn't paint him in the best light, but did the man think he was a womanizer? He rubbed his forehead to regain his composure.

"Disney. The Fox and The Hound?" Ian prompted.

"My bad," Jeremiah coughed. "Ian. I apologize. I've jumped to the wrong conclusion again." His red face testifying to his embarrassment.

"Forget it, Sheriff," Ian said, dismissing the apology. "Truth is, I'd probably be doing the same thing if I were you."

"Thanks for understanding," Jeremiah said. He held up his glass for a toast. "Shabbat shalom!"

"Shabbat shalom!" Grace and Juniper sang in unison.

"What you said!" Ian raised his glass, clinked it against Jeremiah's, and took a deep gulp. The warmed liquid seared his throat before pooling in his stomach. He suppressed coughing, but tears gathered in his eyes from the effort. "I did not expect that."

"Alcohol? We're Natsarim Ian, not prudes," Jeremiah explained, rising from his chair. "Besides, I enjoy a good hot toddy. Helps these old bones rest easier."

Jeremiah stretched and yawned with exaggeration when he finished his drink. Beside him, Joshua yawned also, mimicking his grandfather's stretch. Unable to stop himself, Ian yawned too.

"Ian, time to go to the cabin. I'm bushed, and morning comes early around here."

"You won't get any arguments from me," Ian yawned yet again. He picked up the small jar, lifting the lid. It held a creamy white substance. He sniffed. *Coconut?*

He questioned Grace with a raised eyebrow, unsure how to address her. He didn't want to be presumptuous until he knew her better. She tapped her cheek, showing he should apply the cream to his sunburned face.

"Oh, okay. Thank you."

Ian rose to follow Jeremiah outside before realizing he had forgotten his manners.

"Thank you, Mrs. Johnson, for the delicious meal," he added shyly.

"Call me Juniper, dear. Mrs. Johnson makes me feel ancient," she said, dismissing his formality. "See you in the morning."

He turned to leave once more but remembered Joshua.

"Goodnight, Joshua. Thank you for the entertaining evening."

"Goodnight, Mr. MacGregor," Joshua giggled and jumped.

Ian grinned at his animation. He found the child's innocent and open nature refreshing. Unlike his mother, who remained reserved the entire evening, joy bubbled out of him. Grace kept more to herself, speaking only when necessary. Ian paused before opening the truck's door letting the dogs swarm his legs. She addressed him directly only twice the entire evening.

He started at the sound of the truck's horn. Jeremiah busted out laughing.

"Good one, Sheriff," Ian said, unable to stop his peeved expression from forming.

Jeremiah laughed harder. "Sorry. Couldn't help myself," he said, not appearing remorseful.

Ian chuckled to himself, shutting the truck door. At least Jeremiah was in a better mood. He agreed hot toddies are good for relaxing.

* * * * *

The steep trail, full of deep ruts, wasn't long, and the views were worth the discomfort of the ride. He followed Jeremiah through the door. The log cabin's small size deceived him.

"This is my thinking spot," Jeremiah proudly announced, lighting an oil lamp.

Ian loved the space at once. One corner served as a library with bookshelves and a comfortable reading chair. To his left stood a wood stove and a small kitchenette. On his right was a rustic wooden table with two ladder-back chairs. The queen-size bed on the far wall beckoned him. Across from the entrance, a bank of floor-to-ceiling windows and a door he assumed led to a porch or deck completed the cozy retreat.

"This is amazing, Sheriff. I expected more of a hunting shack, not a mountain retreat."

"Thank you, but credit for the furnishings belongs to Juniper and Grace," he said, deflecting the compliment. "When we first moved here, this place held the table, chairs, a creaky, old metal bed frame, and a worn-out blue tick mattress with questionable stains. They insisted I be comfortable while researching my sermons, so they revamped the place."

"Sermons? You're a preacher too?" Ian asked.

"Well, in a manner. I got volunteered for the position when the pastor passed away last year," Jeremiah explained. "Turns out, I enjoy preaching and teaching the Word."

"Volunteered? I find it hard to believe a man of your size allowed himself to be pushed into doing anything not of his choosing." Ian chuckled. "Tell the truth. Did your wife make you do it?"

"The elder's council suggested I fill in until we find another pastor." Jeremiah sat at the table. "We need to find a replacement soon. Being sheriff and pastor creates an imbalance of power."

"Elder's council? Balance of power?" Ian asked. The tidbits of information he received throughout the day swirled through his brain without making connections. Everyone acted normal, even though Jeremiah's presence domineered everyone around him. He remembered Grace and Juniper catering to him during supper, bringing him things without being asked. They functioned as servants rather than a wife or daughter. The cult alarms triggered again. "Sheriff, precisely what sort of community is this?" he asked.

Jeremiah retrieved a booklet from one bookcase.

"Here you go. This should answer your questions," he said, tapping the cover.

"Covenant Cove: History and Beliefs," Ian read aloud. "Will this tell me how Casey knew I needed a tow without me calling him?"

A grin spread across Jeremiah's face. "Oh, he did? Casey didn't tell me the details of how you arrived. I suspect the Holy Ghost prompted him on where he needed to go. When you live in a Spirit-based community, you hear His voice more often."

A bark of laughter escaped Ian. "Holy Ghost?" he mocked. "As in Father, Son, Holy Ghost? The Trinity?"

"I see you've heard of them," Jeremiah said. "Except, they're not a trinity as taught by the modern Christian churches. 'Hear, O Israel: The LORD our God is one LORD.' Deuteronomy 6:4. There is only one God."

Ian rolled his eyes. *Here we go. Bible lessons activated.* "Sheriff, the entire world believes the entity you call God is three separate, coequal beings. Trust me, I know. I had plenty of lessons and debates over the Trinity versus non-Trinity issue at the Christian academy I attended."

Jeremiah grunted. "And the tone of your voice tells me you don't believe what they taught you, either. Here, I'll show you. It's quite simple." He moved the lamp between them. "The Bible states: 'For our God is a consuming fire.'" He pointed to the flame in the lamp. "The fire is God. Okay?"

"Okay," Ian said, going along with the lesson to humor Jeremiah.

"What do you get from fire?"

Ian shrugged, not putting much thought into the answer being sought. The room grew brighter and darker. "Light. You get light."

"Correct. Jesus is the light of the world. He lights our path, showing us the way," Jeremiah said. "'I am the light of the world: he that followeth me shall not walk in darkness, but shall have the light of life.' John 8:12. Now, what else do you get?"

Again, the answer escaped Ian, and he shrugged. Jeremiah grabbed his hand, holding his open palm over the lamp's chimney. "Ow! Why'd you do that?" Ian asked, jerking his hand out of Jeremiah's grasp.

"Well, what do you get?"

Ian rubbed the palm of his hand. He never realized how much heat those lamps emitted. *Oh, duh.* "Heat. You get heat."

"Correct again. The heat is the Holy Ghost. His warmth fills and comforts us, giving us counsel and instructions," Jeremiah informed him. "Fire cannot exist without producing light and heat. Light and heat cannot exist without fire. The Trinity is One."

"Huh. The way you explained everything makes more sense. Good lesson, Sheriff. No wonder the Elder's Council picked you to be the pastor."

"Thanks, but I can't take the credit. The former pastor passed the fire analogy on to me many years ago." Jeremiah stood. "Okay, I believe I've given you enough food for thought tonight. That door leads to the outhouse. Be careful. There are bears."

"Got it."

"Oh, and one last thing." Jeremiah cupped his hand over the chimney, blowing out the flame. Darkness engulfed them. "Without

God, you've got nothing but darkness. Goodnight Ian. See you in the morning."

"Goodnight, Sheriff."

Ian stood in the dark, listening to the sounds of Jeremiah leaving. The door to his pickup truck squeaked. A hollow slam followed. The engine fired up, then fell into a low rumble. The loud snap of a dead branch told him the truck was in motion. Still, Ian didn't move away from the table. A feeling, a tug, had started in his chest.

He struggled with the concept of the God taught to him. The Bible said there was only one God and a Trinity simultaneously. Plus, he could never reconcile the loving God they taught when He allowed so many terrible things to happen. The more Bible lessons the school gave, the more confused Ian became, so he pushed God away because no one gave him the answers he sought. He led his life without God entering his thoughts.

Ian moved to the wall of windows. He anticipated Bible lessons because of Jeremiah's words while they toured the town. He prepared himself for the onslaught. He expected to leave this place without a change in his opinion of God, but then Jeremiah delivered his little sermon, throwing him off kilter. The analogy awakened his curious nature. He wanted to know more.

He laughed. The Trinity is One. Jeremiah clarified everything in one simple sentence. "But is God really that simple?" he asked his reflection.

"*Yes.*"

The hair on the back of Ian's neck rose, and chills ran over his spine. He clearly heard someone other than himself speak. He spun around the room and checked under the bed. No one. *I must have imagined it.* He kicked off his shoes before falling onto the bed. Sleep found him before he rolled over.

* * * * *

"Hey, Junebug," Jeremiah said, pulling Juniper into his arms and nuzzling her neck.

"Hey." she yawned, turning within his embrace to lay her cheek against his chest. "Do you think he's the one?"

"Maybe." Jeremiah yawned and rolled to his back. "If not, we'll continue to pray until we get an answer. Time to go to sleep. I'm exhausted."

"I like him," Juniper said, ignoring Jeremiah's request for sleep. "Did you see the way he kept Joshua from falling when his booster seat shifted on the chair?"

"Yeah. He has quick reflexes. Don't tell him, but I like him too," he warned. "If he is the one, I need to test him to be sure he can keep his cool under pressure. Right now, I've got him hopping like a Mexican jumping bean." Jeremiah laughed.

"You need to quit teasing him." Juniper rolled to her other side. "Did you see how he watched Grace?"

"Yeah. As if he's been in the desert for a month and she's a glass of water."

"That worries me," she said.

"Grace will quash his advances if they're out of order. No need to worry." Jeremiah rolled to his side, laying his hand on Juniper's hip. "Goodnight, Junebug. I love you."

"I love you too, dear."

18

The brilliant sunrise streaming through the wall of bare windows penetrated Ian's eyelids. He rolled over, but the chatter of birds filled the air. *Ugh*! He slammed a pillow over his head, but soon, the call of nature demanded he rise.

He shuffled barefoot to the side door. A small porch led to a stone path edged with saplings and a massive deck equal to the size fo the cabin.On his left, a long branch, jutting out from the overgrowth, jumped. What kind of creature hid in there? Carefully, he spread the branches apart. A female cardinal zoomed past his face and up into the empty sky. *Awesome!*

Out on the deck, he imagined himself standing on a precipice. Jeremiah's spread lay below him. Behind the house stood a small barn. Beyond it sat a quaint cottage surrounded by an abundance of plant beds. A wooded area separated the yard from a sizeable field dotted with black cows. No one appeared to be stirring yet.

To the south, the land rose gently, giving him a full view of the town's layout. The early morning sun lit up the buildings, making the townscape more picturesque than yesterday evening. He retrieved his phone, ignoring Jeremiah's warning not to take pictures today if they were to generate income. Saturday may be their Sabbath day, but it wasn't his. Plus, almost everything he did was for the achievement of income. He snapped a few photos and sent Abigail a text message. Then ran to the outhouse.

He checked the time on his phone after returning to the deck. Eight o'clock. Didn't Jeremiah say they started mornings early? He hoped someone would show up soon. Hunger knocked. He needed a distraction before he grew impatient. He returned to the cabin, retrieving the booklet he tossed on the table, then settled in the lounge chair to read.

An hour later, back on the deck, he considered the town in a new light. The booklet explained the town's religious beliefs. They used the Biblical Hebrew names of God and Jesus, Yahuah, and Yahusha. They viewed themselves as citizens of the Kingdom of Yah and followed the laws, the Torah, of His kingdom, which included observing the seventh day Sabbath, not eating unclean foods, and keeping the feast days. What most Christians considered burdensome, they considered an act of love.

The booklet explained the custom of wearing head coverings instead of wedding rings. He noticed Grace and Juniper wearing scarves on their heads yesterday but thought they were part of their outfits.

Does that mean Grace is still married?

The booklet detailed the history of the land and the birth of the town as it stood today. The land passed from the original owners, Nate and Apple Dresden, to their descendants until it reached Walter Dresden, their great-great-grandson. After the Vietnam War, he retired from the military and began a new career, transforming the defunct cattle farm into an old-west-themed vacation retreat named Pioneer Cove. He appointed himself as sheriff.

The retreat remained popular until after Y2K. When the threat of technology becoming extinct never manifested, the novelty of living without electricity waned. People wanted exotic vacations at resorts that offered babysitting services. They kept the place operating until the market crashed in 2008. They closed the business, leaving Walter in despair over how to pay the property taxes.

A longtime friend, a Messianic Jew, who lost everything in the crash, contacted him about renting a cabin until he could get back on his feet. Little did Walter know the phone call would change his life forever. Word spread to others with the same belief of keeping the commandments of Yah and having the testimony of Yahusha. Soon, every cabin filled with the demand for more. In the first year, the property taxes were paid, and he added ten new cabins.

Over the next two years, the community grew to one hundred homes. They built the community center. In the year 2012, the fifty-space campground opened. At eighty-one, Walter rededicated his life and land to the service of Yahuah. They renamed the town Covenant Cove. A twelve-member Elder's Council, representing the twelve tribes of Israel, wrote the town ordinances. Then Walter set up the perpetual trust and charity to protect the land for future generations of believers.

In the spring of 2015, doctors diagnosed Walter with terminal cancer. The council compiled a list of candidates to fill his shoes. The trust ensured only a person with a track record of honesty and integrity gained ownership and operation of the town. After much deliberation, the council voted to offer the responsibility to the current sheriff and owner, Jeremiah Johnson.

No wonder he walks as if he owns the place. He does!

Everything operated similarly to apartment contracts. Besides the low-rate rental agreements, the residents signed binding contracts to abide by Biblical laws. If a resident violated the laws, the elder's council voted on whether the offender should receive a warning, fine, or eviction. Jeremiah, the trust beneficiary, performed the legal removals if needed.

Now he understood how an imbalance of power existed. The pastor served as an advisor and thirteenth member of the council in case of a tie. Jeremiah couldn't enforce the laws and also serve as judge and jury.

"Hello? Anybody home?"

"Out here, Sheriff," Ian said. He held the booklet up when Jeremiah stepped into view. "This explains a lot."

"Thought you might understand reading our beliefs better than me preaching them. Plus, the story cuts down on questions." He moved to stand beside Ian, handing him a travel mug. "Here, bet you could use this. Sorry, I'm late. Joshua wanted me to help him with his chores this morning."

"I thought everyone rested on the Sabbath day."

"Still have to feed the animals."

Ian gulped the warming liquid, taking the edge off his growling stomach. He hummed his thanks. He stood silently beside Jeremiah, enjoying the scenery while fidgeting with the flap covering the drinking hole.

"Something on your mind?"

Ian gave Jeremiah a sheepish glance. The man could probably read him like a book. "Yeah, but nothing important."

"You know, there's only one reason people show up in Covenant Cove," Jeremiah said, leaning his forearms on the porch railing. "They're missing something. What are you missing, Ian MacGregor?"

Purpose. The word sprang to the forefront of Ian's mind. Though he didn't want to admit to his feelings, the past few assignments left him disenchanted. He risked his life doing crazy stunts for what? His adventures turned into one endless hotel room after another. He couldn't name the feeling until Jeremiah asked him what he was missing. *What is my purpose?*

"If you had to decide today, which job would you pick? Sheriff or pastor?"

"Many are the plans in a person's heart, but it is the Lord's purpose that prevails," Jeremiah quoted. "Proverbs. It means I'd choose whichever fulfills Yah's will for my life."

Ian bit back a grimace. He needed insight, not a lecture on God. "How can you fulfill God's purpose if you don't know if God exists?" The words rushed out unfettered, exposing his beliefs.

"What makes you think He doesn't exist?"

"Well, how can He?" Ian snapped. "How can a loving God allow children to be abused?"

Ian saw sadness enter Jeremiah's eyes before he turned away. A tickle of satisfaction bubbled up inside him. *He can't answer the question either.* When he asked the same question in theology class, they blamed everything bad on the fall of Adam. *Ha! There's no way one human caused all suffering throughout history.*

"Ian, you see those hawks circling on the updrafts over there?"

"Yeah?"

"Birds are sort of like robots. Yah programmed them to do bird things," Jeremiah said. "They migrate where and when they're programmed to go. They mate, build nests, and raise their young in the manner of their programming, and they eat what they're programmed to eat. There is no free will for them."

"Yeah, so? How is a hawk a factor in child abuse?"

"Humans, Yah's created children, have free will. They have the option of doing or not doing it. Child abuse is an act someone chooses to commit. Most suffering comes through making poor choices."

Ian tightened his lips. Okay. Personal decisions affecting the lives of others was a valid argument. And things out of human control? "What about cancer?" he asked, challenging Jeremiah further. "Are you saying my mother's choices caused her to die?"

He bit back the tears that arose with the memory of his mother twisting and turning in pain while she lay in her hospital bed. They told him to pray for her to be healed. He prayed and prayed. Every night he kneeled beside his bed, praying for her to get better. She still died.

Other memories arose. His father's drinking. Him marrying another woman a few months after his mother's death. He made getting a new mother sound exciting. He gained two stepbrothers to play with him. They wound up destroying his toys. Even the one he kept in the box because it was the last toy his mother gave him. His father began drinking. His stepmother unleashed her anger and frustration on Ian. He told no one. At ten, his father, driving drunk, died in a car accident. The beatings increased. At twelve, his grandparents discovered her abuse, sued for custody and won, but the scars remained.

"Well, Sheriff? I'm waiting."

"I'm truly sorry you lost your mother," Jeremiah said quietly. "There's an answer, but it won't heal the pain of her loss. There are reasons humans suffer from disease, though most don't accept where the responsibility lies. Can you set aside your anger long enough to listen with your head and not your heart?"

"I'm all ears." Ian crossed his arms, daring Jeremiah to change his mind.

"Alright then." Jeremiah leaned against the porch railing, crossing his arms as well. "Have you ever heard of 'forever chemicals?'"

"I think so. Aren't they a byproduct of nonstick cookware?"

"That's one use, but they're in almost everything. Like atomic waste, they take *forever* to degrade. These, and other chemicals, can alter your genetic code and lead to cancer."

Ian's arms dropped. The simplicity of Jeremiah's explanation surprised him. "So, you're saying pollution caused my mother's cancer?"

"Yes. At some point, whether during your mother's life, her mother's, or her great-grandmother's, her genetic code altered because of environmental toxins."

Ian wavered. He never thought of cancer stemming from contamination. Thinking of the disease as a pollutant made sense.

The answer lowered Ian's resentment a few notches, but he wasn't prepared to relinquish his grudge against God altogether. Ian cleared the emotion out of his throat. "How do we end the cycle of contamination?"

"Yah's already provided the answer. All we need to do is follow His instructions. His Torah."

"We're back to that again?"

Jeremiah smiled. "If the goal is to avoid contamination, shouldn't we return to a life where there is none? Where we're in control of what enters our bodies?"

Ian nodded.

"Stand ye in the ways, and see, and ask for the old paths, where is the good way, and walk therein, and ye shall find rest for your souls. Jeremiah 6:16," Jeremiah quoted. "The 'old paths' are following the laws, the Torah, of God. Torah means instructions."

Ian couldn't stop the bark of laughter. "So, you're saying the Bible is a user's manual? As long as we follow the instructions, we avoid pollution?"

"Basically, yeah. Sin is also a type of pollution," Jeremiah said, chuckling. "Torah teaches honest business practices. If research shows that forever chemicals cause cancer, is a business offering products containing them being honest? Can you imagine going to the store and seeing cookware plastered with warning signs that read, 'Warning: Using this pan can lead to cancer in your great grandchildren'?"

"No. Profits would plummet," Ian said. He had to give Jeremiah credit. The explanations he offered were easy to understand. They brought him closer to closure over the ills of his past. *Perhaps there is something to following the Biblical laws.* He wasn't ready to concede, but he wanted to know more. "You know, I don't think I should call you Sheriff anymore. You're definitely pastor material. You've awakened a curiosity in me I thought died long ago."

"Thanks, Ian. Now, let's go eat breakfast. I'm starving."

19

Jeremiah delivered a late morning sermon on the history of Passover and how the Exodus story foretold the death of Yahusha, the Messiah. He said the crucifixion occurred at sunset on a Wednesday, not Friday, as taught in Sunday school. The timeline made more sense than the church's math. Jesus promised to be in the earth for three days and nights. The church claimed it was one and a half days. Being a child, Ian lacked the maturity to pursue the contradiction. He trusted his teachers.

The lecture also revealed that the word Easter in the Bible was a mistranslation of the Greek word Pesach, meaning Passover, and that the pagan symbols of eggs and rabbits related to fertility goddess worship. He reminded the congregation of Yah's command not to worship Him in the way the pagans worship their gods. He implored them to walk boldly in their faith and to run from worldly traditions into Yah's truth.

Jeremiah's words infused Ian with a new understanding of how following traditions can deceive you if you don't know their meaning. In Thailand, he bowed to a statue of Buddha. He did what the monks instructed. Without a second thought, he got on his knees like everyone else. How did his bowing differ from using an Easter egg or Christmas tree?

Speaking of blind following, how did his life choices differ? Before becoming friends with Abigail, he went to church regularly and never doubted God's existence. In the one instance he mentioned God to her, she insisted God did not exist and gave valid arguments for why He couldn't. Did she teach him disbelief? She conceived the idea of his show, pitching it to him as an exciting adventure. He went along with everything she suggested without a second thought. She influenced his beliefs and even his career choice. He didn't realize her persuasive power until this moment. How different his world might be if she had never entered his life.

"How's it going?" Jeremiah asked, sitting on the bench. "Enjoying your day off?"

Ian crossed his arms on the table. Laughter filled the pavilion where the congregation ate lunch. Earlier, many of the town's citizens stopped to welcome him to the community. Casey introduced him to his wife, Rebecca, and his sons, James and their newborn, Rowen Azariah. Ian and James agreed to meet Monday morning outside the repair shop so the boy could show him the trails in the surrounding mountains. Rebecca promised him a few jars of flavored honey before he left. A group of teenagers gathered for an impromptu Bible study two tables over. Children played on the playground. He didn't view the scene through the lens of a camera or his phone. He gained a new perspective of reality from the peculiar feeling of his empty hand. Life wasn't made to be lived behind a lens.

"Immensely."

"Good, good. How are you liking our little town so far?"

"It's great," Ian said. "Everything is so peaceful, but I guess I should expect peacefulness from a place 'where nothing ever happens, and everybody likes it that way.'"

"There are little dramas from time to time. For instance, those two over there," Jeremiah said, nodding toward Casey and Rebecca. "I didn't think she'd ever reel him in, but Rebecca is sweet, like her honey, and she finally caught him."

"He appears happy to be caught," Ian said, watching Casey follow his wife, cradling his infant son in his arms and proudly showing the baby to anyone who asked for a peek. Ian suppressed the unnamed yearning the scene evoked in him.

"And then there's that one over there," Jeremiah growled, pointing towards the man he spoke with yesterday. "As sheriff, I'd kick him out. As a pastor, I'm allowing it since he's here to help his elderly grandparents. They're good people, and I don't want to embarrass them."

Ian tracked the man's movements. Each time Grace moved away

from him, he countered the evasion, slowly closing the distance between them without being obvious.

"He's herding her," Ian hissed, standing to confront the guy.

"Hold your horses, Romeo," Jeremiah cautioned, grabbing Ian's arm. "Today's the Sabbath. We can't have any scenes. Any other day, I'd address his behavior myself."

"Well, what do we do? She's obviously not comfortable."

"Today, I'm the pastor. Juniper and I must stay with the congregation, but Grace can leave. You think you can get her away from here? You can't be alone with her, though. Don't want any wagging tongues."

"Isn't gossip a sin?"

"Knowing what sin is doesn't stop people from doing it. Only a change of heart can do that. And don't change the subject. He's getting closer by the minute."

Ian searched for answers. Grace's stalker could follow them if they walked around the pond. He spotted the white underside of a boat.

"I could take her out on the pond."

"Good idea," Jeremiah said. "But get Joshua to ask her. He can probably coax his mother into saying yes, better than you. Be careful; there are no life jackets. Joshua knows how to swim. Grace? Not so much. She panics."

Ian hurried to the playground, where Joshua and another little boy with sweaty blonde hair raced up a climbing net. Joshua reached the top first with only seconds to spare.

"I won! I won!" he exclaimed, hopping on his toes. "Did you see Mr. MacGregor? I made it to the top first."

"I saw you, Joshua," Ian praised the little boy. "You're an excellent climber, but I have a better idea."

"What kind of idea, Mr. MacGregor?" Joshua asked in excitement before scooting into the spiral slide. He popped out the bottom with a jump at Ian's feet.

"Well, I have two better ideas. The first is to call me Mr. Ian instead of Mr. MacGregor."

"But Papa —"

"I'll take care of your papa. Okay?"

"Okay, Mr. Ian. What's the other idea?"

"Do you want to ride the pedal boat?"

"Yes! Mama never lets me go on it!" Joshua jumped with excitement.

"Good, go get your mother."

"Can Ethan come too?"

"Yes, your friend Ethan can come too, but only if he asks permission."

Both boys raced off to find their parents. Ian turned towards the pond. He pushed the boat into the water. He tied the pull rope around a cleat on the dock to keep it from floating away.

Ethan returned to the dock first, and Ian helped him into one of the back seats.

"Hurry, mama! Hurry!"

Ian turned to see Joshua pulling Grace behind him. He chuckled at the little boy's effort to make her move faster and Grace's more determined effort to take her time.

"Tell her, Mr. Ian! Tell her I didn't ask!" Joshua shouted when they reached him.

"Mr. MacGregor, Joshua," Grace said, emphasizing the name. "You know you're supposed to address adults by their last names. Mr. MacGregor, I'm sorry if Joshua—."

"Ian."

A puzzled expression crossed Grace's face. "I'm sorry, what?"

"Ian. I prefer you call me Ian. Joshua can call me Mr. Ian. He's still being respectful, and I permitted him. He didn't ask me to go for a ride on the pedal boat either."

"Oh, well, then Joshua, I guess you can—."

"You're coming with us," Ian said.

Grace's jaw dropped.

"You can't say no."

"Mr. MacGregor, Ian, I hardly—."

"I have an ulterior motive," he grinned, mischievousness lighting up his eyes before he helped Joshua into the back seat.

"An ulterior… Ian… I don't think…," Grace stammered, stepping backward.

Ian leaned forward to whisper in her ear. "I'm on a rescue mission." An escaped wisp of her hair teased his cheek when the wind caught it.

Her spicy perfume filled his nostrils. He inhaled deeply, trying to name the scent.

"Mr..... Ian, I don't—," Grace said, her tone sharp.

"Don't turn around," Ian said, grabbing her hand. "You'll ruin my hard work. He's coming this way."

Grace stiffened when his words registered.

Ian stepped backward into the little boat, pulling Grace to the edge of the dock, where she froze. Ian saw the fear in her eyes.

"Grace," he said, keeping his tone calm. "I promise I'm a pro swimmer. Lifeguard classes and everything. I won't let anything happen to Joshua or you."

The sound of her stalker's boots on the wooden boards reached their ears.

Bracing himself, Ian grabbed Grace by the waist, plucking her off the dock and into her seat. Her fingers dug into his arms until the wild rocking of the boat calmed.

"Thank you. I don't think I could've done it myself," she said with a quiver in her voice.

Ian leaned over Grace to unwind the rope from the cleat. The angry eyes of Grace's stalker glared at him. Ian shoved off before giving the man a mock salute.

"Mission accomplished," Ian grinned, settling himself onto the molded seat. "Boys! Please keep your hands and feet inside the ride at all times." He placed his shoes on the pedals, pressing each one to set the paddle wheel underneath the boat in motion. Joshua and Ethan whooped their excitement.

"How long do you plan to keep me out here?" Grace asked, her fear evident in her tense posture.

"Umm. I didn't think that far ahead." Ian scratched his head. "Until he tires of waiting and goes home, I guess."

"Everyone should leave within the hour. Do you think you can hold out?"

"Sure. When I was Joshua's age, my grandfather took me to a lake where they rented pedal boats. We stayed out for hours."

"Joshua's been begging me since he learned how to talk to get on this thing. I don't care for boats. Especially ones this small. They're... unnerving."

"Look, mama. Look, Mr. Ian. There's Papa!" Joshua stood up, waving boldly at his grandfather. The boat rocked with his motions.

Grace grabbed Ian's hand on the rudder control. "Joshua, sit!" she admonished.

"Aww, mama. Nothing's going to happen. See," he said, half jumping.

Grace gasped, digging her nails into Ian's hand.

"Joshua, listen to your mother," Ian said in his most authoritative tone. "Standing in a boat is very dangerous."

"Yes sir, Mr. Ian," Joshua whined before plopping back onto his seat.

Ian stopped pedaling. The flapping sound of the paddle wheel no longer polluted the air. Water lapped against the hull. The gentle rhythm created a relaxing atmosphere. He allowed the boat to drift in the breeze. "You can let go now."

Grace jerked her hand off his. "Sorry."

"No worries." He brought out his phone. "Do you mind if I take pictures?"

"No. It is a beautiful day," Grace said. "Not of Joshua or me, though."

Ian chastised himself. He meant to delete her photo last night before exhaustion overtook him. He made a mental note to do it once they returned to land.

While taking pictures, he noticed the number of people outside the pavilion had dwindled. He laid his phone next to him on the seat. He supposed they should start heading back but waited for Grace to suggest it.

"I must admit, I'm enjoying my stay here. This town grows on you with no one trying," Ian said. "Everyone is so friendly."

"I enjoy living here. I find the lifestyle calming."

"When did you move here?"

"Four years ago this month. My father brought me here after… after Passover when the weather was warmer."

Ian didn't miss Grace's hesitation. He wondered what she hid. He turned to check on the boys. Slumped over in their seats, they were sound asleep. Without thinking, he stroked Joshua's wavy hair. He gasped. The painful surge of yearning he felt watching Casey hold his child pierced his heart. He wanted this! He wanted a family. More to the point, he wanted this family. His attachment grew stronger every minute he spent in their company.

"Grace, how does one become a member of this town?" The half-formed idea exited his mouth before his brain finished thinking.

"Why? Are you entertaining the idea of moving here?" Her eyes sparkled with amusement.

"I don't know. Maybe," he said, staring off into space. "The people are friendly and close to one another, but the God and Torah stuff? I don't know."

"Don't you believe in God, Ian?"

"If you asked me yesterday, I'd have said, 'I don't know.' Then this morning happened, and now I'm confused," he admitted.

"And what happened this morning?"

Her calm voice invited Ian to share his feelings. "Your father, of course," Ian said with a bark of laughter, shaking his head. "I've been mad at God for so long. I blamed Him for my mother's death. Your father somewhat diffused my anger. His sermon on blindly following traditions got me thinking about when I first felt anger toward God. I realized someone may have influenced me to blame Him. Now I don't know if I resent God or my friend for making me feel this way." He paused, trying to decide how to word his next statement. He didn't know whether to call Jeremiah a charlatan or a genius. The man possessed great insight, yet he claimed the two-thousand-year-old doctrine of Christianity to be wrong. "Then there's what your father teaches. For Pete's sake, I went to a Christian high school. Do I believe him when almost everything he says contradicts what I've learned about God?" He braced his elbows on his knees. "I'm so confused."

The boys shifted in the back seat. Ian and Grace turned to check on them. Ethan now lay on the floor, and Joshua sprawled across both seats. Grace laid her hand on his back. Ian watched it rise and fall with each breath. The ache clawed deeper into his heart.

"Grace, he's so amazing."

"I know. When he was a baby, I'd sit for hours watching him sleep," she said. She returned to facing forward. "But enough about me. I think I understand your problem. I used to believe the same way you do. My perspective differed slightly from yours, but I questioned Yah's existence before I moved here."

"What changed your mind?"

"I…." Grace glanced towards the back seat. "Never mind. Besides, we're talking about you, not me. Your problem is not whether you believe Yah exists. It stems from not knowing who God is." Grace turned her smile on him. "For he that cometh to God must believe that He is and that He is a rewarder of those who seek him."

"Huh?"

"It means, if you want to know God, you must believe he exists, seek him out, and form a relationship with Him."

"How do I find God if I don't know if He exists? How do I do that with someone I can't see, hear, or touch?" Ian scoffed.

"'Ask, and it shall be given you; seek, and ye shall find; knock, and it shall be opened unto you.' Yah can't answer His door if you don't knock on it. He gave us a lesson book on how to find Him. Believe, read the Bible, and pray. When you appear on His doorstep, He will answer your knock."

Ian clasped his hands together, closed his eyes, and cleared his throat. "Our Father who art in heaven." He peeked with one eye toward Grace. "Am I doing it right?"

Grace stifled her laugh. "Now you're being silly," she said. "Although people recite the Lord's Prayer, I prefer conversations with my heavenly Father. Like he's my best friend."

"Does He ever talk back?" Ian asked, remembering the word 'yes' coming to him from nowhere and no one.

"Sometimes, but not how we're talking right now. When He speaks to me, I feel His words as much as I hear them, if that makes any sense."

Ian understood. He heard the voice from last night the same way. Maybe he didn't imagine it. Could it have been God?

"Oh, look. My father is pointing at something."

Jeremiah stood on the dock, jabbing his hand toward them and yelling. Ian searched the water. Was there a snake? It should be too cold for them. *Oh, no!* His side of the boat sat much lower than Grace's. There must be a hole.

"Wake up, the boys. Have them both sit behind you." Ian started churning the pedals.

"Hurry!"

"Everything will be alright, Grace. The dock isn't that far." Ian kept the panic out of his voice. He hoped the leak didn't get any worse.

Water threatened to spill into the boat by the time they reached the dock. Jeremiah plucked the two boys from the back seat. Ian shifted to even out the weight load. The water sloshed inside the hull, the boat tipped, and Grace fell into Ian. He grabbed her out of reflex, pulling her in with him.

The pond's depth deceived him. He expected the water to be only five or six feet in depth. He opened his eyes and saw blackness. Where did Grace go? He couldn't see her.

He flung his arms wide, moving in a circle. The water concealed her. He should never have brought Grace out here, knowing she couldn't swim. His limbs ached from the frigid water. His lungs hurt. He needed to go up for air. Something brushed his arm. He hoped it wasn't a fish.

He lunged towards the movement. Grace flailed, trying to swim. Ian pulled her into his embrace. With her arms locked around his neck, he jetted upwards, using all his strength to propel them.

They gasped for air when their heads broke the surface. Though they remained underwater for less than a minute, the effects of the icy water were already taking a toll on Ian's limbs. He leaned back in a float, supporting Grace's weight on his chest. He strained his aching arms and legs to reach the grassy shore.

"Smooth move, Casanova," Jeremiah grunted, lifting Grace's weight off Ian by her dress.

Ian rolled and crawled the rest of the way out of the water before standing upright. Mud caked his knees and hands. Someone threw a blanket around him. "It was an accident," he whispered through chattering teeth.

"Grace, honey. Are you okay?" Juniper asked.

"I need my drops," Grace chattered, fumbling with the front of her dress.

Jeremiah lowered Grace onto the ground. She began convulsing. Ian fell to his knees. *What have I done? I killed her!*

20

Joshua pressed back against Ian; the little boy's usual animation was now subdued by the scene before him. Ian laid his hand on his shoulder. Joshua turned to him, hiding his tears. Ian wrapped his arms around him through the blanket to keep him from getting wet. Joshua sobbed into his neck, but Ian didn't know who comforted whom. He hugged Joshua tighter.

"Hurry, Juniper," Jeremiah hissed.

"Got it!" she exclaimed, pulling a vial attached to a string out from the neckline of Grace's dress.

Ian stopped breathing. Juniper popped the top off the container, removing a plastic syringe holding a tannish-colored substance.

"Hold her," she said, positioning the instrument to be dispensed into Grace's mouth. Jeremiah held Grace's head still for Juniper to dispense the liquid into Grace's cheek. In moments, the seizures began diminishing until they ended altogether. Jeremiah gathered Grace's limp body into his arms, and ate the ground up with his steps headed for his truck.

Juniper turned towards Ian and smiled with tenderness. He wanted to ask a million questions, but she turned her attention to Joshua, rubbing the little boy's back.

"Joshua, honey, your mama will be fine. Are you okay?"

The little boy nodded, not lifting his head from Ian's neck.

"Good, let's get home so she can rest," she said, attempting to pull Joshua out of Ian's arms.

"It's alright. I'll carry him," Ian volunteered, wanting to keep the comfort of the little boy's arms around his neck.

"Mrs. John—." Ian cut off his words when Juniper raised one of her eyebrows. She reminded him of his second-grade teacher when he acted up in class. "Juniper," he amended. "What—?"

"We'll discuss everything later, dear," she said. "We need to get Grace and you out of your wet clothes first. Come on."

Ian followed, carrying Joshua.

Jeremiah, Joshua, and Juniper piled into the front seat. Grace lay across the back seat. With no other choice, Ian sat in the truck's bed for the ride home.

* * * * *

Back at the farm, Joshua and Juniper ran to open the door. Jeremiah carried Grace into the house. Ian waited by the idling truck, hoping someone would explain what had happened to Grace. The dogs came out to sniff him before returning to their relaxed positions on the porch. A few moments later, Jeremiah reappeared carrying a bag of unknown contents.

"Get in the truck before you freeze to death. I turned on the heat."

At the mention of warmth, Ian flung the door open. The blanket offered little protection against the wind. None of his discomforts mattered when compared to what Grace suffered. "What…?"

"Get warmed up first. I'm taking you back to the cabin." Jeremiah snarled, shifting the truck into drive.

Ian nodded. Did Jeremiah's gruff voice arise from his concern over Grace or anger towards him? He couldn't blame the man for any irritation he might hold. He would be mad, too, if his daughter got dunked in freezing water and almost drowned. His less than twenty-four-hour stay in this town might end sooner than he wished. He hoped not. He needed to understand all these foreign emotions coming out since arriving.

Jeremiah's phone rang as they reached the cabin. "You go on inside while I take this," he said before answering the phone.

Ian shut the door without slamming it despite his growing impatience. He wanted to know what had happened. He peeled his wet clothes off and flung them onto the floor before pulling a pair of joggers and a long-sleeved jersey from his bag. Two sets of clothes yesterday and two sets today. If this continued, he needed to go shopping.

Once dressed, he sat at the table to wait. He stared at the oil lamp in front of him. The events of the day swirled inside his head. Confused and anxious, he considered discussing everything with Abigail before deciding not to call her. Why give her more ammunition to tease him?

"Sorry to keep you waiting. That was Casey." Jeremiah shut the door. He set the bag he brought from the house on the table before plopping into the lounge chair. "Seems the lawnmower threw a rock, cracking the boat hull."

"I'm sorry, Sheriff. What happened today is my fault." Ian hung his head. "I should've checked the boat before I put it in the water."

"Son, what happened today is not your fault," Jeremiah said. "Accidents happen. Stop feeling guilty."

"If I checked the boat, Grace...." He let the sentence trail off, not knowing precisely what happened with Grace. "I should've checked the boat."

"Ian. Grace's seizure isn't your fault." Jeremiah stared out the window. "It's mine," he said in a hoarse whisper.

What! Ian suspected Jeremiah and Juniper adopted Grace because neither possessed a strand of red hair. Now the man informed him he caused Grace's illness? What kind of relationship did they have? "How—?"

"I need to know your feelings about Grace."

I don't understand them myself! "I don't know if I can explain my feelings," Ian said.

"Try. There's no right or wrong answer."

Ian closed his eyes, recalling each interaction with Grace. "It felt like I woke up from a deep sleep when I saw her. Disoriented but aware at the same time? Then, seeing Joshua and how much Grace loves him reminded me of my mother, and I felt homesick. I guess that's why I was angry this morning. Out on the boat, I realized I miss having a family and don't want to be alone anymore." Ian's voice cracked with emotion. "Then she had her... when she...."

"The seizure," Jeremiah supplied.

"When the seizure started, I couldn't breathe." Ian chuckled under his breath. "At first, I thought I killed her. I felt so helpless and... guilty and...."

"And?"

"I feared I'd never get to know her, and it scared me to death." He battled the lump in his throat. "I think I want something more, and I want it with Grace."

"And if I told you to leave today? How would you feel then?"

Ian remembered pulling Grace into his arms below the water. Her desperate grip awakened a fierce protective instinct he didn't know he had. Then Joshua sought comfort from him, pressing into him, seeking reassurance, and he wanted to protect him too. How could he leave them when he wanted to keep them safe? He rubbed his chest over his heart. "Empty," he choked out.

Jeremiah's penetrating glare bored into Ian. "What I'm going to reveal must stay a secret. Do you understand?" he asked.

"I understand, Sheriff," Ian agreed.

"I mean it. Grace cannot know I told you her secrets."

"I won't tell her," Ian said, promising to keep their conversation private.

Jeremiah's eyes remained fixed on him. The awkward silence agitated Ian, but he returned his level stare, trying to convey his trustworthiness.

"Five years ago, Grace, Juniper, and I were different people. We led other lives and went by other names," Jeremiah explained.

The meaning of the words registered. "So, what? Are you... in a witness protection program or something?" Ian asked in disbelief.

"Well, I guess you can think of it that way, but Juniper and I planned to move here before I encountered Grace. She's the reason we changed our names." Jeremiah leaned forward with his elbows on his knees. "Five years ago, I accepted an assignment to investigate Grace's husband, one of the worst kinds of criminals."

"What—"

"Don't ask what he did," Jeremiah snapped. "I will only tell you why Grace has seizures."

Ian swallowed. He suspected Grace's husband wasn't the most pleasant person but a criminal? He couldn't imagine what magnitude of crime would prohibit Jeremiah from naming them. "Sorry, Sheriff, I didn't mean to be nosey."

"Grace insisted I needed her help in my investigation when she busted me snooping around their house. I refused at first but discovered I did need her help. I started working as her trainer. We developed a way to communicate in code. I didn't know her husband had infiltrated my team. Everything was a setup from the beginning. Her husband knew my identity and used my investigation to target his opposition, so to speak."

Ian clenched his jaw. Did he mean kill? Did Grace's husband murder people?

"The night before his arrest, I assigned someone to tail Grace's husband. I carried Grace home thinking he wasn't there, and my agents were in place if he made an unexpected return. I thought I covered everything."

Comprehension struck. Grace walked into the house blind. Ian clenched his fists in anger. "What did he do to her?" he choked out.

"Tested her loyalty. He suspected Grace of feeding me information when his plans were thwarted, but he couldn't catch her doing it. When he confronted her, she panicked and told him she loved me. She said I treated her better, and she wanted to leave him for me. He went ballistic." Jeremiah turned towards the window again. "She turned his anger towards her to keep me safe. She protected my identity while he beat her with a baseball bat," he said in a pained whisper.

Ian shot to his feet, making his chair fall over. He stood at the table with his fist clenched, unable to release his rage. How could a man beat his wife? With a bat?

"So, you see. Grace's seizure is not your fault. The blame is mine for not protecting her better. In my arrogance, the idea of one of my own men turning on me never entered my mind. My negligence, not yours, caused her to be the way she is." Jeremiah stood silent, staring out the window briefly before clearing his throat. "'Greater love has no one than this than to lay down one's life for his friends.' Grace protected me back then. I'll do the same for her for the rest of my life." He turned to face Ian. "We changed our names. We moved here after the doctor released Grace from his care. When Joshua arrived, we turned into a family."

Ian remained standing, still clenching his fist. Countless questions raced through his mind. How old was Grace now? Twenty-one? Twenty-two? She must have been around eighteen when it happened. His heart ached when he thought of what she must have gone through. "Is there anything that can be done? Medication? Operation?"

"Grace has a traumatic brain injury. She won't get any better. Most times, stress triggers her seizures. We try to keep our lives peaceful and drama free. Of course, being dunked in water when she can't swim isn't something we planned for," Jeremiah said with a smirk of amusement.

"Sheriff! It's not funny. The health and well-being of the woman I—." Ian snapped his jaw shut. Did he really almost say he loved Grace? Could he love a woman he met only twenty-four hours ago? Doesn't love take time? Maybe he just loved the idea of having a family again.

"The woman, you what?" Jeremiah challenged, merriment dancing in his eyes.

Ian shrugged. The way Jeremiah stared at him made him uncomfortable. He picked up the chair, replacing it under the table. The scrutiny continued. Ian shuffled his feet, then cleared his throat. "Is there anything else?"

"Yes, you can help me with something. I promised Joshua we'd have a boy's day out tomorrow. I'm taking him fishing. Normally, leaving the women alone doesn't worry me, but an unwanted guest may come to call. Do you mind hanging around the homestead?"

"Sure, no problem," Ian said, knowing Jeremiah referenced Grace's stalker.

"Grace will push herself tomorrow, even though she needs to rest. Maybe you can lend a hand? Keep her from overdoing it without coddling her?"

"Got it. I'll figure something out," Ian agreed, looking forward to getting to know her better.

"Alright then. Your supper is in the bag. We normally eat sandwiches on the Sabbath. I hope you don't mind eating by yourself tonight. Grace is testy after an episode and won't be in the best mood for company," Jeremiah explained. "You understand."

"Sure, Sheriff. Don't worry. I'm used to eating alone."

Jeremiah hesitated.

Ian realized his statement sounded like a guilt trip more than a platitude. "Besides, I'm thinking I'll study tonight." He walked over to the bookshelves. "Which Bible will I find God in?"

"The King James Version is probably what you know best. Start in the Book of John. I think it contains the most nuggets."

Ian scanned the shelf. "Got it."

"See you tomorrow night, Ian. Hope you like fish."

"Fish is fine, Sheriff. Enjoy your day off."

* * * * *

Hours later, Ian dug into the brown paper bag. He found a couple of individual packs of chips, two turkey sandwiches made with real turkey, not deli meat, a baggie of cookies, two bottles of water, and a thermos of sweet tea. He set each item on the table around the open Bible in front of him. Adhering to Jeremiah's advice to start in the Book of John, he pored over the black and red words, and, true enough, the chapter held little nuggets of information he had never heard before.

Studying the Bible in high school didn't draw his interest. He considered it a chore to get through quickly so he could return to his video games. Now he found himself spellbound. Like a private detective, he checked each cross-reference in the middle of the page, flipping to other chapters of the Old and New Testaments. Words, written hundreds of years apart, connected prophecy with fulfillment. John 1:29 called Jesus the Lamb of God, and the verse associated with Isaiah 53:7, where the prophet spoke of a savior for God's people 'being brought as a lamb to the slaughter.' How many years separated the prophecy from its realization?

When he read, "If you love Me, keep My commandments," the connection to keeping the Torah as an act of love became clear, as the town's booklet explained. He thought they fabricated or misinterpreted keeping Torah, but the words written in red letters attested to their belief. Turning to the cross-referenced verse, he read, "For this is the love of God, that we keep His commandments. And His commandments are not burdensome." *How are the commands not burdensome? There are so many of them.*

One chapter later, Jeremiah's words from earlier returned to him when he read, "Greater love has no one than this than to lay down one's life for his friends." Everything comes full circle back to the death of Jesus. He held no emotional connection with the man supposed to be the savior of the world, but according to His words, to have everlasting life, Ian needed to believe in Him and keep God's commandments. How do you love somebody you can't see, hear, or touch? How can you know they exist?

141

Leaning back on the hind legs of the chair, Ian growled while stretching his stiff muscles. He stood to work out the ache in his knees. *How long have I been sitting?* The setting sun barely lit the small room. The chilly night air seeped through cracks between logs needing to be re-chinked. It wasn't cold enough to start a fire. Perhaps he should light the lamp.

Ian struck a matchstick against the box. The match sizzled as the phosphorous sulfide ignited. *If God is fire....* He touched the flame to the wick. When he replaced the chimney, light filled the room, and he could see better. Seeing how the glass magnified the fire reminded him of something he had read. *If Jesus is light....*

Ian flipped to the first page of the Gospel of John. If he remembered correctly... there. John 1:4-5 "In Him was life, and the life was the light of men. And the light shines in the darkness, and the darkness did not comprehend it." *What did Jeremiah say?* Something about Jesus lighting our paths. The cross-references led him to John 14:6. "Jesus said to him, 'I am the way, the truth, and the life. No one comes to the Father except through me.'"

Do I need to find Jesus first? Ian rested his head in his palms. He needed help to figure this out. Everything went in circles. Abigail said Jesus was a copycat of the Egyptian god Horus, another fictional character of religion. Who should he trust?

Ian moved to stand in front of the windows, placing his hands on his hips. He wanted to know the truth of God's existence without someone telling him what to believe. He turned back towards the lantern. With determined steps, he returned to the table. Maybe he interpreted Jeremiah's analogy too literally. He could feel the heat without seeing it and see the light without touching it. He could see and feel but couldn't touch. *Like emotions? Knowing God is an emotion? Is that how He works?*

"*Yes.*"

Ian froze. Grace said the voice emanated from inside and outside of her. He perceived it the same way. "Is that you, God?" Ian asked the empty room. He received no answer. He recalled Grace's words from earlier. She said he needed to knock on God's door. He rapped his knuckles on the table three times. "God, if you're speaking to me and this isn't a hallucination, I'm asking you to help me find you. I want to know who you are."

* * * * *

Grace knelt beside her bed. Ian MacGregor filled her thoughts. For the first time, she regretted her circumstances. She shouldn't be drooling over a man she barely knew. She tried to ignore her growing attraction but could not stop herself. His shoulder-length chestnut hair and broody brown eyes set her heart racing.

She pressed her face against her bed, using the thickness of the bedding to muffle her scream of frustration. She couldn't keep from replaying the day's events. The puff of his breath when he whispered in her ear still sent shivers through her spine. The tug of his hand urging her into the boat. His strength when he lifted her off the dock because she couldn't overcome her fear. She giggled at the memory of his expression when he realized the boat was capsizing. His capable arms wrapping around her in the water's darkness. She hugged herself, aching to be embraced again. She missed having a husband.

Tears formed. She wasn't free. According to Torah, she couldn't remarry until her husband handed her a bill of divorce. The annulment didn't count. How could Viktor divorce someone legally dead?

She growled in frustration. *Stop. Thinking. About. Him.* He would make a good father. He made Joshua laugh, but Ian's stern voice compelled Joshua to listen to him, too.

Focus! Say your prayers!

"Dear Heavenly Father," she began praying. "Deliver me from temptation." An image of her kissing Ian popped into her head.

Grace shot to her feet. "Oh, Yah help me! I'll never get him out of my mind."

21

The sun once again woke Ian from his sleep. Exhausted from his late-night study, he groaned in protest of the unwanted intrusion. *What time is it? Why aren't there curtains on the windows?* He sat upright. *Where's my phone?* He last remembered using it to take pictures on the pedal boat. He sprang out of bed to check the pockets of the pants he wore yesterday. Nothing. He knelt to look under the bed. He ran outside, scanning the ground. No phone.

Ian hated being tied to the device because he used it so much for his job, so he intentionally ignored it when he wasn't working. The phone served as a tool to earn money and nothing more. He didn't play games and rarely checked his social media accounts. Abigail did everything for him.

After being included in the community activities yesterday and seeing how everyone greeted each other with genuine joy, Ian realized how much his life of travel, his job, caused him to miss. Most of his classmates already had children. His brag-worthy items comprised his car and his now missing phone. Two people were on his contacts list. His grandmother, who, after being diagnosed with Alzheimer's, often forgot he was her grandson and his friend Abigail, but she managed him more than anything. Sure, she checked on him when he stayed out of contact too long, but they rarely interacted outside of their working relationship. *How depressing.*

Ian, now dressed, left the cabin and headed to the farmhouse. A cacophony of squawking birds and chattering squirrels, warning of his presence, filled Ian's ears. The sun's rays, breaking through the canopy, dotted the dry leaves, where small creatures scurried for cover. He slowed his steps, spinning in wonderment at the abundance of life going on around him. The path did not diminish the wildness. Instead, it enhanced the fact he traveled alone. In this exact location, he could see neither cabin nor the house.

He couldn't help but compare his everyday existence to where he now stood. Life happened without him taking part. Couples walked beaches hand in hand. Parents played with their children. Friends celebrated together. He did nothing but watch. Despite constantly being surrounded by people, places, and things, he walked a solitary path, observing without partaking. He shared his experiences and adventures with the world, but he entered his hotel room alone at the close of the day.

Ian's thoughts turned to his near slip of the tongue last night. He couldn't believe he almost said he loved Grace. His mind balked at the notion. He didn't know her enough to announce any declarations of love. Yet, the word nearly slipped out before he stopped himself. Could he love her? He found her extremely attractive, but she wasn't his type. Jeremiah kept him nervous. Grace and her quiet mannerisms soothed him.

The more he analyzed his emotions, the more confused he became. Ian inhaled the refreshing air. His stomach urged him to continue his downhill trek. A break in the tree line exposed the house. Grace and Juniper stood by an old station wagon, talking. *Are they leaving?* Ian raced the rest of the way.

"Good morning, Juniper," Ian said, his breath coming in pants. Grace wasn't there any longer. "You going somewhere?"

"Good morning, Ian. I'm glad you're awake. Grace and I were worried when you didn't come down for breakfast. I was going to check on you when I returned."

Ian's heart skipped a beat. Worried? Did that mean Grace cared about him? "Sorry. I stayed up late, and I overslept," he apologized. "Do you know if Jeremiah found my phone in his truck?"

"No, dear, but I'll call and tell him you're looking for it," Juniper said, opening the door to sit in the driver's seat. "Ian, I've got to run. I'm coming back with a surprise for Grace. I left your breakfast on the table, and lunch is in the fridge. Oh, and Grace refused to tell us what she planned to do today. Check on her for me so she doesn't overdo it."

Ian agreed and waved as she drove away. What made up

'overdoing it?' How hard can housework be? With a shrug, he turned towards the house.

He found a plate covered with a napkin, a jar of strawberry jelly, a glass of water, and an overturned mug on the kitchen table. Before sitting at the empty table, he filled his cup from the still-warm, half-full coffee carafe. He regretted not waking up earlier. After the noisy family breakfast yesterday morning, the silence of eating alone again weighed on him. Oh well. Even though cold, he expected the food to be flavorful. Lifting the napkin, he found a large biscuit, a heaping of scrambled eggs, and three pieces of bacon. Bacon? *I thought they followed the Old Testament laws.*

He shrugged. *When in Rome....* He scooped up a forkful of eggs. Mmmm. Fluffy and still warm. Grace must've waited until he arrived before cooking them. He bit into the crispy bacon. *Wow, this is the best bacon ever.* He smoothed a glob of red jelly onto half of his biscuit. *Huh?* Not strawberry, but cherry. The last time he ate cherry jelly, his mother made it.

Thunk! The noise came from outside the house. Thunk! *What is she doing?* Thunk! Ian gobbled up his breakfast and downed the rest of his coffee. Thunk. Pause. Thunk. He deposited his dishes in the sink. Under normal circumstances, he wouldn't leave them for someone else to wash, but given his instructions to keep Grace from overexerting herself, he needed to stop her from doing whatever chore caused the noise. The racket being created implied she surpassed "overdoing it" by a long shot.

Stepping outside, he determined the sound to be ricocheting off the tree line beyond the barn. He jogged towards the structure. He didn't expect to see Grace wielding an ax when he rounded the backside of the building. She wrestled a large log onto the chopping block. Boy, did her parents know her well. How could he stop her without offending her? He couldn't demand she turn the ax over to him. Then he remembered his breakfast. He ran back to the house to grab a Bible and confront her.

"Ms. Johnson!" Ian hollered, rounding the corner. "I have a very important question to ask you!"

Grace jumped before bringing the ax down on the log before her.

"And what question is so imperative it requires you to startle me while I'm swinging an ax, Mr. MacGregor?" she asked, placing one hand on her hip while leaning on the hilt of the ax handle.

Ian swallowed. She didn't sound mad, but her posture said otherwise. He shouldn't have spoken with the tool mid-swing, but he couldn't backtrack. He had no other plan to stop her from working.

"Your father told me everybody here follows Torah, and I know for a fact the Bible says you can't eat bacon," he said, shaking the Bible in her direction. "Please, explain how you can serve me bacon when the Torah says not to eat it."

He emphasized his statement by tapping on the cover. He hoped she could tell he asked in humor.

Without a word, Grace took the Book, flipped the pages, handed it back to him, and pointed to a verse.

"And the swine, though he divide the hoof, and be cloven-footed, yet he cheweth not the cud; he is unclean to you," Ian read aloud. "Yeah, swine. Pig. Bacon. Thou shalt not eat bacon."

"Ian, the Bible doesn't say bacon," Grace chuckled. "Bacon is any meat smoked and cured with certain seasonings for taste. The animal doesn't have to be a pig."

"Oh, uhh, right," Ian stumbled over his response. That didn't go as he imagined. He hoped his argument opened a debate to distract her. He scratched his head. "So, what kind of meat did I eat this morning?"

"Beef."

"Beef? Bacon?" He didn't know beef bacon existed.

"Yes, beef. How did it taste?" Grace asked, a teasing tone in her voice.

"Honestly? It's the best bacon I've ever eaten."

She chuckled again. "I said the same thing when I tasted it." She propped the ax against the chopping log. "If you excuse me, I have to return to work. I want to surprise my mother. She's been asking Father to chop this wood up for weeks."

Ian watched her struggle to lift a large log onto the stump. He didn't want to say a girl shouldn't be doing hard work. His words might make her more determined. But how to stop her? She lifted the ax to swing.

"I have another question," Ian blurted out.

Grace dropped the ax to the ground. Her hand cupped the hilt while her index finger tapped the handle.

Uh oh. Seeing her irritation, he hesitated. He didn't want to anger her, but he promised her parents. Should he leave her be but watch her in secret?

Grace wiped her brow with the back of her arm.

Ian didn't notice how her curls clung to her forehead or flushed cheeks until now. His promise to her parents won. So what if he angered her?

"So, I studied the Gospel of John last night. It said Jesus is the Word of God, and Jesus created everything, right?"

"Yes, that's correct. Yahusha, being the Word of Yahuah, spoke everything into existence. 'And God said, Let there be light: and there was light.'" She picked up the ax again.

"Wait, I'm not done."

Grace gave up, propped the ax against the log, and placed her hands on her hips.

Oh no. Now I've done it. Despite her obvious annoyance, he pressed forward with his plan. "Why don't we switch places? It will be easier if you're not working. I'll do your chores while you answer my questions. Deal?"

"Ian, did my father ask you to stop me from working today?" Grace asked, narrowing her eyebrows.

"Uh, no. Your father did not tell me to stop you from working." Okay, so he didn't tell her the complete truth, but Ian refused to feel guilty. Both parents requested he *try* to keep her from 'working too hard.' He made them a promise, and he intended to keep it.

"So, your questions are genuine?"

"Yes. I'd ask your father, but he isn't here." He shrugged, pretending not to care who answered his questions.

"And you're willing to do my chores?"

"Yes. Do we have a deal?" Ian didn't know what to do if she declined his offer.

"Have at it," Grace said, handing the ax to him. She opened her palm to receive the Bible with the other hand. A broad grin lit up her eyes.

Ian's jaw dropped. Her eyes sparkled with mischievousness. He suspected she knew he lied and planned to make him pay for his deception through his labor. Regardless, he'd continue to ask her questions to keep her mind occupied and her hands empty of tools. Ian grabbed the ax and sliced the log in two.

"Very impressive," Grace praised. "You've done this before."

"I've split wood a few times for camping," Ian said, shrugging off the compliment. He divided each half into three pieces before asking his next question. "So, later on, Jesus says, 'If you love me, keep my commandments.' His directive is why you follow the Old Testament laws. Correct? To show your love for God?"

"Yes, but they're not Old Testament laws. Yah gave one law. Yahusha followed Torah, and we're supposed to walk as He walked."

Graced flipped through the Book, then moved to stand beside him. "See here. When Yah gave Moses the Law, the Torah, He said, 'One law shall be for the native-born and for the stranger who dwells among you.' Since Yah does not change, there's still only one Torah."

"Then why do preachers teach the Torah doesn't have to be followed anymore?"

"Misinterpretations passed on through the generations. My father is the better person to go to for knowledge on the subject, but I know Yahusha clearly stated, 'Till heaven and earth pass, one jot or one tittle shall no wise pass from the law, till all be fulfilled.' Everybody ignores what He says." Grace shook her head. "I mean, look around you. Heaven and earth are still here, aren't they? People listen to preachers more than they listen to our Messiah."

"My sheep hear my voice, and I know them, and they follow me," Ian quoted.

"Impressive. You did study the Gospel of John last night," Grace said, moving to sit on an upright log. "Are you still entertaining the idea of moving here?"

Ian shrugged and sat beside her. "Maybe."

"Living here requires a change of heart. You must want to follow Torah yourself, not because I, my father, or anyone else said you're supposed to do it. You can't fake loving God."

Ian shook his index finger at her. "See, now, that's where I'm having trouble. I understand how God wants us to show our love for Him, but I still don't understand how to love someone I can't see, hear, or touch. You might as well be telling me to love… air. If God exists, why doesn't he reveal himself?"

"Ian, don't force your relationship with Yah. Learning to believe in and love Him is like… well, it's a lot like being pregnant," Grace said matter-of-factly before her cheeks turned bright red. She covered her face with her hands.

Ian gasped and choked. "Oh, this I gotta hear," he said, laughing.

Grace laughed with him. "I can't believe I said that," she said into her hands.

"You did. Now I have to know. How is loving God like being pregnant?" Ian asked through his laughter.

"Well, what I meant was…." She lowered her hands to her sides and cleared her throat. "You go through stages the same as a pregnancy. It's a labor of love. Since you've been here, you've gone from the stage of doubting to questioning. There are also the stages of learning, growing, strengthening, testing, revealing, trusting, understanding, accepting, and knowing. And when you realize how much He has done for you, it will break you. You will cry like a baby. You can not fake loving Yah."

"I have to go through all that?"

"No. You don't. Loving Yah is a choice. You can turn around and walk away. Your life will stay the same."

"And if I choose the old paths?"

"A life following Yah is the most rewarding thing I've ever known. I have found love deeper and stronger than I ever could've imagined. I am blessed with joy that heals my wounds and a mended heart that has forgiven my worst enemies. You will not regret choosing Yahuah."

Grace stirred up Ian's suppressed longing to quit his show. Whenever he mentioned quitting to Abigail, she always dissuaded him. She promised he would never have money worries if he stuck the job out until he turned thirty. She sent him quarterly financial records documenting the investments she made on his behalf, but he never paid attention to them, trusting her choices. If he moved here, did he have enough to support himself without any skills to replenish his funds?

"Ian?"

"Hmmm?"

"Ian!"

Grace's voice snapped him out of his reverie. "Oh, uh, sorry. My mind was elsewhere."

"You're fine. Did you have any more questions?"

"Well, no. Not at the moment." He needed to think of something quick.

Grace braced her hands on her knees and rose. "Then I have other—."

"But they usually come to me while I'm reading," he blurted out to stop her from leaving. "Could you read to me while I work?"

"You want me to read to you?" she asked, raising her voice in disbelief.

"Mmm hmm," he nodded, realizing he did want her to read to him. He enjoyed her company. "You answer my questions while I do your chores. Isn't that the bargain we made?"

"You're serious? I read to you, answer your questions, and you do my chores?" she sat back on the stump.

"Yep," he nodded again, wondering what chores she had in mind. "Do we have a deal?"

Grace picked up the Bible. "What chapter?"

"Pick one." Ian stood to place another log on the chopping stump.

"Okay," she shrugged. "In the beginning God…."

22

"How's everything going?" Jeremiah asked Juniper when he entered the morning room.

With a teacup cradled in her hands, she pointed towards the window with one finger.

He peeked through the crack in the curtains.

Ian and Grace stood in the root vegetable patch. Ian leaned on a hoe while Grace showed him something in a Bible.

Yes! His plan to bring the two closer together worked. Despite his diligent efforts to expand her social circle to include eligible bachelors, Grace remained reserved around men after the fiasco of her first marriage. After Dean cornered her in the community center last year, she retreated deeper into her shell.

He expected the same reaction towards Ian. Instead, he caught her staring at him with a little smile. Last night, when she suggested he take a thermos of warm soup up to the cabin so 'Ian doesn't catch a cold,' he realized the depth of her attraction. The protective barriers she hid behind appeared to be crumbling.

Contrary to his personal distaste for the animals, he told Juniper to buy the baby goats Grace repeatedly begged for last week. At first, she refused to leave Grace with a man they barely knew, but he assured her they could trust Ian. His promise to split the logs from the tree that fell this past winter secured her agreement to go along with his matchmaking plan.

"What are they doing?" he asked, peeking through the crack in the curtains.

"Near as I can tell, Ian somehow finagled Grace into reading to him while he works. She has him composting the root garden," Juniper explained.

"You're kidding. I can't believe he got her to agree to that."

Jeremiah moved closer to the window, and sure enough, Grace stood reading while Ian shoveled compost out of a wheelbarrow. He then spread the rich soil around with a hoe. He stopped to ask her a question. She flipped through the Book to show him the answer. With a nod, he returned to his hoe, and Grace began reading again.

"How long have they been out there?"

Juniper shrugged. "I'm not sure. I returned around two o'clock, but he arrived at the house at ten.

Jeremiah checked his watch. "Ian's kept her by his side for at least three hours straight? That's a record!" He flashed a grin at Juniper. "It's working."

She pursed her lips. "Jeremiah dear, are you sure?" she asked, frowning.

"Yeah. He loves her."

"He loves her!" Juniper gasped. "He said those words?"

"Well, not in those exact words, but yeah, he told me." Jeremiah continued to watch the couple through the window, congratulating himself. He half expected to return to find the two arguing. Given Grace's penchant for pushing herself harder than usual after a seizure, he thought she'd balk if Ian interfered with her plans. Instead, he persuaded her to stop working altogether. How promising!

"Not in those.... Jeremiah, if he didn't tell you, then how do you know?"

Hearing the agitation in his wife's voice, he turned his full attention toward her. "You're worried," he said, kissing her cheek. "Don't be."

"How can I not worry?" Juniper asked, standing up. "Hasn't Grace already been through enough without you trying to fix her up with someone she met two days ago?"

"I told you he loves her," Jeremiah teased, trying to appease her with a hug.

"How do you know if he didn't say it?" she grilled, pushing against his embrace.

"He feels the same way about her as I did about you. Your braids drew me like a magnet."

"Jeremiah! I hated you when I first met you."

"I know. And look how well we turned out." Jeremiah pulled Juniper closer, this time kissing her. "I love you more than ever, Junebug."

"I love you too, Dear," Juniper said, hugging him back before releasing him in alarm. "Where's Joshua?"

"Asleep in the truck. Where's the surprise?"

"Eating poison ivy on the trail up to the cabin." Juniper picked up her now empty teacup. "Jeremiah, are you sure?" she asked one more time.

"Honey, you know I can't continue being sheriff and pastor. This house goes with the sheriff's position. If I become the pastor full-time, we have to move to the parish house. It will uproot Grace, and she's doing so well here. If I continue being sheriff, Grace will never move on with her life. She'll keep hiding in her cottage, pushing men away. Unless…," he paused for emphasis. "She marries the new sheriff."

Juniper fumbled her empty cup. "You really think Ian's the answer to our prayers?"

"Yes, I believe he's the one."

"Jeremiah! He's a social media star. How is he qualified to be the sheriff of Covenant Cove, not to mention the spiritual leader of our daughter and grandson? Is he ready to change his way of life for her? What if he takes her away? Couples can't be unequally yoked." Juniper took her empty teacup to the sink.

Jeremiah followed. His wife's apprehension over his matchmaking scheme drowned out her normal positive nature. He should've told her the truth of Ian MacGregor's identity when the young man first arrived, but he hesitated, not wanting to raise her hopes if his instincts were wrong. "You remember when I went to visit my old drill sergeant? Right before I accepted the Doroshenko case?"

"Yeah?" Juniper leaned against the counter, crossing her arms.

"Ian's his grandson. He asked me to keep watch over his family for him. He was dying of lung cancer. That's when I started following Ian on social media."

"You're kidding!"

"Nope. I know what Ian is capable of because I know who raised him. He just needs the right motivation, and that's where Grace comes in. A man, who is determined, will do just about anything to win the heart of the woman he loves. If you remember, you made me eat a worm before going out with me."

"I couldn't believe you ate it. I was so mad I had to keep my promise."

"Now, do you trust me?" he asked with unabashed arrogance.

Juniper hugged him. "I should've never doubted you, Dear."

Jeremiah's stomach growled.

"There's my cue to fix supper," she said with a sigh, returning to the sink to wash the dishes left there. "What if I don't want to cook tonight?" A teasing smile lit up her face.

"Bite your tongue, woman! You know I'm a bear to be around when I'm starving," he said, hugging her waist and growling into Juniper's neck.

"Yes, dear. I know." She removed a stack of mixing bowls from the cabinet. "I suppose you'll want spicey tarter sauce and chili lime, sweet potato fries to go with your fish?"

"Ohhh, that sounds delicious. Yes, please," Jeremiah said, rubbing his belly.

Juniper took out a jar of homemade pickle relish and a bowl piled with sweet potatoes from the cupboard. "And you're going to want scones with strawberry preserves for dessert?"

"Woman! You're speaking my love language," he said, spinning her into his arms. "Juniper, you're the best wife ever."

She chuckled. "I know, Dear, you've told me many times, but I still love hearing you say it," she said, puckering her lips for a kiss. "Now, go get your fish. Dinner will be ready within an hour."

Jeremiah peeked out the window again. "Good. Ian will have time to wash. I bet he smells ripe after the work he's done today."

"Why don't you fill your soaker tub for him? While he's relaxing, you can fetch his bag and the goats. I'll keep Grace and Joshua busy helping me."

"Good idea," Jeremiah said, giving her another quick kiss before heading outside to retrieve the cooler.

Jeremiah woke Joshua, telling him to go around back with his mother before taking the fish inside and grabbing a couple of towels.

He then headed to the fenced area on the far end of the house to turn on the on-demand, outdoor, propane, hot water heater to fill the watering trough he turned into a tub. The setup saved him many nights of tossing and turning after a hard day's work.

Nearing the garden patch, Jeremiah noticed Ian and Grace fully engrossed in what Joshua was telling them.

"It almost broke Papa's pole! It was this big!" Joshua stretched his arms to each side.

Jeremiah smiled. He loved his grandson more than he thought he could. He tried his best to fulfill the role of father, but keeping up with the rambunctious little boy exhausted him. Too often disappointment crept into Joshua's eyes when Jeremiah told him he was too tired to play. He needed a younger man to keep up with his activity level. He hoped Ian wanted the position.

"This is a mighty fine fisherman you've trained, Sheriff," Ian remarked once Joshua finished speaking. "A fish the size of a house, no less?"

"You're not a true fisherman if you can't master the craft of telling a tall tale now and then. Don't you agree?"

"Oh, absolutely. How big was your fish really, Sheriff?" Ian taunted, holding his fingers two inches apart.

Jeremiah gave Ian an annoyed grimace.

"Father? Why didn't you ask Ian to go with you today?" Grace asked, crossing her arms.

The men eyed each other in bewilderment.

"Well, I—"

"He asked me," Ian blurted, glancing at Jeremiah.

Jeremiah frowned, wide-eyed. *Oh no!* He taught Grace how to tell if someone was lying.

"Oh?" Grace blinked twice, waiting for Ian to answer.

"Umm, yeah. He asked me, and I said… well, he asked me last night. I said I'd had enough water."

"Mmm hmm," Grace murmured, holding her hand out for Joshua. "Come on, Son. Let's leave these men to their tall tales."

Jeremiah and Ian watched Joshua skip alongside Grace on their way to the house, naming the type of fish he caught in the order he caught them.

"Yeah, she didn't buy that," Jeremiah said, once the back door shut.

"I know. I panicked." He pointed to the towel Jeremiah held in his arms. "I guess that's for me?"

"Don't you think you need it?" Jeremiah held his free hand out. "Give me the hoe. I'll clean up and fetch your bag while you bathe. The tub is inside the fence."

Ian shoved the hoe into Jeremiah's hand, grabbed the towel, and set off in a slow jog. He watched Ian open the wooden door, then turn to give him the thumbs-up sign. Jeremiah imagined he was saying a prayer of thanks for Southern ingenuity as the door shut.

* * * * *

Ian, Jeremiah, and Joshua sat at the table while Juniper and Grace brought several platters and bowls from the kitchen. Ian's mouth watered over the smell of the home-cooked meal. Restaurant food couldn't compare to food prepared with love.

"How'd you like my hillbilly hot tub?" Jeremiah asked.

"Extraordinary invention," Ian said, paying more attention to the food. When Juniper set a plate of steaming cornbread right in front of him, he reached for a piece.

Juniper popped Ian's hand. "You're as bad as Joshua," she said with a teasing grin.

Joshua giggled.

"Mother, let Ian steal a piece," Grace said. "He split the logs behind the barn today. You'll be able to fire up your wood kiln tomorrow."

Jeremiah whistled low and long. "Chopped wood and composted the garden? I bet those city boy hands have some impressive blisters."

Ian grinned, displaying his hands as badges of honor. His palms hosted several open sores. Grace grabbed one, glaring at the angry, eroded divots before throwing his hand away and stomping off toward the bedrooms. He turned a dumbfounded gaze towards Jeremiah, who shrugged. Within seconds, she returned, holding a small jar and bandages. Without a word, she applied cream to his palms, easing the sting of the raw flesh. She covered the sores with a non-stick wound pad and wrapped gauze around his hand.

"This is your fault," she snapped at Jeremiah once she completed her ministrations.

"My fault?" he balked. "How are his blisters my fault?"

"If you didn't ask him to stop me from working today, this would've never happened."

"Grace, I told you, your father didn't ask me to stop you from working. That was my decision," Ian reminded her. "Your father asked me to watch over you, and that's it."

"But he always—"

Ian shook his head at her questioning look.

Grace turned to Jeremiah, who also shook his head. She glanced back at Ian before dropping his hand and running out the door.

Ian, dumbfounded by her extreme reaction, stared at Jeremiah.

"Don't sit there like a wart on a toad. Go after her."

Ian sprang from his chair, racing outside. He glimpsed her going into the barn. He followed at a slower pace to give her time to gain control of her emotions. Another door on the opposite wall stood open. Even though only fifteen feet separated the two entrances, the change in sounds impressed upon him the aura of walking into another dimension.

On the other side, the atmosphere changed. He now walked in Grace's domain. To his right, the yellow blooms of Forsythia hid the stack of wood he chopped earlier today. To his left stretched a hedge of bushes with cones of white flowers he couldn't name. The setting sun cast a glow over rows of raised beds filled with various budding plants. A center fountain bubbled a calming tune. Rhododendrons bloomed along the edge of the woods. A Victorian-style cottage with a screened-in front porch completed the fairytale scene.

Movement on the porch caught his eye. At least she wasn't inside the house where she could keep him shut out. Ian kept his pace slow and calculated while he approached her. He didn't want to alert her to his presence yet. A carpet of dandelions covered one bed. Why would she purposefully grow weeds she could find in abundance in any yard? A squeaking noise from the porch drew his attention away from the bright yellow blooms.

She sat on a swing with her back to him, one leg keeping the swing in motion. Her chin rested atop her crossed arms on the back of the swing. She stared towards the woods behind the cottage. What did she see? He eased to the side, making no noise. A deer munched on something growing near the edge of the woods. He stepped back before he startled the animal and alerted Grace to his presence. A mental image of them sitting on the swing together popped into Ian's head. The now familiar ache whenever he saw Grace told him his thoughts held a deeper significance than a mere daydream. His attraction to her went beyond passing interest, but he still hesitated to call it love.

Taking a deep breath, he pushed the image aside and grasped the door handle. If Grace didn't feel the same way, his attraction to her didn't matter. Her guilt stood between them—time to fix his mistake.

The spring keeping the door shut gave a metallic groan when he pulled on the handle. "Grace?"

She launched herself off the swing, heading towards the front door.

"Grace. Please?" Ian stopped her from turning the doorknob. This close, her peppery scent muddled his thoughts. He didn't know if he leaned into her or if she swayed against him, but when they touched, she gasped and flinched away. He released her hand, stepping back to put distance between them.

Grace hung her head and hesitated momentarily before turning around to face him. "Ian, I want to apologize for causing you injury. I assumed you lied to me today, and I allowed my temper to get the best of me. I'm truly sorry for your pain."

"My blisters are not your fault," he said. "They're mine."

Her head jerked up to look at him. "Your fault? I heaped all that work on you because I didn't believe you. I thought my father was trying to control me through you, and I got mad." She picked up both of Ian's bandaged hands. "My inability to manage my temper caused this, not you."

Are those tears in her eyes? "Grace, I could tell you didn't believe me. I could've stopped working whenever I wanted."

"You could've… why didn't you?" Grace asked incredulously.

Ian hesitated, looking over her head to avoid seeing the moisture gathered there. He didn't mean to make her cry. He needed to tell her the truth. "Because… because I wanted to be near you." The words rushed out, and he finally faced her, hanging his emotions out for her to see.

"Because you…. Oh."

Ian shuffled his feet, hanging his thumbs in the back pockets of his jeans. "Something is going on between us. I've never felt whatever this is with anyone else. Do… do you feel it too?"

Grace dropped eye contact and turned away from him.

I pushed her too far. He wanted an answer. Good or bad, he needed to know where he stood, but he could wait.

"Mama! Mama! Come see the surprise Papa and Gramma June got you!" Joshua yelled from outside.

Grace wiped her face. The screen door slammed shut behind him. His exuberance intruded upon the tension hanging in the air.

He grabbed Grace's hand and tugged. "Come on, Mama!"

Grace's eyes met Ian's, asking him in silence for understanding.

He gave her a compassionate smile before turning towards Joshua. "A surprise you say!" He mimicked Joshua's excitement. He swooped Joshua up in his arms and rushed outside, where he lifted him up onto his shoulders, then turned back towards Grace. "Well, don't just stand there, Mama. Don't you want to see your surprise?"

* * * * *

Grace relived the events of the day while lying in bed. She enjoyed reading to Ian while he worked. His curiosity appeared genuine, but could his words be a ruse to get past her defenses? Wary of any male attention, she often assigned Viktor's unscrupulous characteristics, namely his ability to manipulate her, to other men. She didn't tell Ian, but that's why she got so mad today. She knew she was being manipulated.

Ian asked if she felt the connection between them. She didn't know how to answer. She could admit her attraction to herself but not to him. Unlike him, she'd been down this path before, and it almost led to her destruction. Plus, there were the restrictions of Torah she had to consider. How could she explain the situation to someone who didn't understand why they followed Torah? Should she try? If this was a vacation fling, then everything would blow over by the time he left. Then she wouldn't have to worry anymore. No, best not to say anything.

She rolled over. The image of Joshua's excitement while riding on Ian's shoulders brought a smile to her lips. She followed a few steps behind them, waiting when he stopped in the barn's doorway so Joshua could slap the wall above the door frame. His attention seemed to be focused solely on Joshua. They chatted like old friends. Did Ian fake the attention he gave Joshua to get to her?

Frustrated, she rolled back to her other side. When they reached the backyard, her parents held a sheet in front of her surprise. With a 'tada', her father snatched the sheet away, revealing the two half-grown baby goats she'd begged him to get. Ian's exuberance over them exceeded hers. He got down on the ground to head butt with the little male. His begging to name them reminded her of Joshua. She agreed and he named the female Chevron because of the ring around her middle. The male, he named Sarge. Grace's doubt cracked. She wanted Ian's interest to be real but feared it might be a tactic to get her to drop her defenses.

After supper, her mother's heart ached seeing Joshua cradled against Ian's side while he read Joshua's current favorite storybook, The Mother of All Spiders, to him. Before long, they fell asleep. She silently woke Joshua to put him in his own bed and covered Ian with a blanket before returning to her cottage.

Rolling over yet again, she sighed. Her thoughts remained in turmoil, but she couldn't keep her eyes open any longer. Distant thunder accompanied her into her dreams.

* * * * *

Ian jerked awake at the boom. Ever since getting caught in a tornado a few years ago, he'd been unable to sleep through thunderstorms. Might as well get up. "Ohhh." Every muscle ached. Another nearer thunderclap snatched him upright. He kept himself physically fit, but the workout from doing farm work couldn't compare to anything he did in the gym. The clink of glass in the darkness caused him to jump.

"Sheriff?" he hissed.

"Here. Thought you could use this."

A flash of lighting glinted off the shot glass Jeremiah offered him. Ian took it.

"What is it?"

"Does it matter if it helps the pain?"

"Point taken," Ian conceded before downing the liquid in one swallow. Whiskey. He sighed as the liquid spread its warmth. "Ahh, sure hits the spot."

The men sat in silence as the storm moved over them. Ian broke the quiet.

"Sheriff, did you find my phone in your truck?"

"No, I didn't. If you need to call somebody, you can always use mine."

"I'd have to remember their number first." Ian braced himself for a dressing down. He now had to admit to not erasing Grace's picture in case the image showed up on his social media. "So, I need to confess something."

Jeremiah grunted. "What have you done?"

"You know when you told me not to take any pictures of your family?"

"Yeah?" Jeremiah drawled.

"I took a picture of Grace before you issued your decree. I didn't have time to erase them."

"Didn't have the time or didn't want to?" Jeremiah quipped.

"If I'm being totally honest, I didn't want to."

Ian expected Jeremiah to scold him. Instead, the man walked calmly over to a secretary desk by the window. Jeremiah turned on a lamp and opened the middle drawer. He selected something, shut the drawer, and returned to his seat. "Don't lose this one," he said.

It was a photograph of Grace and Joshua. "You're not mad?" Ian asked, disbelieving Jeremiah's calm reaction to his deliberate disobedience.

"Oh, I'm not happy, but I understand why you didn't erase the picture," Jeremiah grunted. "You've acknowledged your error in judgment, so I won't hold it against you, but Grace's position is... precarious."

"I'm sorry, Sheriff." He gave the man a sheepish look. He never thought his actions might put Grace in danger.

"Don't worry yourself. Everything happens for a reason," he said, yawning. "I'll check your accounts tomorrow once I'm in the office. I'm going back to bed. Good night, Ian."

"Good night, Sheriff, and thank you for understanding,"

Jeremiah grunted again before turning off the light.

23

Ian tossed and turned for hours after Jeremiah returned to bed. He couldn't forget Jeremiah's words. He never thought his actions might bring danger to Grace. Maybe he should leave Covenant Cove. At least he could look forward to a decent night's sleep once he resumed his trip. Plus, leaving would keep Grace safe from any more of his mishaps.

He retrieved the picture of Joshua and her from atop his bag. Their faces, barely discernible in the darkened room, beamed with happiness. Joshua's face nestled against Grace's. What he wouldn't give to be next to them, holding them both in his embrace. With his line of work, any kind of relationship was impossible because of the possibility of exposing Grace.

He stashed the photograph away in a book he kept for reading during layovers. With a heavy heart, he stepped outside to wait for everyone else to awaken. The faint glow of the rising sun hovered above the treetops far behind Grace's cottage. Over the past few days, this family became imprinted on his heart. He didn't realize the amount of pleasure you could find simply by enjoying a meal or reading to a small child. Now he knew, and the mere thought of leaving left him drained and aching. He had little time left to collect enough memories to last a lifetime.

Grace's porch light interrupted the darkness. The screen door squeaked and slammed shut. A flashlight beam bobbed through the bushes, and headed toward the barn. She must be checking on the goats. He ran to meet her.

"Good morning," he said, stepping inside the building.

Grace squealed at the sound of his voice. "Ian! You're as bad as my father sneaking up on people."

"Sorry, I saw your light and thought you might need help." He moved to stand next to her in front of the goat pen. The animals munched happily on hay in the feed rack.

"I wanted to check on them. I've never raised goats." She turned her flashlight on him. "What are you doing up, anyway? After all your hard work yesterday, shouldn't you be sleeping?"

Ian squinted against the bright light. "The storm woke me up," he said. He wrinkled his nose and shoved his hands in his pockets. "I survived a tornado a few years ago. Now I have a touch of storm phobia."

"After such a harrowing experience, I expect I'd feel the same way," Grace said, returning to watching the goats.

Ian wanted her to talk more. He wanted to know everything about her. He rocked back and forth on his feet, dismissing every sentence popping into his head. How do you talk to a girl you're interested in without coming across as having a hidden agenda because you're leaving in a couple of days?

"So, why—"

"I can make you some coffee?" Grace blurted. "Sorry, I didn't mean to interrupt you." The glow from her flashlight flickered as she tapped it against her leg.

Is she nervous too? The thought brought him a level of comfort and boosted his ego. "That sounds great. After my sleepless night, I'll need more than one cup today."

"Okay. We can sit on the porch while the sun finishes rising." The flickering ended when she spun around, taking rapid steps away from him.

Ian followed more sedately, already regretting his hasty decision to leave. If he stayed, couldn't he abandon social media and his notoriety altogether to keep her whereabouts unknown? He paused mid-stride. The thought didn't upset him. Interesting.

The bright yellow flowers in the dandelion bed distracted him. *Why does she cultivate dandelions?* A wry smile appeared on his face as a plan formulated in his mind. Staying meant he didn't need to stifle his attraction. He could find a decent house nearby. Nothing fancy. Something quaint. With a large yard for Grace to grow as many weeds as she wanted. He could have his own family. Liking his new plan better; he turned towards the porch. Time to discover more about Grace Johnson.

"Here you go." Grace offered Ian a cup. "You drink yours black, right? I added a couple of ice cubes, so you won't burn your tongue."

She paid attention to how I drink my coffee? That's promising. "Thank you. Yes. I'm allergic to dairy." He inhaled deeply. "Ahh, fresh coffee smells so good."

"I love it. Especially when it's loaded with sugar and vanilla," she chuckled before leaning against the arm of the swing. "The sun is almost ready to show itself." She curled her legs under her. "What do you prefer, Ian? Sunrise or sunset?"

He sat facing her. "Oh, I don't know. I can't decide. They both can put on a flamboyant display. When you're on a plane, the perspective is quite different. The views are the best part of flying. There have been times when the sun appeared to be a giant orb floating among the clouds, chasing us across the sky." His voice trailed off in memory.

"That must be an extraordinary sight," Grace said in a wistful whisper.

"It is." *One day we'll see it together.* After a few moments, he remembered the dandelions. "Grace, why are you growing a bed full of weeds?"

"Weeds? Oh, you mean the dandelions?" she giggled. "I use them for my business."

"Really? What kind? What's the name?"

"Grace's Teas, Tinctures, and Tonics. I'm an herbalist."

"Huh! The jars of salve make sense now."

Grace chuckled again. "You must've missed the big sign on my store across from Casey's shop."

Well, yeah. I was too busy staring at a stunning redhead. "I guess I did. What made you decide to become an herbalist?" As usual, her attire comprised a knotted scarf, a bohemian style overdress with a long-sleeved t-shirt underneath, and lace-up work boots. From head to toe, she epitomized the stereotype of a naturalist.

"I took after my grandmother. She loved flowers. Especially peonies." Grace sipped her coffee. "After I moved here, I wanted to do something meaningful with my life. To help others. I combined the two," she said with a shrug. "And you? How did you become a professional adventurer?"

"A friend of mine suggested it, and here I am. End of story."

"Nothing more? One day you started recording your travels and became famous?"

Ian drew back one corner of his mouth. "Yep. Pretty pathetic, isn't it?" he chuckled at himself. Up to this point, his greatest achievement was mastering a selfie stick. If he wanted a future with Grace, he must reassess his goals.

"I don't think so. I hoped to see more of the world. It's too late now," she said with a sigh of regret.

"What do you mean?"

"Plane travel can trigger seizures. I wanted to visit Australia. Now I'll never get to go."

How disappointed she must be. Even though she survived what her husband did to her, he still robbed her of the life she should've led. Perhaps he could alleviate her regret about not getting to fulfill her dream. "Do you like spiders?"

"They're my least favorite of Yah's creatures. Wolf spiders especially terrify me. All those babies on their back." She shivered her revulsion. "Why?"

"You'd hate Australia then. They have a whole spider season. I've seen huntsman spiders as big as my hand." He splayed his fingers to show her the size. "They like to hide. Uncovering one really gets the adrenaline pumping."

Grace's eyes bulged. "No, thank you. I'll stick with the little spiders we have around here." She shuddered again.

"Truth is, I've become disenchanted with traveling." He turned towards the now-risen sun. "I didn't realize how much I missed until my car stranded me." He closed his eyes against the bright rays and smiled before turning back to face Grace. "I'm ready for a new chapter."

"Any ideas yet?"

Ian traced the top of his mug with one finger. *Yes!* "I don't know," he said, shrugging. "I'll have to find a different way to earn a living. Math was my best subject in school. Maybe I could become an accountant. I should earn enough to support a family." He stared pointedly at

Grace. "Don't you think?"

She cleared her throat. "Speaking of math, you want to see something cool I discovered in my studies?"

"Sure," he said, noting the eagerness in her voice. He didn't care what she showed him as long as it made her happy and kept her by his side.

Grace hopped up off the swing, sending it rocking. "I'll be right back. You're going to love this."

She reappeared within seconds, hugging a large brown object and wearing a smile that reached from ear to ear.

"Have you heard of the Fibonacci sequence?" she asked, sitting across from him again.

"I don't remember hearing the term before." Ian fell victim to her excitement. "What is the Fibonacci sequence, and what are you hiding?" he asked, reaching for the object she held.

"Not yet!" she said, leaning back.

Ian lowered his hand, more curious now. "Why are you being so mysterious? Show me." He reached for the object again.

"You'll see in a second," she said, pushing his hand away. "The Fibonacci sequence goes: zero, one, one, two, three, five, eight, thirteen, twenty-one, and so on and so on until infinity. The sum of each two numbers equals the next number in the sequence. A sunflower has three numbers of the code." She extended her arms, showing him a dried sunflower head the size of both her palms.

"That thing is huge!"

"I know. That's why I kept it. I'm saving this to teach Joshua when he's old enough to understand. Look," she said. "The sunflower has three sets of parabolic spirals. There are twenty-one large spirals." She traced the seed pattern for Ian. "Then there are thirty-four medium spirals going in the opposite direction." Again, she traced the pattern. "And then there are these short spirals." Once again, tracing the seeds to show him the slope of the spiral. "Can you guess how many there are?"

"Given the sequence, shouldn't the next number be fifty-five?"

"Yes! Isn't flower math the coolest thing?" Her head remained lowered while she grazed the bumps of the seeds with the tips of her fingers. "Yah is so amazing. Not only is He our creator, but He's also a mathematician. This sequence and the Golden Ratio are everywhere. Shells, pinecones, fruit."

Ian bent over the flower, using his finger to trace a set of spirals. No one ever presented God to him as a designer, using measurements and mathematical rules to create patterns. Now that he could see the interlocking swirls, the hidden beauty in the seeds amazed him.

"And to think, Ian. This same attention to detail went into every single one of us. It's even written in our DNA," Grace whispered.

The crack in Ian's disbelief burst like a dam. Seeds could never hold such intricacy through random development. Only intentional design could create the complex pattern before him. *God is real.* His awakening stunned him with its ferocity. He spent the past fifteen years pushing God away. Grace was right. He believed in God; he just didn't know Him. A passion to know Him more overcame him. "Grace?" His voice cracked with emotion, and he cleared his throat. "Is this how you found God?"

Grace gasped. "Ian?"

Ian's questioning eyes met hers. Mere inches separated them. He couldn't stop himself. His gaze dropped to her lips. "Grace, I—" He shouldn't be doing this. He leaned forward.

A rooster crowed its morning greeting.

Grace jumped to her feet, hugging the sunflower to her chest again. "I... um... I need to cook breakfast. It's my turn, and everyone will be up soon."

Ian smiled in satisfaction. Grace's skittishness told him his nearness affected her as much as being near her did him. It might be premature, but his mind raced to their future together. "Do you mind if I help?" he asked, sitting his mug on the side table.

She turned back towards him. A shy smile grew across her face. "No, I don't mind."

* * * * *

"Grace, what are you doing today?" Jeremiah asked, spooning a large helping of fried apples onto a stack of pancakes smothered with melting butter.

"Let's see. I have dried herb cuttings to process. The seed starts need to be separated. I have several orders to fill." She counted her chores on her fingers. "Why? Do you need my help with something?"

"No. I have to help Casey service the battery bank for the campground. A few Passover guests are arriving today. Oh, and two prospective families scheduled tours, and, of course, they had to be at two different times, so I'm busy until supper."

"I'll take the golf cart into town this afternoon. That way, you don't have to worry about bringing Mother and Joshua home."

"Good idea. Thanks." He shoveled the rest of his food into his mouth, took a huge gulp of coffee, then asked Juniper about her plans.

"Well, ten more requests for dough bowls came in over the weekend. I underestimated their popularity when I advertised them for pre-order. Grace, I'm going to mold your spoon ends today. Thanks to Ian, I can do the wood-fired glaze you wanted."

Ian understood why Jeremiah asked where the women intended to spend their day. Knowing their plans enabled him to protect them without being overbearing. The observation inspired Ian to watch how Jeremiah interacted with his family more since he was planning to start one of his own soon. Jeremiah's strategy of nonchalant inquiry achieved a balance of independence and protection. Maybe he wasn't as domineering as he first thought.

"What are you doing today, Ian?" Juniper asked.

"Huh?" He didn't expect to be included in the family's circle of interest, and the question caught him off guard. "Oh. I'm meeting James this morning so he can show me around. I thought we'd go mountain biking, but I'm too sore to do anything other than push the bike," he grumbled.

Without a word, Grace left the table.

"Humph," Joshua said, crossing his arms, leaning back in his chair, and sticking out his lower lip.

What upset him? Ian glanced at Jeremiah and Juniper, but they appeared perplexed as well.

"What's wrong, Joshua?" he asked.

"Nobody cares about what I'm going to be doing today," he moped.

Everybody gushed out their apologies, making Joshua the center of attention. How thoughtless of them! Of course, they cared! Their fawning turned Joshua's pout into giggles.

"What will you be doing today, Joshua?" Ian asked with a crooked grin, expecting to hear how much he would be playing.

"Today, Brother Seamus and Brother Daniel are doing a jiu-jitsu demonstration. The LampKeeper is telling us a new story. And then Moreh will teach us how to write Passover in Hebrew and—"

"Moreh?" Ian asked.

"It means teacher in Hebrew," Grace said when she returned, setting a steaming teacup of tan-colored liquid in front of Ian. "Joshua, you'll be stuck home with me if you don't finish your breakfast and do your chores,"

"Aww, Mom. Do I have to?" Joshua whined.

"You don't want to feed the chickens and the goats?" she asked, returning to her seat beside Joshua.

"I want to feed the goats, but do I have to feed the chickens? King Saul is mean." Joshua scrunched up his face in dislike.

"If that rooster doesn't learn his lesson, I'll add his carcass to the bone broth scraps in the freezer," Juniper proclaimed, standing. "Come on, Joshua. I'll protect you from old King Saul!" she said, holding her hand out.

Ian's jaw dropped. The statement caught Ian off guard. So used to eating in restaurants he didn't connect the food he ate over the weekend to animals raised in the backyard. *Talk about a low carbon footprint!* He drank the tea to distract himself from his shock. "Mmm, honey. What is this?"

"Meadowsweet tea. It helps with muscle soreness," Grace answered.

"Thanks," he said, giving Grace a knowing smile. The quiet interlude they shared this morning was still fresh in his mind.

Grace returned his smile before hiding her blush behind her second cup of coffee.

"Sheriff, are there any sightseeing interests near here?

"There are caves and a waterfall. They're in the next valley."

"Sounds perfect."

"If you're going that far, you'll need food and water. Grace, will you bring Ian one of the small GO bags?"

"GO bags?"

"GO stands for 'get out.' It's a bag you grab when you have to leave your home in a hurry." Grace returned, laying a small backpack on the table. "I set this one up with a one-day supply for hiking. There's bottled water, snack bars, and a few emergency supplies," Jeremiah said.

"Thanks. I didn't think that far ahead."

"James will have a cell phone. After he wandered off and got lost in the woods, Sister Rebecca won't allow him to go anywhere without a way for her to contact him. Watch out for snakes and, of course, bears. What else?"

Ian didn't realize the depth of Jeremiah's protectiveness until it extended to himself. Being included in his circle of concern made Ian feel like part of the family. He cleared his throat. He met Grace's eyes with a mischievous smirk. "Yes, Father," he said, using the same tone of voice she used when Jeremiah gave her commands.

Grace squelched her laugh.

"Oh, haha. Turned into a comedian, have you? I think Grace's tea has taken effect."

Ian stood, bending and twisting from side to side. "I think you're right, Sheriff. I don't ache as badly. Thanks, Grace."

Jeremiah downed the rest of his coffee. "And since you're so full of yourself this morning, you can load the wood onto the trailer."

Ian reached for the bag but noticed Grace clearing the table and grabbed his plate.

She laid her hand on Ian's, stopping his heart.

"I'll clean up. Father needs your help more than I do."

"Grace!" Jeremiah bellowed from the foyer.

She snatched her hand away, her eyes as big as saucers.

Jeremiah returned to the breakfast nook. "On second thought, don't leave the homestead today. Don't take the golf cart. Call me instead." He glanced at his watch. "I'll call to check on you in two hours."

Grace cut her eyes at Ian and smiled. "Yes, Father," she said.

Ian cut off his laughter, seeing the stern look of admonishment on Jeremiah's face.

"You two are full of jokes this morning, aren't you?" Jeremiah half scolded. "Ian quit dawdling. Joshua and Juniper are waiting in the truck." He screwed on his ball cap. "Grace, I'm serious. Two hours. And keep your phone with you."

Graced sighed. "Yes, Father. I'll be waiting."

"You still standing there, Ian? Go load the wood." He walked out the door without another word.

Ian slung the backpack over his shoulder. "See you tonight, Grace."

24

Jeremiah meandered the truck and trailer through the streets, waving to people preparing their gardens for planting. Joshua waved to his friends playing in their front yards. Though the houses varied in style and color, they all appeared to be the same basic square box. Curtained windows in the eaves showed they contained sleeping areas above the main floor. Are there any vacancies? He added the question to his running list. He could be closer to Grace if he stayed in town instead of buying a house elsewhere.

The truck veered into a sharp right-hand swing, bringing Ian out of his thoughts. Jeremiah pulled behind Casey's garage and past the little shed he had escaped sleeping in. On this side of the building, there was a large hole. Thank God he didnt have to sleep there.

They passed the large, open space between the garage and the row of connected shops. He brought the pickup to a stop past a shed-style porch covering the first back entrance. A tall, slender brick box with a chimney stood next to a depleted pile of split logs. Everyone piled out to unload the firewood. Then, Jeremiah drove away.

"Is this your kiln?" Ian asked Juniper while stacking his arms full.

"Yes. I rarely use it, though. I have a much larger gas kiln inside. Grace likes the ash deposits this wood-fired one leaves on the pottery."

"Interesting. I'd like to watch the firing process someday, if you don't mind."

"I'd love to show you," Juniper said, smiling. "We'll mold you your own mug when you return."

"I'd enjoy that a lot." Her words brought him hope for his future with this family. "I wish I didn't have to leave."

"Hey! Mr. MacGregor! We're here!"

Ian turned to see James rolling out of a golf cart. Casey unlocked the shed and pulled out two mountain bikes.

"Duty calls. Catch y'all this evening."

"Have fun and be careful," Juniper admonished. "Come on, Joshua, time to go to school, or you'll be late for the karate demonstration."

"Jiu-jitsu Gramma. Jiu. Jit. Su," he enunciated. "It's better than karate. Okay?"

Juniper's suppressed smirk told Ian she used the word 'karate' on purpose. He exchanged a smile of camaraderie with her.

"Oh, I'm very sorry, Joshua," she apologized. "I didn't realize the difference was so important. Can you ever forgive me?" She squatted to Joshua's level, making a sad face.

Joshua giggled. "Gramma, you're being silly." He hugged her neck.

"Yes, I am, my darling boy," she said. "How shall we walk today? Skip, saunter, ambulate," she asked, demonstrating each movement. "Or run!" She shot off down the alley, holding her full skirt high enough to avoid tripping. Joshua raced after her.

Ian turned back towards James, laughing at Juniper's antics. He desired to be a part of the family more and more. He never wanted to be alone again.

"You ready to be a cameraman?" he asked James when he reached the golf cart. Before leaving the house, he loaded his filming supplies into the small backpack. He pulled out two different harnesses for the GoPro's he used for action footage. "Chest or head?"

"Chest," James said, pointing. "Mom makes me wear a helmet."

Ian set up the harness, adjusting the straps for James' size. "Okay, this button turns on the camera. Your job is simple. Follow me. Oh, and call me Ian. Can't have you calling me Mr. MacGregor when the show's named There Goes Ian. Got it?"

"Got it," James nodded.

"Sheriff said there is a waterfall and caves in the next valley. You know the way there?"

"Yeah, Casey and I go there. The trail switchbacks to the ridge and then curves downward in a wide arc to the falls. There's an outcropping of rocks where Mom enjoys picnicking."

"We should get good footage, then. I want to look for my phone by the pond before we leave."

* * * * *

Searching the park turned up nothing. At James' direction, Ian took the left fork of the path, circling behind the pond. They rode uphill, side-by-side, until the path narrowed to the point of having to travel single file. The hairpin turns somewhat eased the steep ascent, but Ian gave out midway and dismounted to walk his bike to the summit. They grabbed a twenty-minute break, pulling out protein bars and water to keep them fueled for the second portion of the journey. Ian figured only two hours had passed since they began. Jeremiah should've checked on Grace by now. He resisted the urge to ask if he could use James' phone to double-check she was okay.

The trail continued across the ridge for half a mile before descending. They should return to Covenant Cove an hour before sunset if they kept at the same pace. Ian hopped on his bike, his mouth watering for supper and his heart longing for the woman who would prepare his meal.

He stopped to check their brakes before the path made a noticeable decline. He didn't inspect the connections once and almost killed himself when a brake line slipped out of the anchor bolt. Another less-traveled path caught his eye that continued straight across the ridge. Apprehension swelled within him.

"What's through there?" he asked, pointing to the narrower trail.

"Sheriff's cabin. Casey stayed there when he came to live here. It's just a deer path. We hiked through there once. I got covered in poison ivy."

"Then we shouldn't go that way. Don't want to show up for my shoot Saturday with red splotches on my face." Ian checked the camera strapped to James, making sure the device was still recording, then he donned the headgear holding the other GoPro. Abigail would scold him for not filming firsthand footage of the downhill descent. He walked his bike forward, straddled the frame, and placed his foot on the pedal, ready to propel the bike forward.

"Go back."

"Did you say something?"

James shook his head.

Weird. Once again, Ian prepared to set the bike in motion.

"Go back!"

An image of Grace accompanied the voice. Ian didn't question the phenomenon further. He turned his bike around without explanation and barreled through the overgrown path.

"Wait! Ian!" James dropped his shoulders and followed with the camera rolling.

Ian peddled as if a demon pursued him. Leaves and branches slapped him in the face. He didn't know what danger surrounded Grace, but he knew she needed his help. He abandoned his bike in the overgrowth by the outhouse. Grace's shout reached his ears over his labored breathing. Where? Which way? James arrived beside him.

"What's wrong?"

"Shhh!"

A piercing scream coming from below the cabin echoed off the trees. Grace! Ian cannoned down the trail with James in pursuit.

Another shriek rang out, and he pushed himself harder. Around the bend where the descent towards the homestead started, he skidded to a halt. Disbelief over what he saw froze him in place. Grace's nemesis, Dean, loomed over her. Her dress pulled up past her thighs, revealing a long scratch from his rough handling.

"Let me go! Let me go!" Grace struggled against the hands holding hers.

"Scream. No one's here to stop me this time." Dean threw back his head, laughing. He grabbed the neckline of Grace's shift, ripping it in a single motion.

The sound of the fabric tearing broke Ian's stupor. He roared, catapulting himself into Dean's boney form, knocking him off Grace. They tumbled downhill into the dense dead-leaf ground cover. Ian struggled to gain the upper hand against Dean's deceptive wiry build. James helped turn the tables by delivering a strong whack to the back of Dean's head with a tree limb broken off in last night's storm.

Dean howled in pain and turned to grab James. Ian pulled his GoPro harness off and walloped him upside the temple when he turned back around. The disorienting blow gave Ian time to dump the backpack and find a restraint. He reached for an elastic bandage as Dean launched himself into a tackle. Ian used the force of the attack against him, turning the lunge into a somersault with himself coming out on top. He punched Dean twice, bloodying his nose before rolling him onto his stomach.

Dean struggled to extricate himself, but Ian ground his knee into the man's back, wrenching one of his arms at an odd angle. He tied the bandage around one wrist, then wrapped each ankle. The free end he tied around the other wrist, forming an X over Dean's back. Whatever appendage he moved, the opposite arm or leg moved in tandem. Grace's attacker could only rock on his belly like a turtle on its shell.

Ian looked up to see James standing by with the limb, ready to strike.

"Go get Jeremiah," he said before running to help Grace.

He found her clutching the flask she kept chained around her neck, her shaking hands preventing her from unscrewing the lid.

"My… my drops," she mumbled before convulsions overtook her.

Ian removed the lid to find the vial containing her medicine. He emulated the motions of Jeremiah and Juniper, squirting the liquid into her cheek. A few seconds later, the seizure subsided. Relief sagged his shoulders. He did everything correctly.

He gathered her limp form into his arms, carrying her back to the cabin, laying her gently on top of the bedcovers. Her breathing and pulse, though fast, remained steady. He checked the scratch on her leg. Thank goodness it wasn't deep. He found a first-aid kit in the kitchenette and cleaned the wound. He sat at the foot of the bed to wait.

* * * * *

Jeremiah careened over the roots and ruts, racing up the path. Panic over not knowing what awaited him drove him to push the truck to its limits. When James found Casey and himself at the solar panel bank, he gasped, "Grace. Dean. Ian." Then he pointed towards the homestead.

Casey insisted on coming along to serve as a witness. Jeremiah grew angry when they found no one at the house. He told Grace to stay home today. How did Dean slip past him?

"Ow!" Casey complained from the passenger seat. "Slow down, or you'll knock us out before we get there!"

"I can't. We don't know what happened. What if he hurt Grace?"

The driver's side front wheel bottomed out in the wheel basin. Jeremiah's teeth clicked together with the impact.

"I swear, if I have to replace the axle in this truck again, you will not like me," Casey warned.

Jeremiah spotted movement in a patch of overgrowth to the left of the path. He stomped on the brakes, ready to release his anger onto Dean's face. The sight greeting him stopped him dead in his tracks.

"Get a load of this, Casey," he exclaimed in astonishment. "You ever seen anything like it?"

They laughed, watching Dean rock on his belly, trying to reach one of his feet to release the tension on the strained elastic bandage.

"Ian trussed him up like a Thanksgiving turkey!" Casey chuckled. "I have to get a picture."

"Sheriff! Get me out of this! I didn't do nothing!" Dean protested, rolling from side to side. "I can't feel my hands anymore."

"Didn't do anything? Something tells me you're not being honest, Dean."

"I am telling the truth! Grace and I were discussing the mushrooms she picked. See, her basket is up there," he said, pointing with his head. "She said morels are full of antioxidants and planned to make a soup with them. Next thing I know, I get ambushed. Come on, Sheriff! This hurts!"

"So, nothing happened between you and Grace except talking, huh?" Jeremiah squatted next to Dean, taking in the condition of his face. Three parallel scratches ran across one cheek. Blood ran from his nose, covering his mouth and chin. "Is that how you got those scratches? Talking?"

"Okay, so I tried to kiss her too, but I did nothing more than what that social media yahoo did this morning," Dean protested without meeting Jeremiah's eyes. "I'd never hurt Grace."

This morning? How long had Dean been lurking in the shadows around their house? How did he get past the town sentries?

Jeremiah grabbed Dean by the hair, wrenching his head to face him. "So, you've been stalking her too?"

Dean jerked his head away.

"Did you hurt her?" Jeremiah waited for an answer. He pressed Dean's foot closest to him towards the ground, tightening the elastic band even further.

"Ahhh! No! No! Stop!"

"I'm sure this camera will tell the truth, Jeremiah," Casey said, holding up Ian's GoPro, still attached to the harness. "James wore one of these too."

Dean dropped his forehead to the ground.

"Jeremiah, go check on Grace. I'll get him cuffed and loaded into the truck."

* * * * *

"How is she?" Jeremiah asked.

Ian stood, watching Jeremiah test her pulse.

"I think she's okay," Ian said, worry in his voice. "She hasn't stirred, though."

"Sleeping is normal," Jeremiah assured him, touching her forehead. "A seizure is like an electrical storm. The neurons fire all at once with no purpose. It's an intense exercise session compacted into a minute or two. Her body tells her what she needs. When she's done, she'll wake up. She might be a tad disoriented." He noticed the torn bodice of her dress and clenched his fist. "Did he…"

Ian shook his head. "I got here in time."

They both fell silent, watching Grace's chest steadily rise and fall. Each breath calming their frayed nerves.

"Well, you can handle everything from here. I need to go wait for the county sheriff." Jeremiah turned to leave.

"Before you go, I want to ask you something."

"Sure. What's on your mind?"

"How does the Holy Ghost talk to someone?"

"Different ways. Depends on the person," Jeremiah said. "Why?"

Ian scratched his head. "I think He's been trying to communicate with me since arriving. The first few times, I thought I was hearing things. Then I heard the words 'Go back' twice on the trail. A strong sense of dread came over me before I saw an image of Grace in my head. You think He was telling me Grace was in danger?"

"Yes, I believe the Holy Ghost guided you here the same as He guided Casey to go find you. Most people call the experience 'gut instincts.' How does knowing He spoke to you affect your belief in Him?"

Ian stuck his hands in his pockets and shuffled his feet. "I guess… blessed," he said with a shy smile. "I do not doubt God's existence anymore. Grace showed me something this morning that dispelled all my disbelief."

"Her sunflower?"

Ian nodded. "I never considered the designs in nature until she showed them to me. There's no way those mathematical patterns could occur because of a spontaneous explosion billions of years ago."

Jeremiah laid his hand on Ian's shoulder. "Son, I'm proud of everything you've done today. You could protect Grace today because you opened your heart to hearing our heavenly father. Your grandfather would be proud of you, too, if he could be here."

Ian jerked his head up in astonishment. "Wait. You knew my grandfather?"

"Sure did. He was a good man. If it weren't for him, I wouldn't have this job. He recommended me to the previous owner." Jeremiah opened the door. "You don't think I'd allow any old social media star to sleep in the same house with my family, do you?" he said, his chin raised with his grin of superiority. "By the way, I have another question to ask you." He laid his hand on Ian's shoulder again, but this time squeezed it. "What happened on Shabbat and today? Does it change your feelings about Grace? The seizures will never go away."

"What? No! I want to...."

Jeremiah lifted one intimidating eyebrow.

Ian swallowed. Speaking the words out loud was entirely different from thinking them. Saying them to Jeremiah terrified him. "I intend to... marry... Grace," Ian said, uncertainty coloring his admission.

Ian winced when Jeremiah slapped him on the shoulder.

"That's good, son. That's real good."

25

Hands clawed at her, scratching her chest. The faces of Viktor and Dean swam in and out of focus. Hot breath and the onion scent of body odor clogged her airways. Drool dripped and rolled across her neck. Fabric ripped.

"Noooo!" Grace screamed, launching herself forward. Someone grabbed her. "No! No! No!" she raged, swinging her fists at her attacker. "Leave me alone! Leave me alone!" A hand clamped around her wrist. "Let me go! Let me go!" She struggled against her captor, biting the hand holding her.

"Grace. Ow! Grace! Stop!"

The unfamiliar voice penetrated her fight-or-flight response, clouding her awareness. She ceased her struggle. Breath heaved in and out of her lungs. Tender fingers parted the hair covering her face.

"Grace?"

She remembered. *Ian?* "Ian! Oh. I'm sorry." She burst into tears.

He pulled her into his embrace. "Everything is okay, Grace. I'm here. You're safe."

"I'm sorry. I thought you were...," she sobbed into his shoulder. "Did I hurt you?"

"It's okay. It's not your fault," he said, pulling her tighter against him. "Don't worry. He'll never hurt you again. I won't let him."

Grace clung to Ian, taking comfort in the protective circle of his arms. She didn't want him to see her in this state of uncontrollable crying, but her tears persisted. Memories from her previous life flooded her mind, and she couldn't separate her emotions from past and present. She thought she buried the trials and tribulations of her past life after the birth of Joshua. All this time, the sorrows and fear responses of Viktor's conditioning lay hidden within her, waiting to strike.

She wanted to be healed. She yearned to be strong, but Dean's attack rattled the calmness she cultivated along with her flowers and herbs. In a single instant, the memories came flooding back, undoing the progress she had made in forgetting. She wanted to be Grace, stalwart, and resilient. Not whimpering, Tamsin, forever frightened by what hidden dangers lie around every corner. *Stop being scared! Stop crying!*

Ian stroked her hair. Somehow, he now cradled her against his chest, her head resting on his shoulder. His strength protected her, and she relished his embrace of safety. She shouldn't remain here, but she couldn't force herself to pull away from him. Her tears ceased. Ian didn't release her.

She waited a full minute before sitting upright. With a sigh, she braced a foot against the bed to rest her forehead on her bent knee, giving herself time to feel normal again. Ian sat in silence beside her. She spied on him through her tangled curls. He traced the lines in the palms of his hands. *He waits.* Her heart hurt for him, knowing he waited in vain. Nothing could ever come of their attraction. She had nothing to give him except the truth.

"Ian?" He turned his questioning eyes on her without speaking. "I died."

"Wait. What?" Panic strained his voice.

"When I found God. When I started believing he was real. It happened when I died." She watched his shoulders sag with relief.

"Grace, don't scare me like that," he said, moving her hair out of her face to wipe her tears away. "What do you mean you died?"

She flashed a smile. Falling in love with this man would be easy. "The person I was before I moved here... died. She has a death certificate and everything. Joshua's father killed me. I went to Sheol." She scooted to sit beside him on the edge of the bed. "You know how everyone says the 'pearly gates of heaven'?" she asked, mystery tainting her voice. "Well, they're not pearly. They're gold. And huge! I couldn't see the top of them. Scores of people are waiting to enter. My grandmother greeted me. 'Go back,' she said. 'It's not your time.' So, I came back." Grace shrugged her shoulder before rising to stand in front of the windows. "I don't know why I'm telling you this. Even my father doesn't know."

"Jeremiah doesn't know you died?"

"Oh, he knows about my clinical death. He's the one who performed CPR. I've never told him what I saw when I died, though. In fact, no one knows except you."

Ian came to stand in front of her. *Why am I so attracted to him?* Though handsome enough, he didn't have Viktor's blonde Adonis look that made her swoon with desire. He possessed a pensive expression until he smiled. Then his face lit up, crinkling the corners of his eyes. *I know next to nothing about him, but I want to share everything with him.* Oh, why did he have to show up disrupting her peace?

He picked something out of her hair before using his index finger to brush the curls away from her face. She became lost in the tranquility of his soulful eyes. The palm of his hand cupped her jawline. She closed her eyes, tilting her head into his reassuring strength. *Oh, how I've missed this.*

"Thank you for sharing your secret with me," Ian said, his voice barely above a whisper. "Do you think my mother is there? Waiting for me?"

"I'm sure she is."

The pad of his thumb brushed against her bottom lip. The yearning the movement evoked brought her out of her trance. "I want to go home and shower." She hurried across the room, exiting the cabin.

"Right now, a shower sounds good. I'll get my bike," he said, walking towards the outhouse.

"Stop!" Grace shouted.

Ian searched the ground for danger. He turned questioning eyes on her.

"Did you come through there?" she asked in horror, pointing to the overgrown trail.

"Well, yeah. James said the path is a shortcut. My bike is on the other side of the outhouse." Ian stepped in the direction he had pointed.

"No! You have to shower right now," she said, dragging him away.

"But I have to return the bike to Casey." He scratched his cheek with his free hand.

"Casey can get it himself," Grace said, still pulling him. "He's not allergic to poison ivy."

"Grace, there is no need to worry. Besides, I'm wearing pants. Poison ivy grows on the ground."

"Ian, there are vines in there thicker than my wrist," she said, holding up her arm for emphasis. "They grow on the trees and are overhanging the path. If you don't shower right now, you will be covered in blisters by nightfall."

Ian's eyes grew large before he darted off. He kept ahead, stopping whenever he lost sight of her. She shooed him forward but loved that he waited, more concerned with her well-being than his own. He would make someone a great husband. *Just not me.*

Once they reached the bathing enclosure, Grace made quick work of the knobs and levers, diverting the water supply from the tub to a shower head.

"Strip and toss your clothes out so I can put them in the washer. I'll leave your bag, a bar of soap, and a bottle of alcohol outside the door for you to rub down with after you shower. I'm going to throw the kitchen sink of home remedies at you. Hopefully, we'll prevent most of the blistering."

* * * * *

Ian nodded his understanding while shooing Grace out of the enclosure, willing to do anything she told him, even if she demanded he remove the top layer of his skin, to avert the horrible case of poison ivy rash already prickling to be scratched.

He followed her bathing instructions twice to be safe before he entered the house—the hum of a washing machine droned in the background. Grace stood beside the kitchen table, a pleasant smile pasted on her face. She pulled out a chair for him.

"Welcome to my office."

"You're doctoring me again?" Ian teased, sitting. A round wooden container, a pair of soft stretch gloves, and a roll of gauze bandaging lay in a line. He removed the lid of the container, revealing a greenish-gray cream. He sniffed. It didn't smell bad.

"Yes, and you're going to be grateful I did," she said, holding out her hand. "Arm."

Ian complied. Happy to be her center of attention. He held the container for her. "What are the ingredients?"

"Plantain, bentonite clay, and jewelweed, along with a few minor others. Jewelweed is the most important one, though. It's the antidote to poison ivy."

"So, the pink calamine lotion my grandmother slathered me with?"

"Worthless."

"What does the other stuff do?" he asked, warming to the subject. He found her way of viewing the world fascinating. Instead of seeing a weed, she saw medicine.

"The humble plantain is nature's secret weapon. The plant possesses many properties for all kinds of healing, but for this mixture, it serves as an anti-inflammatory. Bentonite clay is a drying agent," she explained while swaddling his arm with the gauze. "It will dehydrate the blisters when they form. Here, put this on," she said, holding the wrist opening of one of the gloves apart for him to slide his hand into.

The glove over the ointment stimulated his yuck factor. Ian grimaced.

"At least you'll have use of your hands. Once everything dries, you can wash again."

He switched the container to his gloved hand while she worked on his other arm. Starting at his shoulder, she slathered on the cream before wrapping his arm with a bandage.

"The gauze is thin enough for the air to permeate and allows you to use your arms without the cream coming off." She reached for his hand, hesitating when she saw his wounded knuckles. "Thank you for saving me today. You were very brave. The plantain will help heal these abrasions, too," she said, slathering the cream across his knuckles.

"You're welcome," Ian said, beaming under her praise. "It's not every day you get to be a knight in shining armor."

Grace gasped, dropping his hand. She stared at Ian in bewilderment. *Oh, no!* Did he say something wrong? His stomach muscles clenched. His heart pounded in his chest. He wanted to say, 'I'm sorry,' but he didn't know what he had said wrong. He waited for her to make the next move.

Seeming to reach a conclusion, a languid grin spread across Grace's face. "Hand!" she said, almost bouncing with happiness now.

Ian's breath caught in his throat. Did her smile mean what he thought? He'd gladly fight a million battles to see the way her eyes sparkled now. *God, please don't let me mess this up.*

"You're lucky you didn't wear shorts today," Grace said, dabbing the cream that was in his gloved hand onto his face.

Ian wasn't sure, but her voice seemed to hold a lilt of happiness not present a moment ago. Her smile remained in place. Ian dropped his eyelids, suppressing the hope rising inside him. "Why?" he asked, his voice cracked.

"Because, with your legs wrapped also, you will look like a mummy and frighten Joshua."

Ian raised his gauze-covered arms before him and rose from the chair.

"Uhh," he moaned.

"Quit playing and sit back down," she scolded with a laugh. "I still have your neck and face to do."

Ian obeyed and closed his eyes, tilting his head back, anticipating the feel of Grace's fingertips any second. Nothing happened. He peeked to see why she had stopped.

Grace stood frozen. With his head tilted at this angle, her parted lips hovered mere inches above his. If she leaned forward a little more... He suppressed the thought. Ian closed his eyes and clenched his jaw, chastising himself. After what she went through this morning, he shouldn't be thinking of kissing her. He wanted to build a family with her. To achieve his goal, he needed to prove his attraction ran deeper than physical desire like Jeremiah said.

"The cream," he said, reminding Grace of her task.

"Oh, right," she said as she swiped the ointment across his forehead and on his cheeks.

Ian inhaled his resolve. He could stay until Friday. Before he left, he intended to divulge the depth of his affections. He resolved to broach the subject of marriage with her at the first opportunity. He didn't expect her to answer immediately. Maybe not for months. He waited this long to find the right woman to marry. He would wait forever for her to say yes.

"I'm telling you, Isaac. Yah gave the commandment of stoning to prevent repeat offenders," Jeremiah said.

"Oh!" Grace squeaked, dropping the container of cream.

Ian shot to his feet.

"Oh, good grief! What happened to you?" Jeremiah asked before bursting out in laughter. "It looks like an avocado exploded in your face."

* * * * *

Grace snuggled beneath the heavy quilt, protecting her against the chilly air. Her father and mother insisted she sleep in the spare bedroom for the next week after having two seizures so close together. If she had stayed in her cottage, she could've started a fire in the little pot belly woodstove to stave off the cold. In her parents' house, once the night temperatures neared fifty degrees regularly, her father shut down the wood furnace, relying solely on the wood stove in the morning room for heat. The warmth never quite reached the bedrooms.

She could dig out a sleeping bag from the hall closet but didn't want to risk waking Ian, who slept on the living room couch. Grace rolled over, re-tucking the blanket tightly around her neck so no cold air could seep into the warmth of her cocoon. The day was enjoyable despite the horrible events of the morning. Ian's constant attention and concern shrouded the memory of Dean's assault before it could grow roots.

She knew his affection for her grew by the moment. She also knew she shouldn't encourage him because she couldn't marry anyone without obtaining a Biblical divorce. Knowing didn't stop her from enjoying his tender care or quell her attraction. His presence brought the contentment of security she pined for. For the rest of the day, he stood steadfastly beside her while she worked in her garden beds, keeping her distracted with his stories and questions. His voice calmed her. She rolled back to her other side. One thought chasing after another.

His feelings for her should die once he left at the end of the week. She could allow his attention until then, provided they didn't cross the boundaries of respectability. What did it hurt to enjoy his company for a few more days?

Even though he professed to be considering moving to Covenant Cove, she believed he'd choose to stay once he returned to mainstream society. A single tear escaped her eye. No matter how much she might wish the circumstances to be otherwise, any relationship with Ian remained hopeless. Once the novelty of his attraction wore off, he'd never look back. Plus, the specter of Viktor loomed. He'd stop at nothing to get to her if he found out she still lived.

When Dean snuck up on her this morning, he whispered, "Somebody's been looking for you," in her ear. At first, his words struck terror into her heart. Did Viktor somehow find her? Then he said he tried to ask her on Shabbat what to give his grandmother, afraid she contracted the Covid virus circulating the globe, but between Ian and Jeremiah, he couldn't get close enough to her. Dummy her, believed him. She lowered her guard and placed her clippers away in her basket. Once she no longer held a weapon, he pounced.

Then Ian showed up to rescue her. One minute Dean's leering face loomed above her, and then wham! Grace giggled. Dean didn't know what hit him. Too bad the seizure aura started. She would've enjoyed seeing Dean hogtied.

Alright, Grace. Enough for tonight. She needed sleep. Closing her eyes, she prayed.

<h1 style="text-align:center">26</h1>

The noise of wheels rolling back and forth on the coffee table woke Ian. Joshua's heavy breathing while he played with his toys and the rhythmic ticking of the grandfather clock in the hall lulled Ian into a state of domestic bliss. If Grace accepted his proposal, this could be his life. No more sleeping on planes or eating alone and on the go. The corners of his mouth twitched at the unmistakable sound of a finger snap, followed by a gasp. *Somebody's in trouble.*

"Joshua, I told you not to be in here. Let Mr. Ian sleep in peace," Grace whispered.

"Momma? Why does his face look funny?" Joshua asked in a loud whisper.

Oh, no! Joshua missed his mummified state the day before, so they didn't tell him what had happened. He didn't see any spots last night before Grace applied a small amount of argan oil to combat the drying effects of the bentonite clay while he slept. She promised to apply more salve this morning. Might as well get this over with.

"Good morning, Joshua," Ian drawled, opening his eyes.

"Mama! He's awake!"

Grace sat on the coffee table and gave Ian a knowing smile. "How'd you sleep?" she asked, checking his arms and hands for signs of the rash.

"I've had better nights," Ian said, raising up on his elbows. "Is it that bad? I tried not to scratch."

"You didn't escape completely, but we diverted the worst," she said. "Here, sit up, and I'll apply more cream to the places on your face. Hopefully, this will be the last time." She turned to Joshua. "Bring me the container and paper towels off the table, please."

Joshua took off and returned before Ian finished sitting upright. He reclined against the arm of the couch, leaving room for Grace to sit on the edge beside him. Taking the container from Joshua, she dabbed the contents onto Ian's face.

"He looks like a Dalmatian Mama," Joshua giggled.

Grace smeared ointment on Joshua's nose. "There. Now you're a Dalmatian too."

Joshua jumped with high-pitched barking before dropping to his hands and knees, pretending to be a dog. Grace wiped the excess off her finger and closed the container, a loving smile lighting up her face over Joshua's antics. Ian watched her. For a few seconds, she lost her joy before her smile returned. What could've caused that? He curled his fingers into Grace's empty hand, locking their hands together.

"He's amazing. I'd give anything to have a son like him."

Grace turned toward him. His heart swelled with the love he saw there. His breath caught. *Does this mean?* He squeezed her fingers tighter. She placed her free hand on top of his. *Yes!*

"Joshua, you shouldn't tease Mr. Ian. He rescued your mama from a dangerous villain yesterday," Grace said, never taking her eyes off Ian.

"He did?" Joshua asked, popping to his knees.

"Yes, he did. He's a proper knight in shining armor, the same as your Papa."

Grace rubbed the pad of her thumb across the abrasions on Ian's knuckles, kicking the beat of his heart into high gear. The gesture squelched any doubt he held over Grace's feelings. He'd ask her to marry him tonight. They could go for a walk with the moon almost full.

"Did you jiu-jitsu him, Mr. Ian?" Joshua asked, rolling around on the floor, wrestling with an imaginary opponent.

Embarrassment colored Ian's cheeks. It appeared self-defense ranked high on Joshua's required skill set. He didn't want to disappoint the little boy with his lack of skills. Besides a few evasive maneuvers his grandfather taught him, he knew nothing about self-defense. Did rushing Dean like a linebacker count? "Well... I... um."

"Joshua, jiu-jitsu is not the only form of self-defense," Grace admonished. "Mr. Ian did an excellent job of protecting me yesterday."

The corners of Ian's mouth turned up with her praise. He thanked Grace for the compliment with a gentle squeeze and laid his hand on top of hers.

She smiled.

He beamed back. Their silent communication was an assurance of her affection towards him.

Grace disengaged her hand, laying it against his cheek, and leaned towards him.

Ian's heart throbbed. Was she going to kiss him? Oh, he hoped so. He forced himself to be still.

"Now. Why don't you be a good little doggie and get washed up for breakfast," Grace said before getting up and leaving the room.

Ian's jaw dropped. A squawk of protest escaped his throat. She left him hanging! He did not expect such dry humor from her. Though unexpected, he rejoiced in the knowledge of her feeling comfortable enough to joke with him. Their life together would be full of happiness. Hmmm. Two can play this game. If she liked surprises, he could think of quite a few to knock her off her feet.

"Hey, Joshua," Ian whispered, motioning for him to move closer and keep quiet.

"Yeah, Mr. Ian?" Joshua asked in the same loud whisper he used earlier.

"Shhh," Ian cautioned, glancing at the open doorway. "Do you want to surprise your mom with flowers?"

"Yeah. Yeah. Yeah." Excited, Joshua hopped with each word.

"Good. Where can we find some flowers?" Ian said, keeping his voice low.

Joshua thought for a moment. "In Mama's garden," he blurted.

"Shhhh, you don't want her to hear us," Ian reminded him. "We can't pick those. Think of somewhere else."

Grace poked her head in the doorway. "Oh, Ian. I meant to ask you earlier. Do you mind delivering a couple of containers of poison ivy cream to Sister Rebecca this morning? I'm sure she needs more. James is highly allergic."

"No problem. Where does she live?" Ian agreed, willing to use her unwitting excuse to leave the house.

"Take Joshua. He knows the way. In fact. You'll be doing me a favor if you keep him out for a while. I have chores to do, and they'll be easier without him underfoot."

"Sure. We'll make an adventure of it." He pasted on a placating smile, waiting for her to leave. He couldn't believe his good fortune.

"Great. Well, then. I'll have your breakfast done shortly," she said with a nod.

"Thank you. I'll be there in a couple more minutes."Ian held up his hand for Joshua to give him a high five.

* * * * *

Down a gravel drive, past the solar panel bank and a field full of ripening barley, lay a large meadow of wildflowers full of feeding bees. *Jackpot!* Gigantic oaks separated Rebecca's apiary from her cornflower blue cottage. James, covered in the greenish-gray salve, sunned himself by the hives to hasten the drying effects.

"Hi, James. Sorry to drag you into everything yesterday. Grace sent some cream over for you."

"It's okay. It was for a good cause." James gestured towards the table behind him. "You can put them beside the jars the sheriff and Mrs. Juniper delivered this morning."

At that moment, Ian realized why Grace commandeered him for the delivery and asked him to bring along Joshua. She must've overheard their plans. So much for surprising her. He should've known she schemed an ulterior motive for sending him to the beekeeper's house.

He grimaced at the bouquets Joshua and he held. The tiny flowers weren't what he had in mind but would do. "You know, Joshua, your mother is one smart lady. She knew what we were looking for without us saying anything."

"Yeah, she knows a lot of stuff I don't tell her," Joshua agreed. "One time, I lied to her, and she knew I was lying, but I don't know how she knew."

"Why did you lie to your mother, Joshua?" Ian asked incredulous Joshua knew how to lie at such a young age.

"I ate the last piece of coconut cream pie she was saving," he confessed.

"Your mother likes coconut cream pie?" Ian asked, storing the information away for later.

"Mmm hmm, it's her favorite." Joshua stopped walking and looked

192

up at him. "Mr. Ian, how'd Mama know it was me and not Papa or Gramma June?"

"I don't know, Joshua," Ian answered. "The world's greatest detectives are mothers. My mother always knew when I lied to her, too. She said it hurt her feelings when I lied."

"Do you think I hurt my mama's feelings when I lied to her?"

"Probably. When you lie to someone, it's the same as saying you don't care about them."

"But, I love Mama. I just didn't want to get in trouble," Joshua protested.

"I know, but lying always makes everything worse. You should tell the truth no matter what. Okay?"

"Okay," Joshua said, taking hold of his hand.

By the time they reached the house, Ian's stomach rumbled from hunger. Joshua pulled him to the backyard, where they could hear Grace and Juniper talking. Fresh bed linens hung on the clothesline.

"Mama! Mama! Look what me and Mr. Ian picked for you!"

Grace knelt, holding her arms wide for Joshua to run into her embrace. "Oh, my goodness Joshua. What lovely flowers!" she gushed before kissing him on the cheek. "Thank you for surprising me."

Juniper sang her own praises over Joshua's thoughtfulness. Ian's heart ached witnessing the love shared. *This is the family I choose.*

When he lived with his grandparents, although they lavished him with affection, he did not feel the same desperate need to be a part of their family that he felt now. In his teenage mind, he believed they didn't want him. They left him with his stepmother to be abused instead of trying to get custody of him. His emotions colored any gesture of love they gave him. Not until after his grandfather passed away and his grandmother had to be put in a nursing home did he learn they tried to get custody right after his father died. The judge sided with his stepmother so she could keep receiving support from his father's social security surviving child benefits.

Ian dismissed the unpleasant memory. He didn't want to invest another minute ruminating upon things no longer worth his time and energy. He would not let unwelcome memories bog down his happiness. His future was with Grace, Joshua, Juniper, and even Jeremiah, despite the man's penchant for intimidating him.

Grace turned her smile on him, and Ian's breath caught. *God, please don't take this away from me.* He swallowed before speaking. "Joshua, aren't you forgetting someone?" Ian asked, holding out the bouquet for Joshua to take.

"Oh, yeah." Joshua grabbed the flowers and shoved them toward Juniper. "Here, Gramma. These are for you."

"Joshua," she gushed. "Where did you find so many colorful flowers?"

"It's amazing what you can find in a beekeeper's front yard," Ian said, crossing his arms and staring Grace in the eye.

She blushed, suppressing the grin his accusation brought.

"Mama, can I play with the goats?"

Grace broke eye contact with Ian. "Yes, but you know the rules. After you do your chores."

"But—."

"No buts. Chickens then goats," Grace said, using a firm tone. "Mother, we should put our flowers in water. Ian can watch Joshua." She smiled at him before turning towards the house.

Ian watched her go, confident of Grace's growing affections. All he needed to do was work up the courage to ask her to be his wife.

"Aw!" Joshua scraped the ground with his foot.

Joshua's displeasure interrupted Ian's musings.

"It's chickens, Joshua. How hard can it be?" Ian asked.

"It's easy, except for King Saul. Come on," Joshua said, grabbing Ian's hand. "I'll show you."

He led Ian to the barn, filled a bucket with feed, and proceeded to the chicken coop. There, he unlatched the door, pushing it wide open. The chickens flooded out of the enclosure, followed by a strutting rooster.

"That's King Saul," Joshua said, pointing to the large, brownish-red bird. "Don't turn your back on him, or he'll attack you."

Ian smothered a snicker. The way King Saul strutted reminded him of Jeremiah the first time he saw him. "Duly noted," Ian said. "What's next?"

"You take this feed," Joshua said, grabbing a handful. "And throw it everywhere." The chickens rushed after the little nuggets where they fell.

"That's it?"

Joshua threw another handful. "Yep."

"Alright, then I'll do your chore, and you can play with the goats." Ian took the bucket from Joshua.

"Thanks, Mr. Ian," Joshua hollered over his shoulder, running towards the barn.

Ian chuckled. Oh, to be young and carefree again. He returned his attention to the chickens. With timid movements, he spread the feed with a fanning motion. The birds rushed to the new area where it dropped. This isn't so hard. He repeated the gesture several more times, each time growing in confidence until he emptied the bucket.

He set the bucket on the ground and turned his complete attention toward the trio at play. Joshua kicked a ball, and the baby goats chased it. Child's laughter bubbled out of Joshua, and Ian laughed along with him. Sarge and Chevron competed to reach the ball. Over and over, the goats tripped when their little legs became tangled together.

A wild kick caused the ball to roll under the hanging laundry. The fluttering sheets didn't deter Sarge. He darted under the first row only to run into the corner pocket of a fitted sheet. Blinded and frightened, he jerked and bucked until he pulled the sheet off the line, then raced unseeing towards Ian and the flock of chickens with the linen trailing behind him. The frightened sqwaks of the birds set the dog to braying.

Ian dove, bringing Sarge's wild flight to a halt. Before he could untangle the goat from the now-soiled sheet, King Saul's spurs sliced across his back. His beak sank into his scalp with vicious pecks. He made the mistake of turning his back on the bird, leaving himself open for attack. Ian leaped to his feet and kicked the rooster away. King Saul strutted off, unperturbed by Ian's treatment.

"Crazy bird," Ian said, cutting his eyes in anger. He picked the sheet up, checking for damage.

"Mr. Ian, are you okay?" Joshua asked, running up to Ian. "You're bleeding!" Joshua gasped. He ran to the house, hollering for his mother.

Grace and Juniper rushed out the door, worry written on their faces.

"Joshua! Are you okay?" Grace asked, inspecting him for injuries.

"Mama, King Saul attacked Mr. Ian, and he's bleeding," Joshua cried, tears pooling in his eyes. "I didn't mean to kick the ball into the sheets."

Ian, the corner of his mouth pulled back in a grimace, joined them, displaying a large tear in the grass-stained sheet. "There's been a goatastrophy."

"I can see that," Grace chuckled before cutting off her laughter. She grabbed Ian's head, pulling it to her level to comb through his hair.

"Grace, what are you doing?"

"You're bleeding!"

"I'm fine. It's a few scratches and pecks." Ian assured her, drawing away and standing upright. "No need to fuss."

"Regardless, they still require tending," she said, moving behind him. "There's blood on your shirt, too."

Ian twisted out of her reach. He was not ready for her to see the scars on his back. He needed more time before revealing those secrets. "I'm sure they're minor scratches."

"Ian quit moving! I need to see how deep they are. What if you need stitches?" She went for the hem of his shirt.

"I don't need stitches. I'm fine," he said, turning out of her reach again. Grace made another dive. Ian grabbed her hands. "Honestly, I'm fine. I'll check them when I shower later."

Grace pursed her lips. "Ian MacGregor, this is a farm. Without proper treatment, your wounds could develop infection and lead to sepsis, which means you could die. Do you want to die, Ian?"

Her words left him speechless. Of course, he didn't want to die, but he didn't want her seeing his back, either. "Uhhh... no," he admitted when he couldn't think of an excuse to counter her argument.

"Good, then I'll hear no more arguments. Mother, help me pick fresh plantain leaves. Joshua, quick, fetch me the box of large bandages."

Joshua returned before Ian could think of another excuse. Grace grabbed him by the wrist, pulling him towards the barn. "Come on, Ian, everything else I need is in my cottage," she said with a broad smile.

The smile finished him. If tending to his injuries brought her happiness, what gave him the right to deny her? He hoped to have more time to reveal his past, but here he was, taking the plunge, all because Grace smiled at him. Dreading her reaction he sighed. He wanted her love, not her fawning sympathy like his past girlfriends gave him when they found out. *Here goes nothing.*

27

Ian entered Grace's domain with trepidation. Though no one spoke the words, he understood entering her private quarters to be forbidden to him. In his mind, he painted a picture of an ethereal fairytale cottage decorated with the bits and bobs she treasured. Instead, a workroom lined with shelves full of neatly labeled jars of dried substances, bottles, jugs, burners, pots, and other tools of her trade greeted him. Centered in the room was a round table covered in a crocheted lace tablecloth, its femininity incongruent with the other furnishings.

Grace flipped the cloth up to expose the worn wood underneath and turned out a low-backed chair sideways. "Sit," she said, taking the handful of greens to the kitchen.

Ian complied, straddling the seat and crossing his arms over the back of the chair to watch her putter around, assembling the supplies she needed to doctor him. She filled the sink with water, adding vinegar and the plantain to soak. Then she made a saline solution in a bottle with a nozzle.

"This is not what I expected," Ian said.

"Oh? What did you expect?" Grace asked, still smiling while she opened drawers and cabinet doors, taking out supplies.

Not to fall in love. The silent admission brought him a sense of peace. Why did he fight against his heart when Jeremiah confronted him? Why did he want to hide his past from her if he loved her? He trusted Grace with his heart. He could trust her with his wounds, both old and new. Ian's misgivings over her reaction to the scars on his back fell away.

"Not you," Ian said, his voice raw with emotion.

Grace gasped, staring at him wide-eyed. "Me?"

"Joshua, Jeremiah and Juniper, Covenant Cove. I didn't expect any of this," Ian added to ease her apprehension over his words. "I haven't been this happy since before my mother passed away."

"I'm glad you're enjoying your visit," Grace said, practically singing the words. She deposited a tray full of tools on the table. "Having someone my age for company has been a pleasant change. Most of our houseguests are nearer to my parent's age group. How long are you staying?" she asked, returning to the kitchen. She began grinding the plantain leaves with a mortar and pestle.

"Until Friday. My first shoot is at a barbeque joint on Saturday in Chattanooga," Ian answered. "With most of the festivals canceled because of this Covid virus, my manager set up one-on-one recording sessions with restaurants off the beaten path. I'm not looking forward to all the traveling. After staying here these few days, I know I'm ready to settle down."

"I think you're doing a good thing. So many have lost their source of income because of the government shutdown. Maybe your notoriety will help keep businesses open, which might've closed," she said. "Hey, can you grab the shampoo and a couple of towels? The bathroom is behind this wall."

Ian flipped the light switch, illuminating the windowless room under the loft's stairway. He grabbed an unlabeled bottle from the shower. The towels were behind the door. He turned to cut off the light, and his hand paused in mid-air. Above the sink, the painted mirror read: "For if anyone is a hearer of the word and not a doer, he is like a man who looks at his natural face in a mirror." A shiver ran through him. He was guilty of hearing and not doing.

"Did you find the shampoo?" Grace poked her head through the door. "Oh, good. You did." She grabbed the bottle from Ian and cut off the light.

"Why did you paint that verse on the mirror? Don't you need to see yourself?" Ian asked, following Grace into the kitchen.

Grace turned on the tap. "I was a vain person in my previous life. I believed Yah had turned his back on me; therefore, I didn't need him. Clothes, makeup, cars, houses. Those were my gods, and I had to have the best. I was trying to fill His absence with things of this world. The verse reminds me that I don't need stuff to make me happy. I use my Bible as my mirror. We cannot buy its gifts."

"Okay. I'll bite. How is the Bible a mirror, and what gifts?" He leaned against the counter. Jeremiah and Grace never ceased to amaze him. The way they described God kept him curious and coming back for more. They didn't lecture when discussing their beliefs; they imparted knowledge.

"Unlike man-made mirrors, which show nothing more than our reflections, the Bible shows us our truth. It reads us while we're reading it. It tells us who we are instead of who we think we are. Water's ready," she said, moving aside for him to lean over the sink.

"I can wash my hair myself," Ian said, sticking his head under the running water.

"Humor me." Grace wet his hair, cupping her hand to pour water where the faucet didn't reach.

"So, how does the Bible read us?"

"By revealing our spiritual selves," she explained before squirting shampoo into her open palm. She worked the soap into a foam, massaging his scalp with the pads of her fingers.

Ian could get used to this.

"The Bible exposes how Yah sees us. It reveals our strengths and flaws through the stories it contains. The thoughts of our hearts, even the private thoughts we hide from everyone else, are laid bare. Character flaws such as greed, lust, and jealousy are brought to light so we can bring every thought captive. It teaches us to walk as Yahusha walked. It makes us better people."

Her words hit Ian with a splash. At present, the thoughts of his heart involved a passionate kiss with Grace. God probably shook his head in disappointment at some things that raced through his mind. "How do you stop yourself from thinking random thoughts?" Ian asked. "Sometimes things pop into your head."

"Well, we are only human. Everyone has stray thoughts. Giving in to them is what leads to sin. We should bring to heal thoughts not aligning with scripture before they take root." Grace turned off the tap. "All done." She squeezed the excess moisture from his hair before draping a towel around his shoulders. "Sit at the table so I can finish drying your hair."

Ian complied. Grace used the towel like a mitt, applying pressure to wick away the moisture in his hair. Within moments, his thoughts returned to kissing her. He conjured up the sound of a needle scraping across a vinyl record. Change the subject. He caught a whiff of the shampoo. The scent, though familiar, eluded him. Its astringent qualities stung the wounds where King Saul pecked him. "The shampoo you used is quite invigorating. Did you make it?"

"No, another sister makes our soaps, shampoos, and other self-care products. This is my favorite. The smell of the eucalyptus is refreshing and has antibacterial properties, which is why I insisted on washing your hair."

What else are you planning to do to me? What's this paste stuff?

"It's a mixture of honey, tea tree oil, and yarrow. I'll use it on your head. The scratches on your back require a poultice. Not only is plantain an anti-inflammatory, but it's also antibacterial, antimicrobial, and antitoxic as well," Grace said, singing the plant's praises.

Ian tilted the bowl of dark green pulp towards him. "This weed does all that?"

"Mmm hmm," Grace murmured, laying the towel on the table. "Lean your head forward. I think you're dry enough now. I'll place a small piece of cotton over each wound, so the rest of your hair won't get stuck in the honey." She quartered the cotton ball with scissors, then used the popsicle stick to apply the salve.

Ian checked himself before his thoughts strayed too far into another fantasy. Grace's words convicted him to bring his mind under control. He believed himself a good person until she spoke of how private thoughts should align with scripture. He wasn't prone to lying, nor did he cheat or steal, and he donated to charities. However, he took part in self-indulgent daydreaming often. He considered his fantasies benign because he never contemplated making them real. Like when he dreamed of beating the tar out of David Duncan after he shoved Ian's 'pizza face' in the toilet. Ian revisited that fantasy several times before ninth grade when the school finally expelled his nemesis for spray painting a teacher's car.

Now, analyzing his daydreams from the perspective Grace presented, he admitted the desire in his heart to do violence contradicted who he portrayed himself to be. His teachers praised him for his amicable and easygoing nature. What words could they have used if they knew the darkness of his secret thoughts? Fake? Charlatan? Hypocrite? Ian's stomach knotted. He decided to do better now that he knew.

"I can't believe you're using weeds. My grandmother destroyed every weed she could find. Her yard was her pride and joy," Ian said, returning to plants for a topic to distract himself.

"Tell me about her." Grace searched his scalp for wounds.

"She used to walk from one side of the yard to the other in rows, carrying a grocery bag, a trowel, and a bottle of weed killer, searching for forbidden grasses and weeds. She dug up or squirted everything that wasn't the Kentucky blue fescue grass carpet she loved." The memory of his grandmother hunched over, walking back and forth, back and forth, brought mixed emotions. During his teenage years, Ian thought her nuts. Once he reached adulthood, he realized her ritualistic obsession was a harbinger of Alzheimer's. He should've spent more time helping her instead of brushing her off as a fanatic.

"Isn't grass just grass? How do you tell the difference?" Grace asked before raising Ian's shirt. Her hands stilled before pushing the garment over his head, leaving his arms in the sleeves.

"No clue, but my grandmother seemed to know them all," Ian continued his story, expecting Grace to ask about the scars on his back any moment. How much should he tell her? "She hated Bermuda grass and wild violets the most. In the backyard, she planted tons of flowers. In the beds, she tucked in garden gnomes in funny poses."

"I've always thought those statues cute. My grandmother liked them as well. I'm more into insects myself."

"What kind?" Ian asked, glancing over his shoulder. He wanted to know her favorite things. That way, he could surprise her. Once, he gifted Abigail a vintage-style Batman t-shirt for her birthday, and she marveled for weeks because he remembered her favorite comic character. Would he get the same reaction from Grace when he surprised her with a well-chosen gift gleaned from their casual conversations?

"Oh, I like dragonflies the most, but butterflies and moths are nice, too. I stopped liking beetles when I discovered where the grubs killing my plants came from." Grace squirted the saline water on his back.

Ian flinched.

"Sorry. I should have warned you. Did it sting?" She blew gently on the wounds. "Some scratches are deeper than I expected."

"You're okay. It didn't hurt. Just cold." Ian clenched the rungs of the chair. *Think of anything besides what she is doing.*

Grace dabbed the washcloth against his wounds. "Tell me more about your grandmother and her garden."

Oh yeah! The statues. "There was one statue of a man and woman facing each other. They held an umbrella angled so you couldn't see their faces," Ian continued the memory. "I asked my grandmother why they hid behind the umbrella. She told me it was a secret. I never looked. I rented the house when she could no longer live alone and had to be put in a nursing home. Now the statues are gone." He made a scoffing noise. "I still wonder if they were whispering, kissing, or what. I'd know their secret if I'd been smart and more inquisitive like Joshua."

"Personally, I think you're smarter than Joshua."

Ian half turned in the chair. "Oh, yeah? How so?"

Grace forced his shoulders to face forward again. She began placing the bandages over the wounds. "Because you understood what secrets are and didn't go prying. Most people live their whole lives and never learn such a valuable lesson. I'd say you possessed wisdom and maturity far beyond your age."

Ian realized her words were her way of saying she didn't intend to ask about the scars on his back. His heart swelled over her thoughtfulness. "I never thought of it that way. Thank you for the compliment, Grace."

"You're welcome." She lowered his shirt. "I'm through doctoring you now. I'll change the bandages tonight before you go to bed."

Grace gathered the empty wrappers while he loaded the tray with her tools. His heart beat the rhythm of a hundred horse hooves thundering across dry grounds. They were alone. This was his best opportunity to bring up their future relationship.

"Grace," Ian croaked with nervousness. He cleared his throat to try again. "Grace, can I ask you a personal question?"

"Sure. What do you want to know?" She turned on the water to wash the utensils.

Ian waited for her to finish. Once he started down this road, he had to complete the journey, and he didn't want her distracted. After so many speculations, he needed to end his lovesick musings. Either he stood a chance, or he didn't. His heart couldn't stand this turmoil any longer.

Grace turned to Ian with an expectant expression. She dried her hands on a dish towel. The corners of her mouth tilted in a slight smile.

"Why do you wear a head covering?"

"My scarves symbolize my submission to Yah's order of authority," she said, turning back towards the cabinets. "Do you want tea? I can brew dandelion tea with honey."

"Order of authority? What do you mean?"

"Yah is a God of order. You saw it in the Fibonacci sequence. There's a family order too. Children are to love and obey their parents. The duty of wives is to comfort, teach, and nurture the family. The husband protects, leads, and provides for all who live in his house. Above him is Yahusha, our king of kings. His authority is Yahuah, our creator. Each layer is a covering of protection," Grace explained, using her hands to show the different levels before filling a teakettle with water.

Ian latched onto the word husband to use for an opening to suggest she find a new one. Before he could speak, Grace interrupted him.

"My head covering also deters men who might wish to pursue a relationship with me," she continued, removing a blue and white porcelain tea set from the cabinet.

Wait. What? "Why? Don't you want to remarry?" Ian asked, pressing further.

"It's not a matter of what I want. I'm not free to remarry." Grace opened another door, removed a tin, and shook it. "There's roasted dandelion root." She placed the container on the counter. "Or I can pick fresh."

Grace's words dumbfounded Ian. *Not free!* Did he misunderstand the sheriff? Grace walked by him to go outside. He grabbed her arm. "What do you mean you're not free? Aren't you divorced?" Ian choked out. There had to be a miscommunication somewhere.

Grace bowed her head. "I annulled my marriage before.... Civil law doesn't equate to Yah's laws. In His eyes, the marriage is still in effect."

Ian's hand spasmed. He let go of her arm. Her words angered him.

All this time, his dreams and plans for their future were fruitless. Why did Jeremiah approve of him asking Grace to marry him if she wasn't free? Was he missing something? "What requirements need to be met for a divorce, according to God?"

"My husband must hand me a certificate of divorce, but it cannot be for any other reason than if I commit adultery." Grace heaved a sigh. "If I remarry without a certificate, my new husband will also sin. No matter how much I might love someone, I can't allow my desires to cause another person's sin."

"There has to be an exception," Ian pressed. He grasped both of her shoulders, willing her to look at him. "There's a way. Right?" he asked in desperation. She shrugged off his touch. Ian's hands fell empty to his sides. The shards of his shattered hope pierced his heart. He couldn't marry Grace.

"Ian, don't ruin the rest of your stay. Please?" She turned away from him to lean on one worktable.

"But Grace, it's not fair," Ian said, his voice gruff with emotion. "It's not fair to you. It's not fair to… it's just not fair!"

Grace huffed a laugh. "Fair according to whom? You? Me? Or Yah? His thoughts are not our thoughts. Our ways are not his ways. We live by His laws because they are instructions for us to lead happy and healthy lives." She returned to the kitchen to exchange the tea for a different tin. "We follow His commands because we love Him, not to get everything we want. If we allow our fleshly desires to override our love for Him, we do not truly love Him." She removed an ornate silver tea infuser from the cabinet. "'And thou shalt love the Lord thy God with all thine heart, and with all thy soul, and with all thy might.' I won't let anyone, or anything, come before Him." Grace said with fierce determination.

Ian sat in the chair. He didn't understand any of this. How could a loving God require a woman as wonderful as Grace to spend her life alone? "I don't know what to do. I thought. Never mind." Ian fell silent for a moment before speaking again. His happy-ever-after daydreams were ruined. "I don't understand how God can institute laws forcing people to be alone for the rest of their lives. Why? Your first marriage not working out wasn't your fault. Your husband abused you." His anger spilled over with his words.

Grace rushed to him. She pulled out a chair to sit in before taking his hands in hers. "Ian, I know this is hard to comprehend because you don't have a firm foundation of faith yet, but you don't need to understand. Now is the time to trust Yah. He knows what is best for us. If I can trust him after everything I've been through, you can trust him too. He will create a way if He wants us together. Don't allow this setback to destroy your faith. Trust him."

Grace's eyes and voice begged him. He didn't know about trusting God yet, but he loved and trusted her. If she could trust God despite her trials and ordeals, he would also try to trust Him. Ian nodded his head, acquiescing to her plea.

"Great. Let's change the subject. Instead of dandelion tea, I think we need chamomile to calm our nerves. I'll put on the kettle."

Ian smiled. She loved taking care of people. No matter how much something bothered her, nothing stopped her from nurturing. How wonderful it must be to live with the conviction her faith gave her. A thought popped into his head. A setback didn't mean he had to quit. She said if God wanted them together, He would make a way. Well, Ian believed he belonged here. All he needed to do was wait. "I have another question."

"I'm listening." Grace lit a match to ignite the propane burner.

"If you could remarry, what qualities would you look for in a husband?"

Grace blew out the match without lighting the burner. With measured movements, she laid the charred stick on the edge of the stainless-steel sink. "You are determined to put me in the hot seat today." She turned to face him, leaning against the counter. "Okay, I'll bite." She crossed her arms. "He'd be kind and generous. Loving. Attentive. Honest and faithful. He'd like to laugh and have fun but be strong and assertive in times of trial." Grace returned to her chair, taking hold of Ian's hands again. "He might be clumsy and unsure but still possess confidence enough to laugh at himself and be brave even though he's frightened. Oh, and he must love Joshua as his son because he will be the man to teach Joshua what it means to love his wife as himself. And if he didn't know how to love Yah, he'd have the heart to learn so he could become the spiritual leader of our family." Tears threatened to spill from her eyes.

Grace tried to pull her hands from Ian's. He held them tight, waiting for her to meet his gaze. He wanted her to see him speak his following words with sincerity. She tried to pull away again. He tightened his grip. She raised her eyes in alarm. "If that man asked to be part of your life without marriage, would you push him away?" She wanted someone to love Joshua and be a man of God. He could fulfill that role without marrying her.

"You'd do that?" she gasped in disbelief. "Ian! Do you know what you're saying?"

"Yes. I know exactly what I'm saying." Ian softened his expression. "It means I won't be alone anymore. It means I'll have a family who loves me as much as I love them." Ian inhaled a bolstering breath before continuing. "I can still be a part of this family without marrying you. Can't I?"

"But Ian, you—"

"Grace, even the Holy Ghost knows I belong here. Yesterday, He sent me down a path filled with poison ivy almost half an hour before Dean attacked you. He could've sent any other person, but he sent me. If I didn't belong here, why did he pick me?"

"I don't know, Ian. Whatever the reason, it changes nothing. I can't let you throw your life away. You will feel different when you find a woman you can marry. You'll understand—"

"Grace, this concerns more than my feelings for you. Since I've been here, I've felt whole again. I want this to be my home. I mean, yeah, your father enjoys intimidating me, but I understand and respect him. Your mother reminds me of my grandmother, who doesn't remember who I am. Do you know how it feels to be forgotten?" Ian pressed. "And Joshua? When I look at him, I see myself at his age. I want to give him everything I didn't have growing up."

"Joshua has his grandfather," Grace insisted.

"A grandfather can't replace a father's love. I know."

"Ian, you can't waltz into our lives, play daddy for a few days, and then waltz out again whenever—"

"I'm asking you not to push me away. Nothing more. Give me a chance. I'm asking because I don't want to be alone anymore. We can work the details out later. Grace, please," Ian whispered.

"Hey, Mr. Ian. Gramma June told me to bring you a clean shirt," Joshua hollered, pushing open the door.

Grace shot up out of the chair, returning to the kitchen. Ian watched her wipe the tears from her eyes before Joshua saw them. He knew he asked more than she may be ready to give. If she said yes, he could suppress his emotions to gain everything else he wanted. "Hey, buddy." Ian wrapped his arm around Joshua's shoulder, taking the shirt from him. "Did you pick this shirt out yourself?"

"Yep. Did I pick a good one?"

Ian glanced towards Grace. Her face held a passive expression, but he could see in her eyes she analyzed Joshua and his exchange. "Not only did you pick a good one, but you also picked my favorite t-shirt," Ian praised Joshua, bringing a smile to the little boy's face. "If your mom lets me, I'll tell you the adventures this shirt, and I have been through." He turned his attention back to Grace. "What do you say, Mom? Can I?"

"Please, Mama," Joshua begged. "Mr. Ian tells the best stories."

Grace returned to the chair. She tried to brush Joshua's curls into order with her fingers. "You enjoy spending time with Mr. Ian, don't you?"

"Yeah, we had a lot of fun this morning."

Grace turned her attention to Ian. "Then Mr. Ian can tell you about his adventures."

"Yay!" Ian and Joshua shouted at the same time.

Grace cleared her throat, interrupting their celebration. "As long as he promises me one thing," she continued when they fell silent.

"Anything," Ian whispered.

"You must promise me, no matter what, no matter how, no matter where you are, you will tell Joshua a story every single day until he turns eighteen. You have to be there for him, no matter what. Can you make that promise to his mother Ian MacGregor?" Grace asked, narrowing her eyes.

Ian wrapped Grace's clenched fist in his free hand. When she relented to his request, he understood she fought against her mother's instinct to protect her child. He met her eyes while he tangled his fingers with hers. He saw her uncertainty. "Grace, I promise. I will never abandon Joshua," he said, hoping she heard his resolve. "One story, every single day, no matter what."

Grace heaved a shuddering sigh and nodded her head.

"Awww, Mama! He's already told me a story today," Joshua

complained.

Grace laughed her relief. "Since today is the first day, he can tell you two stories."

"Yay!" Ian prompted Joshua with a high five. He exchanged his blood-stained shirt for the one Joshua brought him. "Come on Joshua. I'll tell you how I got duped into boxing a kangaroo."

"Actually." Ian and Joshua turned back to her. Grace hesitated. "Do… do you mind saving the story for later? I want to hear it, too."

Ian's heart soared. He'd follow Grace's suggestion and place his trust in God to make a way for them to be a family. "I don't mind." He picked Joshua up in his arms. "Joshua and I will do something else. Won't we?" he asked, turning towards Joshua for confirmation. "Let's find your Papa. We can build a pen where you can play with the goats without having to worry about old King Saul."

"Oh, he won't bother us anymore. Gramma June chopped his head off."

Ian's jaw dropped. He looked to Grace for confirmation Joshua spoke the truth. He didn't fault Juniper for keeping her promise, but he never expected her to carry it through.

Grace's laughter followed Ian out the door.

*****

Graced picked up the shirt Ian left behind, winding the stretchy fabric around her hands. She didn't give a thought to the significance of picking up after the man willing to fulfill the role of father for Joshua. She stepped onto the porch, watching them walk away, her apprehension fading with each step they took.

The words she spoke to Ian about loving Yah were more for her benefit than his. She wanted Ian, but to have him, she would have to turn her back on Yah and everything she believed. Yahusha said, "If any *man* will come after me, let him deny himself, and take up his cross, and follow me." Why did Ian have to be the one thing denied to her?

Then Ian asked to tell Joshua stories. She knew it was an excuse to stay close to her. At first, she wanted to say no, but seeing his arm wrapped around Joshua's shoulders made her realize she couldn't remember the last time her father held Joshua.

Though Jeremiah tried to hide his infirmities, she recognized the tell-tell signs of his deteriorating health. She already added anti-inflammatories to her parents' breakfasts and lunches to help with their complaints of arthritis. In recent months, she noticed her father's face becoming more flushed than usual when he exerted himself. She suggested he see the town doctor, Brother Seamus, but he refused, proclaiming, 'I'm healthy as a horse.'

Joshua would grow into a teenager while her father's health continued to decline. The knowledge compelled her to agree to Ian's request. Her son needed guidance and advice from a dependable male figure who could keep up with him. So, she said 'yes,' despite her misgivings.

Ian reached the barn with Joshua sitting on his shoulders. Again, Joshua smacked the building at Ian's encouragement before they disappeared out of her sight. Seeing their camaraderie, Grace knew she had made the right decision.

28

Passover morning, Ian woke early. Being careful not to disturb anyone, he prepared coffee. He needed copious amounts of caffeine and time alone after yesterday's emotional roller coaster. First, Grace nixed his proposal before he made one. He skated through the fiasco instead of slinking away to lick his wounds. He didn't understand the Biblical laws Grace cited, but he respected her decision to follow them.

Then Jeremiah briefed him on what to expect today. Passover came with a frenzied day of welcoming guests, shuffling them to their registered campsites, and preparing enough lamb for everyone to have a taste at mealtime. They expected around one hundred visitors. They planned for two hundred. Ian volunteered to help wherever needed. Jeremiah assigned him to the port-a-potty delivery.

Before supper, Grace invited him to her cottage for a private talk. At first, he thought she might've changed her mind. Instead, she revealed the magnitude of her ex-husband's depravity and her plans for opening a safe house for underaged victims of human trafficking. He pushed aside his initial shock over the evil her husband forced her to take part of. Jeremiah was right. Her ex was the worst kind of criminal. Instead, he focused on the portion of the conversation where he thought she was asking him to be a partner in the safe house. Except she didn't ask for his help in building the charity. She didn't want his money. She reduced him to the status of a sales gimmick by asking to use his notoriety to drum up donations.

The highlight of yesterday was spending time with Joshua. They grabbed a couple of fishing poles once they decided where to put the goat pen, then set off towards a small pond near the cow pasture. A picnic area with a firepit and covered table indicated the family regularly used the tranquil spot. Joshua showed Ian the tree where Jeremiah agreed to build him a fort once he turned six. They dug for worms and, even though Ian fished in every ocean and on every continent, he let Joshua instruct him on how to bait a hook. They ended the day with the promised boxing kangaroo story and him tucking Joshua into bed for the night. All his pent-up frustrations drained away when Joshua's little arms hugged him goodnight. The uncomplicated love of a child could fix the most wounded of hearts.

Ian sighed, remembering the feeling, while he waited for the sun to rise. Letting go of the life he created in his mind with Grace as his wife would take more time than it did to imagine it. Although, after thinking everything through, a platonic relationship based on commitment might be just as good. He could provide the stability and support of a marriage and be a father figure to Joshua without sleeping in the same bed with her. In fact, not being married displayed more dedication than any piece of paper could ever do. His magnanimous sacrifice showed his devotion. The thought lifted Ian's despondent mood, and he congratulated himself.

Across the yard, Grace's screen door slammed shut. The hound beside him only raised an eyebrow. Time to get the day started. Ian waited for her to come to him. He wanted to tell her the things he couldn't bring himself to say yesterday.

"Good morning," Ian said when she reached the porch, a smile lighting up his eyes.

"Good morning," she replied, ascending the steps. "You're grinning from ear to ear. Is there something you're not telling me? Do I have something stuck on my face?"

"Nope. I'm just standing here, getting a new perspective on life."

Grace sniffed his coffee. "Did you get into my father's stash? It's too early to be philosophical."

"I woke up feeling sorry for myself. Yesterday, when you asked me for help with your charity, I assumed you told me because you wanted me to be your partner. Then you refused my money, and I began to think you were using me for my fame like everybody else. I mean, I understood why. My channel is popular, and I could rake in thousands of donations." Ian leaned against the porch railing. "Then, this morning, I realized if you wanted nothing more than to take advantage of my celebrity status, you didn't need to agree to me helping you raise Joshua to gain my cooperation. You really want me to stay? Don't you?"

"Oh, my gosh! Ian! Of course I do and I'm so sorry if I made you think otherwise. I refused your financial support because I didn't want anyone thinking I'm using you for your money." Grace sat across from him. She picked at a button on the bodice of her dress. "To be honest, I've been afraid my confession might've caused you to change your mind. I didn't realize how scared I have been of being alone for the rest of my life until you offered to keep me company."

Ian took her hands in his. "Grace, I should've told you this yesterday. I love you and I don't say that lightly. I will never leave you. Everything that I am, everything that I have, is yours. I want to use my assets for something good. You have my pledge to make your safe house a reality. Let me be your partner."

Grace burst into tears. "I don't know what to say. How can you give me so much when I have nothing to offer you in return?"

"I'm going to spend the rest of my life raising a precocious little boy with a beautiful woman who has an overabundance of love. She's steadfast in her convictions and possesses a strength that enables her to forsake her own desires. I've watched you. You care for everyone around you and ask for nothing in return. Grace, you're an amazing woman and you're making my dreams come true. You're giving me a family. You're giving my life purpose. I need nothing else."

"It's Passover! It's Passover!" Joshua's voice sang through the window.

Grace wiped her tears away.

"Mama? Mama!" Joshua called, searching for his mother inside the house.

"Ian isn't in the living room. He better hope I don't find him at Grace's," Jeremiah said, his voice raised.

"Don't go jumping to conclusions, dear."

"I'm not jumping to conclusions. I don't enjoy waking up and finding people missing from my house." Jeremiah opened the back door. Still buttoning his shirt, he stepped onto the porch. "Why did I agree to her staying in her cottage last night?"

"Good morning, Sheriff." A smirk of satisfaction appeared on Ian's lips when Jeremiah jumped. *Got him!*

Jeremiah stared daggers into Ian before shutting the door.

"That's my cue to help Mother fix breakfast. When Father stops speaking, it means he's reached the end of his patience. We'll discuss everything later. Okay?" Grace squeezed his hand.

Ian acknowledged her leaving with a nod. The question Jeremiah asked him not long after he arrived came back to him. Ian rubbed his lower lip with the pad of his thumb lost in his thoughts. What are you missing, Ian MacGregor? Purpose, his subconscious answered. The way the word popped into his mind; he wondered if the Holy Ghost were not speaking to him even then. A slow smile spread across his lips. No matter. Grace provided the solution for everything missing in his life. She filled every void. She completed him.

Ian finished his mug of now cold coffee before sticking his head in the door. "Joshua! Get dressed and put on your shoes. We're going to do your chores before breakfast."

* * * * *

Everyone except Juniper, who stayed home to finish the Passover meal preparations, rode into town. Ian noticed several campers and tents being set up around the pond. Children scrambled over the playground equipment. He didn't expect this amount of commotion so early. Jeremiah parked his truck at the service center.

"Mama, can I go play?"

"Not right now, Joshua," Grace said, taking the basket of herbs she packed out of the backseat. "I didn't recognize any of the mothers. Once I process my orders, I'll take you over there. Okay?"

"Awww!" Joshua whined, dropping his shoulders and arms as if they were the heaviest burdens in the world. "That will take forever!"

"Here, let me carry that for you," Ian said, holding his hand out for the basket.

"I'll get it. It's not heavy and I'm just going right over there," Grace said, pointing to her shop across the street, next to the post office.

"Okay. I can stop by after the port-a-potty delivery and take Joshua off your hands."

"Oh, that will be great. I don't enjoy keeping him cooped up when he's so full of energy," Grace said. She braced the basket against her hip, turned, and held her hand out for Joshua. "Come on Joshua. I have a surprise for you in the back room."

With the promise of a surprise, Joshua fell into step beside his mother. At the curb, they paused, looking both ways before crossing the street. He didn't know why, but seeing Grace perform the motherly act seemed more special because the woman he loved was the one doing the instructing.

Jeremiah came to stand beside him.

"She's an excellent mother," Ian said.

"Yeah, she is. She'll be a good wife, too. You mention anything to her yet?"

"She knows how I feel." Ian didn't care to elaborate.

"She turned you down, didn't she?"

"What? You encouraged me knowing she'd refuse? Wow! Thanks for nothing, Jeremiah." Ian turned to walk away.

"Hang on. I wasn't done," Jeremiah said, grabbing Ian's arm to stop him.

"I don't get it," Ian said, his agitation showing. "Why did you give me false hope?"

"I didn't. Grace's situation falls into a gray area. The elders are divided on the interpretation of the law," Jeremiah explained. "Half believe she cannot remarry because of what the Torah says. The other half believe she should be able to remarry because of what the Torah doesn't say. The law doesn't account for what to do in the case of an abusive husband."

"So, Grace is siding with the first half?"

"Unfortunately for you, yes. I hoped her feelings for you would be enough to change her mind."

"Whose side are you on?"

"Yours."

Ian braced his hands on his hips challenging Jeremiah's claim. "Really? From where I'm standing it looks like you set me up for a fall."

Jeremiah grimaced, "I understand how you came to that conclusion, but it's not the case. Look, let's finish this discussion in my office."

Ian fell in step with Jeremiah. The sound of their shooes thunking on the wood plank sidewalk reminded Ian of the town's old west-themed origins.

An SUV pulling a pop-up camper drove by, followed by a truck towing a round, wooden gypsy caravan painted in a bright paisley pattern. They waved to each vehicle. In this community, the past merged with more modern conveniences, creating a harmonious way of life. Ian looked forward to becoming a full-time resident.

Jeremiah unlocked the corner building. "Before we head to my office, I want to show you something. You're going to get a kick out of this," he said before throwing the doors open.

Ian crossed the threshold. An Old West saloon, complete with a bar, spittoon, a dance stage, and rooms upstairs, greeted him. "This is amazing, Jeremiah. It's a time capsule into the past."

"This is my favorite building in the whole town."

"I can see why."

"Right now, we're using it for a daycare center and school, but we're thinking of turning it into a bed-and-breakfast for overnight visitors."

A man and woman appeared in the doorway. Jeremiah introduced the couple as Daniel and his wife JessaMae, Grace's friend. Daniel brought the completed plans for the new schoolhouse. He unrolled blueprints of the building across one table to review the details with Jeremiah.

"Did you finish the cost analysis for the final phase of Grace's project?" Jeremiah asked once Daniel finished his report.

"Yes. I'm waiting until after the feast to submit everything to her."

"That bad?"

Daniel nodded with a grimace.

"Y'all are discussing the restoration house? I'm her partner. How much will the project cost?" Ian asked, eager to help Grace.

"She told you?" Jeremiah asked his expression one of disbelief.

"Well, yeah. We have somewhat of an understanding." Irritation flashed across Jeremiah's face. Ian's defenses rose. Why did Jeremiah always jump to the worst conclusions?

JessaMae cleared her throat. "I'm surprised Grace mentioned her charity project to you, much less being a partner. She possesses an overdeveloped independent streak and has shunned our offers of assistance. How did you get her cooperation?"

"I begged." Ian scratched the nape of his neck, a sheepish grin on his face.

Everyone laughed. Ian glanced towards Jeremiah. The laughter did not reach his eyes. Ian's smile died.

"Well, everything is on track. The library renovations are almost complete, and we'll have a schoolhouse by fall. Then we'll be ready for the housing expansion. Thank you for your hard work, Brother Daniel," Jeremiah said, herding everyone out the door. Once the couple were out of hearing range, he turned on Ian. "You have some explaining to do," he said before marching across the street to the rec center.

Ian followed, bracing himself for Jeremiah's tongue-lashing.

Before entering the building, Jeremiah grunted a good morning to the teenage girl sitting behind a folding table with a 'Check In Here' sign taped to the front.

Panic rose in Ian. Grace said when Jeremiah stopped talking is when you had to worry.

Once they entered the office, Jeremiah shut the door and strode straight to the coffeemaker. He poured two mugs, holding one to his lips while extending the other towards Ian. "Tell me more about this understanding between Grace and you. What exactly have you talked my daughter into doing?"

Ian took the cup without sampling the contents. His nerves quaked too much. How could he explain his intentions as generous when they appeared self-serving? "We haven't worked out the details yet."

Jeremiah sat behind his desk, tilting his chair back. He crossed his ankle on top of his knee. His index finger tapped his mug. "Well, of course, you haven't. Neither of you discussed your understanding with me before it became understood."

Heat flushed Ian's face. The calm Jeremiah now displayed made him more nervous. He expected anger. He coughed before taking a cautious seat on the other side of the desk. "I can safely say you'll be seeing quite a lot of me in the future."

"In what capacity?"

Ian gulped.

Jeremiah leaned forward, setting his mug on the desk. "I'm going to say this to you once. You're talking about my family. When it comes to my family, I don't play. Now you're going to explain the agreement between you and Grace, or I'm going to wring it out of you. Have I made myself clear?"

The undercurrent of suppressed anger in Jeremiah's voice reminded Ian of when his grandfather caught him sneaking out of the house. He never tried to break the rules again, fearing an unnamed retribution intimated by the drilling tone of his grandfather's words. *Here we go.*

"The restoration house isn't the only partnership between Grace and I. I'm going to help her raise Joshua."

"What?" Jeremiah smacked his open palm on the desk.

Ian jumped in his seat.

"Are you crazy?" Jeremiah rose to his feet. He braced the palms of his hands on the desk. "You can't play father to Joshua while you're off gallivanting around the world."

Ian leaped to his feet. "Now, hang on a minute. First off, I'm not playing—"

"I'm not done yet! You're putting Grace in a precarious position. The elder's council will think you're coveting another man's wife and that she's encouraging the behavior."

"Coveting another man's wife? How am I coveting another man's wife? Grace said she got an annulment. You told me the guy was out of the picture. Come to find out, the man's rotting away in a federal penitentiary for murder and human trafficking. Why are you still calling him her husband?" Ian turned away from the anger on Jeremiah's face. He ran his fingers through his hair. He needed to control himself. "Husbands don't...." He turned back to Jeremiah. "What is so wrong with me wanting to be the man who provides Grace with security? Why can't I be the one who makes sure Joshua and she have a roof over their heads and food on the table? When Joshua needs advice, why can't I be the man he comes to? Why can't I be his father?" Ian deflated back into the chair. "Why does God's law prevent us from getting married? I don't understand."

Jeremiah returned to his seat. "Yah's law isn't preventing Grace from remarrying except for one tiny detail. Her husband didn't write her a bill of divorce. Even though Torah doesn't name abuse as a reason for divorce, it does mention neglect. If a man isn't treating his wife in the manner he should, he's commanded to release her from the marriage to find a husband who will treat her properly. In my book, improper treatment includes abuse. I side with the half of the council who believe Grace's death at the hands of her husband, even though she survived, released her from the marriage covenant. The other half requires the written divorce agreement. It's a legal formality Grace must decide for herself." He leaned back, rocking his office chair. "See, when people realize Torah isn't only for the Jews, and they've been doing a huge amount of sin, they feel guilty. To absolve themselves of their guilt, they fall into the trap of legalism. They're trying to prove they're worthy of Yah's grace by keeping the letter of the law to perfection without considering the spiritual side." He leaned forward, grabbing Ian's undrunk coffee. "Knowing Grace's story, you can imagine how much guilt she carries."

"But I thought everyone here kept the law because they love God."

"We do. Grace hasn't come to terms with the guilt she carries. Until she does, she will always try to prove herself worthy of Yah's grace by keeping the letter of His law. She doesn't realize she's being legalistic."

"Isn't there something you can do? Try to make her understand?"

"Teaching Yahusha died for our sins is entirely different from accepting His forgiveness. We must work out our own salvation with fear and trembling. Absolving yourself of your sins is personal. If Grace can't forgive herself, she may never move past the trap of legalism. Which means she may never agree to marry you."

Ian leaned forward, resting his folded arms on the desk. "Jeremiah, I may not understand your ways, and I don't know how to follow God's laws, but I do know the past few days have been the happiest I can remember. I've been part of a family again. I didn't realize how much I've been missing until I came here. Thank God my car broke down where it did. If it hadn't, I would never know Grace, Joshua, Juniper, or you existed. Now I can't imagine my life apart from any of you, and I'm not willing to give up what I've found because of a piece of paper or what the elder council thinks, or even what Grace thinks of herself. If I must wait the rest of my life for Grace, I will. She's worth the wait."

"And your job?"

"After this assignment is over, I'm quitting."

"You know I'm going to be dogging your every step."

"I would be suspicious if you didn't."

The phone rang.

"Sheriff's office," Jeremiah said, his tone now upbeat instead of angry.

"Ginger! Glad you got back with me so soon. What did you find out?"

Ian, more focused on the change in Jeremiah's disposition before the phone call, only half listened to the one-sided conversation. Did the change mean he approved of Ian staying?

"What do you mean, he's out?"

If Jeremiah approved, he needed to decide where to live. It might be best if he didn't live too near to Grace. Even though he didn't care what the rest of the community thought about their relationship, he didn't want to cause her any difficulties.

"Oh? They're calling it a clerical error? Well, imagine that."

He didn't want to live too far away, either. He should be close in case Grace or Joshua needed him. Maybe he could stay in the cabin? The heating system would have to be upgraded, and a water supply needed to be installed.

Jeremiah slammed the phone receiver on the desk. "What else can go wrong?"

A sinking feeling erupted in the pit of Ian's stomach. Of all the questions Jeremiah could've asked, he had to ask the one that always brought Ian to disaster. "What happened?"

"This Covid mess. You heard they released non-violent criminals to stop the spread in prisons?"

"Don't tell me they released Dean."

"No. Worse. They released Viktor Doroshenko. Grace's ex."

Ian shot to his feet. "Did you check my social media accounts?"

"Of course, I checked them. I spoke with Abigail. Nice girl. The picture wasn't up for more than a few hours. The odds of Viktor finding Grace are slim to none." He held his mug towards Ian. "Pour me another cup of coffee. It's going to be a late night, and I'm not as young as I used to be."

"You've already drank mine. Don't you think three cups are enough for today?"

"Now you're beginning to sound like Juniper and Grace. Always fussing over me. Go ahead." He wiggled the cup. "I promise, this is my last one."

"Papa! Papa! Papa!" Joshua yelled, rushing into the room.

Ian knelt. "Joshua, what's wrong?" he asked, wiping away Joshua's tears.

"Mama said danger nuffing!" Joshua wailed, fresh tears pouring from his eyes.

Jeremiah cussed. He flung open a drawer, pulled a notebook out, grabbed his phone, and left the office.

Ian followed, carrying Joshua with him. "What's 'danger nuffing' mean? What's wrong?" He hadn't heard a curse word since coming here. Something must be terribly awry for Jeremiah to break character.

"He means fig newton. It's Grace's code word for if Viktor shows up."

"He's here! What do we do? We have to help her! I'll go to the shop."

"No, you won't!" Jeremiah growled, shoving open the front door. He slammed the notebook and phone on the table. "Sarah, start the phone tree. Operation ARK. Also, call Isaac. Tell him I said to get here now and have an ambulance on standby. Then call Brother Seamus. Tell him we need the MFAK. Then get those kids and campers in the rec center and lock the door." He turned to go back inside the building. He hesitated seeing Joshua. "Here, watch Joshua too. Don't let him out of your sight. You. Come with me," he said, turning on Ian.

Ian followed Jeremiah. "What's going on? What's Operation ARK? What's MFAK?"

Jeremiah unlocked a door behind his office.

Ian gasped. An arsenal of weapons lined both walls of a room the size of a walk-in closet.

"Operation ARK is code for everyone to seek shelter. And MFAK stands for multiple person first aid kit." Jeremiah handed a rifle with a scope to Ian. "Take this rifle to Casey. Tell him: roof, building three, nothing out. Use the back alley. Stay in the garage once you deliver the message."

Ian hesitated, wanting to ask more questions.

"The longer you stand there, the longer Grace is in danger. Go!"

29

Grace hummed while walking towards her store. The scattered puzzle pieces of her life were finally coming together. Marrying Viktor was the dumbest decision she ever made, and she paid the price for the mistake. When she first moved to Covenant Cove, the long-term prognosis of her seizures was yet unknown. Scared and pregnant, she leaned on Jeremiah and Juniper for everything. Worry kept her from making plans for future independence. She fell into depression; sure her child would die with her at any moment.

Her father, the optimist, searched for alternative treatments to bring her debilitating convulsions under control. The family went on a ketogenic diet with high hopes. Within a week, they voted to abandon the restrictive diet when Juniper's carb cravings overruled her normal, pleasant demeanor. Next, they turned to acupuncture and meditation with little success. De-stressing sessions at a local spa led to a reduction in the number of her seizures, but not enough for her new parents to feel comfortable leaving her alone. Seamus, the town doctor, suggested they try cannabidiol oil after she gave birth to Joshua.

Grace's world transformed immediately. After a month of treatment, the frequency of her seizures went from several a day to occasional. With a cell phone and the promise to check in every half hour, she strapped Joshua to her back to go exploring on the trails surrounding the valley. The hikes relieved the monotony of doing nothing but being a mother inside a house where she felt like a burden. On one of her longer excursions, she met the herbalist who became her teacher. On another, she discovered an abandoned plantation home hidden among the woods of Covenant Cove.

While exploring the relic, an idea bloomed in her heart. She could open a safe house for underage victims of human trafficking. Nothing could erase her past, but she could assuage her guilt by giving hope and a future to children rescued from the sex trafficking industry. After discussing her plan with Jeremiah and Juniper, she used the money returned to her from the sale of her grandmother's house to repair the roof and for additions to each side of the Neoclassical structure. She ran out of funds halfway through the renovations.

She apprenticed for two years, staying up late and rising early, while she memorized how different herbs interacted with the body systems. Every bit of knowledge she gained, she turned into a profit to finish the house. She began with simple, molded cough drops made with horehound and marshmallow root. Once her training advanced into foraging and nutrition, she developed her own recipes. She worked with Brother Seamus on holistic treatments for his patients. He encouraged her to open an online shop. Her income soared.

She poured the proceeds into the plantation home to complete the building, but it still wasn't enough to meet state public housing standards. She took a gigantic leap of faith yesterday and discussed with Ian the sordid details of her past and her plans. Bless him. The man tried to give her his credit card. After explaining she didn't want his money, only his name and face to bring in donations, he agreed. Then she stayed up late brainstorming names for the safe house. She didn't make a final decision but still had plenty of time. With her thoughts on the future, she forced herself to walk when she wanted to skip the rest of the way to her shop.

With just enough room for two display windows and an inset door, you might miss her little store sandwiched between the post office and her friend JessaMae's clothing shop. She loved the charm of this town. Covered wooden sidewalks created shade for her to place tea tables outside to visit with friends. She opened the door, inhaling the pungent mixture of herbs greeting her.

An old-west aura of worn wood and glass mixed with shabby chic décor produced a cozy environment for guests to the town to browse her ready-made merchandise, but most of her business generated from custom orders placed through her online shop. She stored her herbs in jars on the shelves, reaching the ceiling behind the divided front counter. Her hands itched to fill orders. Nothing satisfied her more than seeing a pile of neatly packaged products to be sent off on the next mail run.

Grace settled Joshua in the back room with the marble run toy she bought for his birthday before she decided he needed something more challenging. Perhaps Ian knew what a four-year-old boy might want more. Then she chastised herself for the thought while tying her work apron. She couldn't start depending on him for every little thing.

She brought her computer up to print out purchase orders. Grabbing the stack, she returned to the front of the shop, leaving the door to the back room open so she could hear Joshua. A minivan pulled up, blocking her view of the street. Customers already? I'll never get these orders filled. She closed the pass through of the folding countertop. Sometimes customers didn't honor the boundary of the counter. When no one entered, she returned to work, climbing a rolling ladder to retrieve her more costly herbs. Regardless of how many people might come in, the back orders needed to be completed before the noon mail run.

A good half hour or more passed before the bell above the door rang. Heavy footsteps thudded across the wooden floor.

"Just a minute," Grace said, descending the ladder. She set a jar on the back countertop and turned to face her customer. She gasped in horror.

"Hello, Tamsin," Viktor Doroshenko drawled. He leaned on the counter. "Long time no see."

"Wh… what are you doing here?" Grace stammered. She wiped her sweaty palms on her apron. Her chest tightened. The air she inhaled seemed not to reach her lungs. *How did he find me?*

"I came to collect my wife," Viktor replied in an even tone. "Were you not expecting me?"

"I annulled our marriage." She kept her voice low, not wanting to alert Joshua.

"We're married until I say we're not married." Viktor lunged for her.

Grace dodged his hand, picked up the jar behind her, and threw it at Viktor's face before exiting the front of the shop. She slammed the door to the back room, throwing the deadbolt in place before Viktor reached it. Thuds of him trying to break through the wooden barrier grated on her tense nerves. The aged wood could not hold for long.

Joshua stood frozen, staring wide-eyed at the vibrating door.

Grace grabbed his arm, dragging him to the back exit. "Like we rehearsed, Joshua. Run to Papa as fast as you can. Tell him 'Fig Newton.'" She opened the door, shoving her terrified son into the alley. "Run, Joshua!" she exclaimed before slamming the door shut and locking it to give him time to escape.

The wood splintered. She pressed her back against the exit, looking for a weapon. Her father advised her to always keep a gun near her, but she never felt comfortable having a firearm where Joshua might find it if left unsupervised. She regretted not taking his advice.

"Where do you think you're going?" Viktor taunted.

"You need to leave, or you'll never get out of this town alive."

"You're my ticket out of here."

"I'm not going anywhere with you!" Grace inched to her left, where she kept a straw broom.

"Oh, you're leaving alright. I have big plans for you. You'll pay for what you did to me." He reached for her.

Grace grabbed the broom in time to knock Viktor's hand aside. She grasped the handle low with both hands to swing it against his head. He snatched it from her, breaking the slim handle over his knee. Grace backed towards the doorway leading to the front. The snarl on Viktor's face haunted her dreams. The last time she saw the amount of rage his face now held, she woke up in a hospital. She knew she would be dead before nightfall if he left with her.

In her retreat from his anger, her foot hit Joshua's little chair. She flung it before turning to run. She passed the counter before he caught the back of her dress. Grace strained away from him, reaching for the nearest thing she could reach to throw at him. A quarter-pint-sized porcelain jar of cream for eczema broke upon impacting his forehead.

Viktor touched where it hit. His fingertips came away with blood. He roared in anger. "I loved you, and you betrayed me. You ruined everything!"

"That wasn't love! Just go away and leave me alone."

"If only it were that simple." He lunged.

Grace picked up jar after jar, throwing them without aiming, creating a barrage of porcelain projectiles until Viktor needed both hands to defend himself against the onslaught. Grace moved on to the next table that held tins of lip moisturizer and foot balm she had created using beeswax she got from Sister Rebecca. Metal pinged off the walls and windows.

Next, closest to the door, came a table with bottles of witch hazel and aloe vera face wash. The heavy glass smashed through the front windows. Grace edged around, putting the table between Viktor and her until she could reach the doorknob. She flung the door open to escape. Viktor caught her and pulled her back against him.

"You're going to regret this," he fumed in her ear, twisting her hair in his hand.

"Let her go, Viktor," Jeremiah said from beyond the open doorway, his handgun ready for use.

Viktor produced a pistol from behind his back. He pressed the muzzle into Grace's temple. "Well, if it isn't Mr. White Knight, come to save the day," he mocked. Using her as a shield, Viktor pulled her past Jeremiah towards the van parked on the road.

"I said let her go. You're not leaving here with her," Jeremiah warned.

"I beg to differ." Viktor pressed the cold steel barrel of his gun into Grace's temple until she cried out. "How will you stop me? You shoot me, she dies." Viktor said, laughing. He leaned against the front door of the van. "Open it," he commanded.

Grace obeyed, pulling on the handle of the sliding entry to the passenger compartment. She recognized the van as the one having pulled up earlier, which meant he had picked the most opportune moment to enter the store. If not for her deciding to keep Joshua with her this morning, her absence may not have been noticed until later. Dean's words floated back to her. "Somebody's been looking for you." Was Dean involved in this? How were they connected?

"You'll never leave this town alive if you don't release her."

"Watch me," Viktor said, stepping in front of the gaping passenger doorway, the gun still by Grace's head, though no longer pointed towards her.

Bullets rained, ripping holes in the hood of the vehicle. The hiss of air escaping from tires filled the air. Viktor froze.

"I told you to leave, or you wouldn't get out alive," Grace quipped, speaking the words without thought.

"Not another word! You never could keep your mouth shut!" Viktor ground out, jamming the pistol into her flesh.

Grace winced. She shouldn't have said anything. Her scalp burned where Viktor clutched her hair to pull her away from her father into the empty street. Despite her dire circumstances, she forced herself not to panic. They planned for the remote possibility of him finding her. With the moment upon them, she remembered her father's instructions if she fell into Viktor's clutches again. 'Don't get him riled. Let him think he's in control and keep your head out of the way.'

* * * * *

The commotion coming from Grace's shop brought Ian from the safety of the garage. He didn't know what generated the deluge of destruction. Was Grace being attacked, or did she do the attacking? The shade of the overhang prevented him from seeing through to the inside. Several green and brown bottles sailed through one window. Ian took a few steps forward before he spotted Jeremiah closing in on the entrance to the store.

Grace appeared for a brief second in the doorway before being pulled back inside the building. The breath dried up in Ian's chest. He wanted to run across the street to protect the woman he loved. He fought the instinct, knowing his inexperience might compound the situation. Instead, he paced in his helplessness. Right now, Grace needed a warrior, not an accident-prone globe trotter whose primary talents comprised eating exotic food without getting sick, smiling for a camera, and how many days of clothing he could pack into carry-on luggage.

A few seconds later, Grace reappeared, coming out the door. Viktor, the coward, using her as a shield, held a gun to her head. Ian's breath caught. One wrong move and—. He squelched the thought. Jeremiah and Viktor exchanged words. Then Grace disappeared behind the minivan. Shots rang out. Ian ducked.

Once the noise ended, he lifted his head. Holes riddled the engine area of the minivan, and the tires were flat. He recalled the instructions he delivered to Casey. Ian checked the rooflines. Casey stood on Juniper's roof with his rifle still aimed toward the van. 'Nothing out,' the sheriff said. Relief flooded through Ian. Grace's ex couldn't leave Covenant Cove with her, but it didn't mean she was safe.

Shouts from across the street regained his attention.

"I'll kill her, Tony! I swear, I'll kill her!"

"Let her go, Viktor. You're out of options," Jeremiah replied in an even tone.

Viktor, now in the middle of the street, shook his head. He spun in a circle. Ian saw he weighed his escape options. He pulled Grace towards Jeremiah's truck. Knowing Jeremiah had left the keys in the ignition, Ian raced to reach the truck before Viktor. He threw the keys into the bed of wildflowers beside the shop.

With no other way to escape, Viktor stopped.

"Release her," Jeremiah said yet again. "You're finished, Viktor."

"If I let her go, you'll shoot me anyway," Viktor said, refusing to surrender. "No. If I die, she's dying with me."

"If you release her, we won't shoot you. You have my word."

Viktor spoke into Grace's ear. He pointed his gun toward Jeremiah. Grace strained against his hold. Ian blanched when Viktor turned the gun towards him. Grace twisted under Viktor's grasp, biting him on the chest until he freed her. Viktor slapped her to the ground.

"Mama! Mama! Mama!" Joshua screamed, running from the alley.

"Noooo!" Grace screamed, jumping to her feet.

Ian grabbed Joshua, turning to protect him with his own body. Gunfire rang out behind him. He turned to see Grace standing with her arms straight out to her sides, placing her body between Viktor's gun and Joshua. Viktor lay on the ground, a bullet hole in the center of his forehead.

"Nice shooting Kemosabe!" Casey yelled from the rooftop.

Jeremiah waved in acknowledgment before bending over and grabbing his chest.

"Sheriff, you alright?" Ian asked, releasing Joshua to check on Grace, who still stood with her arms out.

Jeremiah nodded, lowering himself to one knee.

"Grace?" Ian asked, walking around her arms to stand in front of her. A flower of blood bloomed on her chest. "Grace!"

"Remember your promise," she said, collapsing into his arms.

30

Grace stood in front of the washstand mirror in her recovery room. She struggled to bring her curls into order. Her confinement in the hospital left her hair in an unruly mess. The sleeve of her gown hung empty where they strapped her arm to her chest to keep it immobile. With the use of only one hand, she wasn't having much luck untangling the massive knot behind her head. She huffed her displeasure. Each attempt to break free from Viktor resulted in scars, but this time, she finally succeeded. She no longer needed to live her life looking over her shoulder. Viktor was dead.

Almost five years ago, she stood in front of a different mirror, imagining herself as a warrior, throwing off the chains of Viktor's bondage. Determined to go where no one knew her history and the abased things she did to survive, she packed her bags. The decision resulted in a scar on her temple, the death of her child, and her loss of courage.

A few weeks later, the man who became her father broke into her home and her heart. He replenished her adventurous spirit and her dream of escape by showing her the life she missed. With his support, she resolved to break free of Viktor or die trying. The encounter left her with a scar on her brain, Joshua, and a new identity.

She didn't become the stalwart she-goddess she imagined. Instead, she changed into something better. She became what the Bible called a Natsarim, a follower of the Way, walking in the footsteps of Yahusha. Her near-death experience awakened her spirituality. She wanted to be a part of the world that came after this life. She opened the Bible Jeremiah gave her and asked questions. With patience, her father led her to understand the stories it contained were instructions to gain wisdom and to learn from the mistakes of their forefathers.

The night Joshua took his first tentative, unassisted steps into her outstretched arms, she cried.

"You know how happy you are right now, Grace?" Jeremiah had asked.

"Yeah, it's the best feeling in the world," she said, gazing upon her sweet son's smiling face.

"That's how God felt when you took your first steps back toward him."

Grace burst into sobs. She finally understood the depth of Yahuah's love for His children through the love of her own son.

Before long, she ran into the arms of the heavenly father the way Joshua ran into her arms, without restraint and at maximum speed. She studied to show herself approved, memorizing the Torah lest she offend. She obeyed the Sabbath laws. Never working for profit or buying anything on Shabbat. Meals were prepared in advance, and she spent the day in fellowship and study. She did everything she could to prove to Yah how much she loved and appreciated His sacrifice.

Then Ian showed up and turned her peaceful world upside down. She tried to keep her distance. She failed. Whenever he turned his adorable smile in her direction, she wished for things she could not have. Hugs, kisses, and the love of a husband. A father for her son.

She thought she learned to make decisions using wisdom and logic. However, like the giddy schoolgirl she was when she agreed to marry a man twice her age, she let her heart overpower her mind. She encouraged Ian's affection, enjoying their flirtations while writing them off as fruitless, knowing he'd leave before the end of the week. Her selfishness, assuming his attention was only a vacation romance, caused him pain. She couldn't forget his look of disappointment when she informed him she wasn't free to remarry. She used him for her own pleasure, killing his hope the same way Viktor killed hers.

Grace covered her mouth to muffle her crying. She thought herself more virtuous than Viktor. He murdered people who got in his way. She helped them. She honored the man and woman who saved her life. Her compassion drove her to pour her money into the restoration house. She forgave her mother for her childhood traumas and her father, who abandoned her before she was born. She even forgave Viktor. Her love of Yahuah inspired her to walk in righteousness, doing no evil against her neighbor. Then the devil dangled the one thing she couldn't have in front of her. She devised a wicked scheme for her own pleasure, and her feet rushed toward the evil. Trying to control her gulping sobs, she leaned against the wall for support, gasping for breath. She wasn't better than Viktor. She was worse.

* * * * *

Ian marched up the staircase in the community clinic. A bag of gifts for Grace and Joshua dangled from his hand. After Viktor shot her, time passed in a blur. Something large and orange knocked him away from Grace before they hauled Jeremiah and her off in ambulances. Juniper and Ian, not permitted in the hospital because of government restrictions, waited silently at home, wondering if their loved ones lived or died. The large orange thing turned out to be Seamus, the town's doctor. He called after midnight, alleviating their worry.

This morning, he transferred Grace to the community clinic to finish recuperating. Jeremiah gave Ian one hour alone with her. His own confinement in the hospital because of a mild myocardial infarction prevented him from seeing Grace as well. He was eager to learn the condition of his daughter for himself.

Ian quickened his pace. He had to leave soon to make his first appointment of his Barbecue Hop tour. He didn't want to go, but he signed the contracts weeks ago. If he backed out now, he risked a lawsuit from his sponsors. Much needed to be said before he left, and he wanted to say it in person.

With Grace's ex dead, nothing hindered their marriage. He couldn't wait to tell Grace. He pushed open the partially opened door. The smile plastered on his face fell.

"Grace! What's wrong? Are you in pain?"

She turned, tears streaming, chest heaving. "Go away," she said between sobs, shoving him backward.

Ian's heart sank. Not this again.

"Grace, tell me what's wrong."

"Nothing. You need to leave." She turned her back on him. "I release you from your promise."

Her words stunned Ian. She released him? What did she mean? "Grace, I—"

"Just go!" she choked out, refusing to face him.

Ian set the bag of gifts on the floor. He did not know how to get her to listen. Maybe once she calmed down, they could work through what bothered her. He hesitated a moment more, hoping to hear her say she had changed her mind. She didn't even turn around. "I love you," he said before shutting the door, clicking the latch in place.

* * * * *

Grace grabbed the front of her gown, where her heart shattered into a million pieces at the sound of the door closing. Her mouth hung open in a silent scream. The weight of her misery pulled her to her knees. She did it. She sent him away where she could never use or hurt him again. Better she caused him a small amount of pain now than later when the blinders of new love couldn't hide her faults anymore.

The image of Ian carrying Joshua on his shoulders flashed through her mind. Fresh tears poured from her eyes. No more memories would be added to the ones she already cherished. Nothing but empty loneliness stretched before her. She might feel different in a few years when the pain wasn't so sharp. Right now, she just wanted to go to sleep, so she didn't have to suffer the crushing emptiness in her heart.

Strong arms snatched her backward. She sat on Ian's lap. She pushed against him, but he tightened his embrace, trapping her palm against his chest.

"Grace, I don't know what's wrong, but you're killing me," Ian said, his chest heaving. "Please, tell me why you're crying. I can't help if you don't tell me."

She ceased struggling against the confines of Ian's embrace. The rise of fall of his shuddering breaths calmed her raw emotions. One arm cradled her against him, his other hand stroked her hair. Closing her eyes, she warred within herself. His patient love conquered her resistance. When their breathing became one, she slipped her free hand to his back, returning his embrace.

* * * * *

"I knew it!" Ian gasped. Her small hand splayed against his back told him everything he needed to know. They could overcome whatever troubled her, so long as she didn't push him away. "I knew you didn't want me to leave."

Grace leaned back, looking up at him from his chest. With her hair disheveled, the tip of her nose red, and tear tracks across her freckled

232

cheeks, Ian thought her more beautiful than the first time he saw her.

"If you had any sense, you would've left while I had the strength to push you away," she said, wiping the moisture from his eyes. "Now you're stuck with me."

Ian stood, still cradling her in his arms. "I lose every bit of sense I possess where you're concerned." Ian placed her on the bed, pulling the blanket over her legs before sitting next to her. "Why did you want me to leave?" he asked, taking her hand in his. "You need to tell me, so we don't have any future misunderstandings."

Grace sighed. "Because I'm a selfish person."

Ian's jaw dropped. "Wait. What? I'm confused. For one, you're the least selfish person I know. And two, how does your supposed selfishness result in you pushing me away? Shouldn't being selfish make you want me closer?"

She pursed her lips and sighed. "Not when it causes people to die."

Ian halted his thumb from caressing the ridges of her knuckles. "Grace, I'm still not following you. Start from the beginning."

"My greed started the chain of events leading up to Wednesday. When I agreed to marry Viktor, I didn't really love him. I loved what he promised to give me. Clothes, jewelry, a car. I didn't care where the money came from. I only cared for the monetary things he provided. People died because of my selfishness." Grace lowered her head. "If I refused your attention as I should've instead of... well... I gave you false hope. I used you because I wanted to feel loved again. You could've died because of me." Grace played with Ian's fingers before speaking again. "Can you forgive me?"

A bubble of laughter escaped Ian.

Grace pursed her lips. "It's not funny," she said. "Viktor could've killed you."

"I'm laughing about the part where you used me."

"That's not funny either. I'm pouring my heart out, and you're laughing at me?"

"You're right. I'm not being nice." Ian cleared his throat. "Tell you what." He took hold of her hand again. "I'll forgive you on the condition you forgive me as well."

"Forgive you? What have you done that needs forgiving?"

"When you spoiled my marriage proposal, my mind leaped on the first thing it could."

She thought for a moment. "Joshua?"

"Yep. I'm selfish too. Totally used your love for him against you."

"You did, didn't you? Ian MacGregor, you should be ashamed of yourself, using a little boy for such nefarious purposes," Grace laughed.

"I should be, but I'm not because I love Joshua's mother very much, and I'm not letting her go."

"I love you too, Ian."

"Good. I'm happy you're finally admitting it because I have something to give you, and I have very little time left." Ian retrieved the gift bag, removing a rectangular box the size of a sheet of paper. "I went shopping yesterday. This is for you."

Ian held the bottom, enabling Grace to lift off the cover with her free hand. Inside lay a golden fox pin atop a cream-colored silk scarf with shimmery yellow and brown flecks woven into the fabric.

Grace caressed the silky fabric. "It looks like coconut cream pie," she said in a whisper.

"Grace, you told me to trust God. You said if He wanted us together, He would make a way." Ian gulped. The next questions he asked scared him enough to hesitate in asking them. What if she said no again? What if she said yes? With a sharp inhalation, the words gushed out of him. "Will you wear this scarf for me? Will you be my wife?"

Grace pushed the box away.

Ian's heart sank.

She then tapped on his knees, urging him to move them out of her way. Once standing, she took the box from him. "Are you going to sit there, or help me put this on?"

Yes! Ian shot to his feet, coming to stand behind her at the washstand. "Show me what to do," he said, holding out his hand for the scarf.

Grace instructed Ian on how to wrap and tie the fabric so that the tiny lace tassels draped against the side of her head below a large knot. Once completed, Ian attached the fox beside the knot. He wrapped his arms around her waist from behind and lowered his chin to rest on her uninjured shoulder. She placed her free hand on his forearm.

"Let's make a deal," Ian said, meeting her smiling eyes in the mirror.

"What kind of deal?"

"A starting over deal. It's time to put our past lives behind us. We forgive the people who hurt us, and we forgive ourselves for the things we did or didn't do."

Grace broke eye contact with him.

"No," Ian said. "Look at me."

Grace returned his stare with a shadow of guardedness.

"I'm a little rusty, but if I remember correctly, there's a Bible verse that says something to the effect of, 'In Messiah, all things are made new.'"

"Therefore, if any man be in Messiah, he is a new creature: old things are passed away; behold all things are become new."

"That's the one." Ian turned his head and kissed the scarf covering her ear. "The way I see it, we're a new couple. As a couple, we move forward. Together. Okay?"

Grace averted her eyes again.

"Come on, Grace. Forgive yourself." He squeezed her waist. "For us? I want nothing from our past to come between us ever again."

The corners of Grace's lips turned upward. "I am going to have a lot of trouble with you."

"Oh yeah? Why do you think so?" Ian asked, angling his head to see her face.

"Because whenever you beg, I can't resist you." Grace turned in his arms to wrap her free arm around his waist. "You are a wise man, Ian MacGregor. You're going to be a wonderful husband and father," she said, laying her head against his chest.

Ian pulled her closer. "Grace, I don't think I can be happier than I am right now."

Grace leaned back to look at him. "Oh, no? Wait until we have children." She said with a chuckle.

A jolt of electricity surged through him. He didn't think that far ahead. Children? "I have a request," he blurted.

"What kind of request?"

"I want our first child to be a daughter. A beautiful and fierce redhead, the same as her mother." Ian leaned in for a kiss.

Grace burst out laughing. "Daughter. Maybe. Redhead. Probably. But fierce? Ian, who are you kidding? I'm a big chicken! I cry at every little thing."

"Grace, you stood in front of a bullet to protect Joshua," he said, concentrating more on how to get past her defenses. He wanted one kiss before he left, and his time alone with her drew closer to the end by the second.

Her laughter died. "Ian, I wasn't protecting Joshua."

He dropped his arms in disbelief. "Not… if you weren't protecting Joshua, why were you standing with your arms out like that?" he asked, demonstrating her stretched arms when Viktor shot her.

A look of pure love lit up Grace's face. She stepped into him, reaching up to cup his cheek. "I was protecting the man who protected my son," she whispered.

Ian forgot how to breathe. She protected him? He didn't deserve this kind of love. He licked his lips to say something, but the words didn't come. "Grace… I…" All he could do was pull her in tight. "Grace, I love you."

"I love you too. With my whole heart."

"Can I kiss you now?"

Grace leaned back, chuckling. "I've been waiting for you to ask. Yes, you may kiss me."

Ian leaned in to claim her lips.

"Mama! Mama! Mama!" Joshua exclaimed, bursting into the room to wrap his arms around Grace's legs.

"Looks like we got here just in time," Jeremiah said, a wide grin on his face.

Ian groaned his frustration. "Has it really been an hour?"

"Close enough."

"Jeremiah, stop it," Juniper said. "I don't know why you have to tease him so much."

"Because it's fun."

Juniper rolled her eyes. "I'm sorry, Ian. The older he gets, the more incorrigible he is."

"It's okay, Juniper." Ian winked. "There will be plenty of time for payback."

"Bring it on," Jeremiah said, slapping his arm around Ian's

shoulder. "Congratulations," he said under his breath.

"Thanks."

"Grace, honey, I brought your most comfortable clothes and the toiletries you requsted." She set a bag on the bed.

Joshua climbed up on the bed and began jumping.

"Oh, Joshua, don't—"

Ian caught Joshua mid-jump. "I have something to keep this little monkey occupied." He retrieved the bag with Joshua's present. "Here, dig into this." He sat on the foot of the bed, handing the bag to Joshua.

"Oh, cool! A tablet!"

"Joshua, I have to leave. It's time for me to go back to work."

"But I don't want you to. You promised to tell me stories." Joshua said, poking out his bottom lip.

"I did, and I will. Every night. No matter where, no matter how, and no matter what. I'll call you on this tablet and tell you a story before bed." Ian called the tablet to show Joshua how to answer. "At the end of the summer, I'm coming back, and your mama and I will get married. What do you think of that?"

Joshua stared at Ian for a second. "Does that mean you'll be my daddy?"

"Yes, it does. Do you want me to be your father?"

Joshua turned towards Grace, looking for confirmation Ian spoke the truth.

Grace nodded her head, encouraging Joshua to accept Ian's proposal.

He turned back, throwing his arms around Ian's neck. "I love you, Mr. Ian," he said with tears in his voice.

"Awww, I love you too, buddy."

"Uh, Ian," Jeremiah said, clearing his throat. "I need to speak with you about something before you leave."

"Sure, Sheriff." Ian set Joshua on his feet. "I have to go now. I'll see you tonight on the tablet, okay?" He kissed Joshua on the forehead.

"Okay, Mr. Ian."

He turned to Grace and sighed. "I have one request."

"Anything."

"Figure out something else for Joshua to call me before I return. I will not spend the rest of my life being called Mr. Ian by my children."

Grace laughed, pulling Joshua into her lap. "Oh, I'm sure we can come up with a very special name." She turned to Joshua. "Don't you think?"

"Yeah," he giggled.

Ian kissed Grace on her forehead. "There's a phone in the bag for you, too. I'll call you when I stop. I love you."

"Be careful. I love you too."

Ian turned to Juniper.

"You kiss my wife; you're going to be in big trouble," Jeremiah said, breaking the tension in the room.

"Juniper, thank you," Ian said with a laugh, exchanging a knowing look with her.

"Ian, you take care of yourself." She squeezed his arm.

Ian turned, pausing in the doorway to take one last peek at the people he came to love in such a short time.

"Grace? Did he say the end of summer?"

"Yes, he did, Mother. Do you think we'll finish the dress in time?"

"We'll be cutting it close. Oh, and there are Ian's clothes, too. We're going to need help."

Jeremiah cleared his throat. "I'll take good care of them for you while you're gone."

"Thanks, Jeremiah. These will be the longest five months of my life."

31

Ian followed Jeremiah outside. Grace's admission weighed on his mind. He assumed she stood in front of a bullet because of her motherly instincts. The entire time, she protected him. He could not reconcile her willingness to sacrifice her life for his. He turned, stopping dead to stare up towards her room.

A horn tooted.

"What are you trying to do? Get yourself killed?" Jeremiah asked, yanking him by the arm. "We parked the truck over at the garage."

"How do you live with it?" Ian asked, still walking backward.

"How do I live with what?"

"Knowing Grace could've died protecting you?"

Jeremiah stopped to stand beside Ian. "Humbling, isn't it?"

"I could understand if she stood in front of that bullet for Joshua, but she said she did it for me. I'm nothing special. My life isn't worth hers."

"That's because you don't see yourself through the eyes of Grace," Jeremiah said, cupping Ian's shoulder. "You may not consider yourself worthy, but the price of your life lies in how others value you, not how you value yourself. You will always be worth more to the people that love you."

"There is no greater love..." Ian whispered, trying to remember the verse. He turned questioning eyes on Jeremiah.

"Greater love has no one than this, that he lay down his life for the sake of his friends." Jeremiah prompted Ian to face him. "There is one who died for you. He saw your worth two-thousand years ago," he said, conveying the solemnness of his words with an intense stare.

Ian's heart skipped a beat. Goosebumps rose on his arms while his increased heart rate brought sweat to his back and brow. Blood roared through his ears. Everything he learned during his stay in Covenant Cove fell into place.

Jesus died for him. The image of a man, bloody and beaten, hanging with his neck bowed on a cross filled his mind.

If you love me, keep my commandments.

Ian sucked in a dizzying breath when the words came to him. Tears formed and spilled over his cheeks.

The abstract concept of Jesus dying for his sins always struck him as implausible. He figured the story to be a fabrication for the church to control its followers through guilt. No way would somebody volunteer to die for people they didn't know.

Before he loved Grace, he didn't understand how deep a person's love could be. Before Grace stood in front of a bullet for him, he never perceived sacrifice. Now he knew. The things he did during his disbelief came back to him with ferociousness. He denied God, blasphemed His name, and laughed over other people's delusions of a savior. How heartbroken God must've been over his behavior. Ian hyperventilated.

"This hurts," Ian said, clutching his chest.

"Ian? Are you okay?" Jeremiah asked.

"Yeah," Ian croaked. He swiped away the tears with both his hands. "I don't know what to do with this."

"With what?"

Jeremiah's obtuse remark brought a bark of laughter from Ian. "Everything, Jeremiah. The depth of His love. Guilt. I've said awful stuff about God."

"Ian, everybody has said and done things they're not proud of. That's why, when we repent of our sins, when we turn away from doing our own will to do His, he gives us His grace. He forgives us. The blood of Yahusha blots out our sins." Jeremiah turned. "Let's go sit in the truck. I'm getting tired standing here."

Ian and Jeremiah slammed the doors shut and rolled down the windows. Ian stared out the front window. Jeremiah leaned against the door, letting the overhead sun warm his face.

"What do I do now?" Ian asked, breaking the silence.

"You live. Same as you always have, but now you live keeping Yah's commandments above everything else. You put Him first." Jeremiah sat up straight, turning his back to the door. "Actually, now that you understand why we're so adamant about following Torah, it makes what I'm going to ask you easier."

Ian didn't like the tone in Jeremiah's voice.

"I have an inherited heart condition. My father didn't make it past the age of fifty-five. I've denied the symptoms for the past year. They say if I make some lifestyle changes, I can live another five to ten years," Jeremiah said.

"What changes?"

Jeremiah rolled his eyes. "Stupid stuff like cutting out caffeine and alcohol."

Ian whistled. "You don't drink too much alcohol,

but caffeine? How will you give up coffee?"

"I know. That will kill me before anything else," Jeremiah said. He crossed his arms atop the steering wheel, leaning forward. "They said I need to reduce my stress level, too. What they really mean is work less, rest more." He leaned back in the seat again. "You're going to need a job once you return to marry Grace. You could be the new sheriff."

Ian scoffed at the suggestion. "Me? Sheriff?"

"Sure. Why not? You'll need training, of course, but I have faith you can do the job. You've proven to me you have the qualities to be a leader."

"Jeremiah, I'm a social media star. My only talent is smiling at the camera. I'm in no way qualified for law enforcement in any town, much less the leader of a God-fearing community. I need to figure out how to care for my family first. No. No, you must've suffered brain damage or something to consider me."

"Why? Don't you think you're worthy?"

Jeremiah's words returned to him. 'Your worth lies in how others see you.' "You really have a way of getting to the heart, Jeremiah," Ian said with a half sneer.

"Only because I've been where you're sitting." Jeremiah shook his head. "When the last sheriff approached me and proposed I take over the position, I thought him crazy. An ex-marine? Sheriff of a religious community? Ian, I've taken lives and seen atrocities so vile; I'll never speak of them. I turned him down." He shook his head again, this time accompanied by a bark of laughter. "That old dog. He reminded me of the story of Moses. He killed a man and looked at what Yah did with him. Shoot, Jonah spent three days and three nights in the belly of a giant fish denying Yah's calling."

"Are you trying to say God is calling me to be sheriff?" Ian asked in disbelief. "I hardly think my car breaking down is a calling."

"You remember when I asked you what you're missing?"

"Yeah," Ian nodded.

"What was your answer?

"Purpose," Ian replied. "And I've found my purpose in Grace and Joshua."

"Are they Yah's purpose or yours?" Jeremiah continued to speak, not giving Ian a chance to answer the question. "Think. What are the events of your life? The things you've been through, learned, and done. Have they led you to this spot? They may not have been what you wanted, but they served a purpose. You believe your car broke down where it did because of Grace and Joshua. I'm telling you it happened because I've been praying for a replacement, and you are what showed up."

Ian thought. His mother died. Then his father died. His stepmother abused him, causing him to be given into the custody of his grandparents. If none of the previous had happened, he never would've gained the skills he learned from his grandfather. He honored his mother's last wish to attend the Christian Academy. Even though he despised being forced to learn the Bible, the classes gave him a Biblical foundation he could now draw from to understand the people of Covenant Cove. If his grandfather didn't die, he never would've been driving the car that broke down outside of town. And if Jeremiah didn't already know his grandfather, Ian never would've stayed in Covenant Cove.

Every path, every twist, every turn led him here. If his life didn't contain challenges and hardships, he couldn't have become who he is now. The person Jeremiah said possessed the qualities to take his place.

Ian chuckled. "I told Grace the Holy Ghost knew I belonged here. I only half believed what I said. But you knew He sent me here all along, didn't you?"

"Well, you're not the only one He speaks to." He leaned forward. The aged seat creaked with his movement. "Does this mean you're saying you'll take the position? It'd make Juniper happy if you did."

"I'm scared to say yes. Given the story of Jonah, I'm more scared to say no," Ian said with a laugh.

"Good. That's real good."

"I have one question."

Jeremiah turned a smile on his face. "What's that?"

"How do I become the leader Grace and Covenant Cove deserve?" Ian asked, his apprehension returning.

"Oh, that's the easy part, son." Jeremiah picked up the Bible he kept on his dashboard. "You just look in the mirror."

32

The story of Tamsin is a work of fiction. Unfortunately, for too many, it is their reality. Whether for the commercial sex industry or domestic trafficking, sexual exploitation of minors is a pandemic. In 2021, 66% of the victims of new criminal sex trafficking cases were minors. Since 2000, 55% of sex trafficking victims have been recruited online.

Organizations to educate parents and children about grooming techniques before they become victims are on the rise, but residential facilities offering rehabilitation services to victims remain few.

Grindstone Ministries is a non-profit working to fill the gap. In 2021, they announced their rehabilitation facility project, Kaleb House, to provide "a covering for abused and trafficked children," which will "allow them to grow and learn in a safe home-like environment."

Cries for help came before they could build the facility. That didn't stop them from aiding victims as young as one-year-old. You can join their mission by making a tax-deductible donation at www.KalebHouse.org.